Another Sea, Another Shore

Another Sea, Another Shore

Persian Stories of Migration

*translated and edited by Shouleh Vatanabadi
and Mohammad Mehdi Khorrami*

Interlink Books

An imprint of Interlink Publishing Group, Inc.
Northampton, Massachusetts

First published in 2004 by

INTERLINK BOOKS
An imprint of Interlink Publishing Group, Inc.
46 Crosby Street, Northampton, Massachusetts 01060
www.interlinkbooks.com

Library of Congress Cataloging-in-Publication Data
Another sea, another shore : Persian stories of migration / edited by
Shouleh Vatanabadi and Mohammad Mehdi Khorrami.—1st American ed.
p. cm. — (Interlink world fiction)
ISBN 1-56656-511-1 (pbk.)
1. Short stories, Persian—Translations into English. 2. Persian
fiction—20th century—Translations into English. 3. Emigration and
immigration—Fiction. I. Vatanabadi, Shouleh. II. Khorrami,
Mohammad Mehdi. III. Series.
PK6449.E7A56 2003
891'.5530108355—dc21

2003013525

Mehri Yalfani's story, "Without Roots," was originally published in the author's *Parastoo:
Stories and Poems*, and is reprinted with the kind permission of the Women's Press, Toronto,
Canada.

The painting on the cover, *Homage to Apollo* by Saliba Douaihy, is courtesy of The Royal
Society of Fine Arts, Jordan National Gallery of Fine Art, Amman, Jordan

To request our complete 40-page full-color catalog,
please call us toll free at **1-800-238-LINK,** visit our
website at **www.interlinkbooks.com**, or write to
Interlink Publishing
46 Crosby Street, Northampton, MA 01060
e-mail: info@interlinkbooks.com

PART ONE

PART TWO

PART THREE

Acknowledgments

We would like to thank all the writers who submitted their stories for consideration in this collection. Our special thanks go to the following friends and colleagues who in many ways have been of invaluable assistance throughout this project: Cheyda Abadian, Janet Afari, Bahman Amini, Mirza Agha Asgari (Mani), Roshanak Bigonah, Mehdi Bozorgmehr, Miriam Frank, Ahmad Karimi-Hakkak, Sorour Kasmaï, Fatemeh Keshavarz, Nasrin Rahimieh, Majid Roshangar, Leyli Shaygan, Ella Shohat, and our friends at Irannewswatch.com.

We are also grateful to members of our families, Zari, Yousef, Yasha, and especially Sharareh, who helped us enormously in all stages of this book. We are particularly thankful to our copyeditor, Patia E. M.Yasin, who went through every single page of the manuscript with diligence and precision and enriched this collection with her suggestions. Our thanks go also to our students at New York University whose insightful comments have been helpful in developing many of the ideas for this book.

This project was supported in part by a grant from the New York University Research Challenge Fund Program. Our thanks go to Dean Steve Curry, Dean David Finney and Dr. David Garcia for their support and assistance.

We are especially grateful to Farkhondeh Hajizadeh, an Iranian writer, our friend, and colleague who has been instrumental in the materialization of the book from its inception. She has helped us in the process of collecting and selecting many of the stories especially those from Iran. We thank her sincerely.

—The Editors

Introduction

Throughout the early part of twentieth century, a number of Iranians were part of the wave of immigrants to different corners of the world. Their experience has been reflected in the works of the writers among them, such as Sadeq Hedayat, Mohammad Ali Jamalzadeh, and Bozorg Alavi, who all produced their major works while living abroad. Although the works of these writers are among the most celebrated in modern Persian literature, they have not constituted a special representational mode resulting from the literary and social characteristics of Iranian migration. Such a mode did not take shape until the massive migration of Iranians after the 1979 Revolution.

The Iranian migration to different places over the past twenty years and the literary texts stemming from the Iranian diaspora prepared ground work for the carving out of a place for the Iranian literature of migration in the general context of diaspora literature. This collection, an attempt to map the characteristics of this space as it is still forming, brings together stories by migrant Iranian writers living in different geographies, including Iran, whose literary works have been influenced by the experience of migration. The inclusion of works produced in Iran was essential, since we believe migration is not a one-way street: it influences both the host and the home societies. Furthermore, the inclusion of these texts indicates that multicultural encounters, which are often the result of migration, do not take place only in the metropolitan centers of the West to which most migrant Iranians have moved. Like many Middle Eastern countries, Iran is a culturally heterogeneous society and is itself host to many migrant groups, including Afghans. To consider the metropolis of the West as the only site where the migrant subject is exposed to heterogeneous notions of identity and culture would impose a reductionist linear and fixed dichotomy of "East" and "West" on the discourse of migration. The stories of migration in this collection, then, represent an example of a literary space that by its nature transcends and collapses such binaries.

Written in the various languages of the host societies, these stories reflect a variety of narrative and linguistic styles. In order to show the multiple layers and dimensions of the stories in this collection, we have avoided a traditional thematic categorization. Instead, our method of organization is an attempt to reflect the different moments in the process of re-constructing the self in diverse times and spaces. Though the stories are grouped under three headings, in many instances they share common themes, such as nostalgia for home, challenges the immigrant subject faces in the new home, and assimilation into a new culture, and many delve as well into issues of gender, race, ethnicity, sexuality, and class.

And when migrant birds
Paddle in the moonlight lake[1]

The experience of separation from home and the rupture in the process of identity construction in the new place influence the narrative strategy of many works in the first part of this collection. One of the most important themes in the stories in this section is the construction of identity through a profound preoccupation with the past. These stories, although written in the environment of the host society, allocate a large textual space to the specific time and place of the homeland.

In many of the stories, references to the host society take the form of highlighting the contrasts of self and other, cultural differences, geographical, political, ideological, and gendered issues of power. The process of identity reconstruction is primarily informed by memories and by imagining the past, although the elements of the new environment are present. In this process, however, these elements are not pronounced enough to be taken into account as an independent narrative voice.

This characteristic appears not only in stories such as Marjan Riahi's "After a Kiss" and Farideh Kheradmand's "Sylvia, Sylvia," which were written in Iran, but also, at times in a more complex fashion and to a different degree, in all of the stories of this section. The narrative strategy of these works underlines a particular space (e.g., political or cultural) by emphasizing a specific event or moment in the imagined past. Thus the protagonist of the story is defined in relation to that space. Because of the practical needs of the narrative, though, elements of the new environment are also present. In this context, Dariush Kargar's "The Last Scripture" and Azar Shahab's "The Return" take into account the political dimension, while Sirus Seif's and Ghodsi Ghazinour's stories deal with cultural realms. Pari Mansouri's and Mahasti Shahrokhi's stories also treat the notion of identity in a similar way, in the sense that, although the border that divides the timeline and locales is recognized, this recognition does not contribute to the conversation between the elements on the two sides of that border. For example, the stories by Shahrokhi, Mansouri and, in particular, Farkhondeh Hajizadeh, present the real and imaginary elements on both sides of the border, yet these elements do not contribute to the process of forming an identity that is created by the simultaneous presence of both sides of the border.

Another dream,
in another marsh!

The stories in the second section lay out the process of formation of identity for the migrant subject who is aware of and has internalized a simultaneous understanding of the notion of the border and the "other." This awareness provides the characters with new tools of representation, shown through a wide range of literary structures and techniques. Unlike the stories in the first section, Nasim Khaksar's "The Road to Arizona" and Mehri Yalfani's "Without Roots," employ traditional forms and structures to create independent voices representing a cultural divide. These voices, whether presented in a confrontational or parallel manner, do not yet interact fully. This demonstrates not only the hybrid quality of many of the characters in the stories but also, more importantly, the setting within which the search for identity is being conducted. Reza Baraheni's "Close Encounter in New York," takes the reader into a space where the cultural divide is further highlighted by a historical awareness. This is demonstrated through the interaction of an Iranian character, carrying an oil can, with the American cops and FBI agents during a night of a New York city blackout. No one but he is able to carry the can. As the Iranian character explains it, the oil can contains his heritage and the past. Mehrnoush Mazarei's "Farrokh-Laqa, Daughter of Petros, King of Farang" goes even further. The narrator of the story, who after years of living abroad has returned to Iran for a short stay, looks for a servant who lived in her childhood home. When she was very young, this servant used to read to her and her siblings from a famous heroic romance, the atmosphere of which is what the narrator is really trying to regain. The space in the story taken up by sections of this heroic romance gives a timeless, spaceless, and historical/legendary dimension to the story. In this fluctuating, fluid place, the protagonist's search for herself is materialized. Clearly, the process of construction of the character's identity and even her existence is at a stage well beyond the simple confrontation of yesterday's and today's societies. Her search for identity requires new elements that cannot be found necessarily in either of these spaces.

Tahereh Alavi's "Original Position" sets out a similar

approach, but in a more symbolic fashion. The action takes place during the short flight from France to Iran, and the narrator/protagonist simply expresses her thoughts about the place she has left and the place where she is going to live. The neither-here-nor-there space of the plane seems to be the only location where she can actually conduct her search, without necessarily finding a conclusive answer. Goli Taraghi's "The Wolf Lady" chooses a thematic approach to a similar quest. It seems the protagonist is trying to construct the proper site for her search by invoking a variety of themes. She is an Iranian woman who, apparently in order to get away from Iran and in particular the dangers of the Iran-Iraq War (1980–1988), has come to France with her two young children. She becomes acquainted with different components of life in exile such as nostalgia about the past world, the language barrier, and feelings of inferiority in the foreign land through the continuous harassments of her neighbor—nicknamed the Wolf Lady by the narrator's children—and through the letters she receives from Iran. But contrary to many similar cases, she does not find any of these discourses suitable for her search, and in the end she finds herself beyond the customary frames of reference to the point where she even gives the impression of identifying herself, as a woman, with the Wolf Lady, who had once symbolized many of her challenges.

How joyful flying

Going beyond defining the self through customary frames of reference is characteristic of the stories in the last part of this collection. The process of the search for identity by the characters in these stories takes place in a domain where time and space are being destabilized.

Kader Abdolah's "Marcia" is the story of an Iranian who has come to Holland and works in a library as a cataloguer of old books. His acquaintance with Marcia—a young intern—becomes a pretext to remind him of his sister, Marsi, and his past. His reminiscing about the past, which includes the assassination of his brother by government agents and his own political activities, does not however amount to the construction of a space where the relationship between the elements of his present identity and those of his past interact in a linear fashion, as happens in many of the stories in the first section of this book. On the contrary, this reminiscing contributes to the deconstruction of the idea of linear relationship between past and present. Indeed, by the end of the story we are led somewhere beyond yesterday and today to a very old book by a Portuguese poet of the Middle Ages in whom he finds a strange likeness.

Hushang Golshiri's "Zarathustra's Fire" chooses another form of this "going beyond" as its narrative strategy. A number of artists are gathered at the Heinrich Boll Foundation. For the most part, their conversations and arguments are about the political conditions of their respective countries and their political, ideological beliefs. These conversations serve to undermine in a very clear manner the absolutism usually associated with ideological stances, emphasizing once more that absolute values, when they go through specific historical experiences, quickly fade. Thematically, Fahimeh Farsaie's "No Comment!" follows the same path, but in a more descriptive fashion. The narrator, an Iranian woman who lives in Germany, is involved with progressive movements. Though active in those causes, in her description of their programs, beliefs, and plans she employs a wryly cynical tone that undercuts those same programs and beliefs. By dismissing definite ideological and political affiliations, these stories problematize fixed spaces and identities.

In all the stories in this section the place appears to expand very rapidly. Said's "he will come" is one such example; the domain of the story is so vast that the protagonist finds himself in an ambiguous atmosphere where questions of tangible reality do not seem to matter. Similarly, Mohammad Asef Soltanzadeh's "We Disappear in Flight" embodies the effect of the removal of familiar or "real" references. It floats in the limitless world of the individual's mind and identity. The story's main character, like the author, is an Afghan refugee who lives in Iran. Throughout the story, the character is consciously shrinking his "real" world while expanding his individual, subjective world. He removes the familiar references in such a conscious and systematic way that at the end he does not even recognize himself.

This is the same predicament confronted by the protagonist of Ali Erfan's "Anonymous." Sarcasm and irony are the two main devices through which the familiar points of reference are first quickly established and then immediately dismissed. Consequently, a self-referential and subjective universe is constructed in which the borders of reality and imagination are no longer just blurred, but completely collapsed. The overarching structure of "Anonymous" is a conversation between a writer and an anonymous person. The conversation takes place in a café in Paris. At the end of the story, after it is implied that all this is taking place in that self-referential, unstable space, the conversation finds a different meaning: in this conversation, the writer—or Anonymous—is alone, and the reader cannot tell which of the two leaves the café, drunk and sad. And the question of "Who am I, and where?" remains unanswered.

Indeed, in all the stories, in all their moments in the process of reconstructing the self in different temporal and spatial settings, this question functions only as a guiding star. The space for a Persian literature of migration is an ensemble of places migrants discover and invent, in their quest, in their voyages, without necessarily finding definitive answers.

PART ONE

And when migrant birds
Paddle in the moonlight lake

After a Kiss

Marjan Riahi

I said to him, What would you do if you wanted to give me your heart? He said, I would kiss you, and he kissed me without hesitation. Even the man I was in love with didn't have such affection. I couldn't understand how such a big thought had come from the curly head of that sweet four-year-old.

Departure began when I thought of the kiss and found an old set of keys that couldn't open any door. Because of those keys I had to go through the metal detector twice.

I didn't expect so many people to come see me off. My kisses were just to be dutiful; the kisses I received spoke volumes. My aunt's kiss was saying that all her wonderful words came from the bottom of her heart, and my cousin's kiss was saying that she hoped to goodness she would never see my face again. My older sister's kiss was full of hopes of marriage, as if I could find a great husband in a few hours. My sister-in-law's kiss was full of special effort, and a sickening magnanimity that was meant to show that the grave family problems were less than they seemed.

My best friend's kiss revived the memory of a year in political prison. That year had happened ten years ago. The moment I wanted to say goodbye to my prison mate and kiss her, she just shrugged her shoulders. Kissing? What for? Not kissing was a sign of strength.

My brother's kiss was not a kiss at all; it was a smooch. Something that needed a lot of work to become a kiss. It smelled of cigarettes and old paper money. A smooch that wanted me to pay attention to my passport and money and documents. A smooch that wanted me not to let go of my purse for a single minute. A smooch that wanted me not to trust anybody and to call him as soon as I arrived.

My niece's kiss was full of the wishes of a seventeen-year-old and maybe they could be realized through me. Her kiss was depressed by wearing a long dress and headscarf every day and wanted to ride a bicycle under a sun that caressed her hair.

I don't know which kiss was lost now that I am sitting in this airplane seat.

We were playing hearts. I said everyone should give whatever they have in their hearts. One of the kids took from his pocket a paper boat he had painted himself. Another a few pistachios stacked inside one another, and a third a few scraps of a paper tissue. Kids' hearts were always in their pockets. I always filled my pockets with chocolates filled with hazelnuts, and the kids loved those chocolates so much that I always ended up being short on hearts and had to divide them.

Then it was time for them to sleep, then time to wake up. Then they kissed me and left, and whoever kissed me the most showed off more.

I couldn't kiss my mother. We just hugged. My father's kiss landed on my face like the droppings of a dirty animal. He was not a bad man; he never did anything wrong. He never did anything.

On the eve of departure, the man I was in love with wanted to kiss me. We brought our faces close to each other. I felt his breathing on my face. His cell phone rang and he forgot what he had brought his face close for.

A kiss only transfers microbes. Every New Year's Day I kept saying that and pretending I had a cold so I could keep myself away from all those different kisses and then the pieces of my life stuck together like a dream without an interpretation.

The sky behind the plane window curves and reaches the ground. I have not started yet, but many things have already ended. This curved sky is exactly what I want to buy with a kiss. A kiss connects me.

The key chain is at the bottom of my pocket and a four-year-old boy with a head full of curly hair has taught me the proper way to play the game of hearts.

My passport is stamped. They press the stamp down on the page as if it is an endless kiss.

Anxieties from Across the Water

Pari Mansouri

It was early September. The morning mist, like outspread remnants of silk, came from the green fields with a gentle breeze, passed over the hills and faded away in the sky.

A middle-aged woman was sitting in an armchair beside a window that opened onto a small garden with low hedges linking a mild incline to the hills and fields. She was listening to nature's most magic symphony in the songs of robins, buntings, swallows, sparrows, and nightingales praising the rising sun, and in the ecstasy of that sacred tranquility, with the magic of a dream, she was stepping into the faraway years, the years of her youth. She had once directly encountered the field, the sky, and the silk of mist in those summers when she went with her parents to her aunt's house in Kelardasht.[1] And now for a few long moments she found herself once more, swift-footed and full of energy, in that lost paradise, which was like this quiet, peaceful village of Highworth near the town of Swindon. There, every morning the sun opened like a flower in the middle of the colorful silks of jugglers, and swarms of butterflies disappeared into the raspberry bushes. Grasshoppers in darting flight broke the crystal of the open air, and dragonflies with their quick leaps reflected with their small colorful wings the sunlight on the pool and the water lilies.

It had been a few days since she left hot, dusty Tehran with its heavy, polluted air and come to this corner of the world, to the house of her daughter Sadaf. Her son-in-law had been sent to the Far East by the company he was working for, and she was cherishing this sweet private time with Sadaf. It was a few years since the mother and daughter had seen each other. For the mother this felt like a few centuries. The first two days she was so excited and confused she couldn't even speak properly.

Instead of talking, she had just looked around. Maybe she thought that if she started talking she would wake from this wonderful dream. The daughter was quite excited, too. She had filled the whole sitting-room table with dishes of chocolates, cookies, and cakes, and yet every other moment she went to the kitchen to bring more sweets from the refrigerator and cupboards. The mother followed her around all the time, watching her every move, and the daughter urged her to go back to the room and sit down. She made tea for her, poured her coffee, sat down beside her and leaned her head against her mother's shoulder with a sigh of satisfaction. She asked her about her father and the family, and the mother told her more about her father—he's worn out, but even in this state he keeps working. The idea of taking a rest makes no sense to him. There is not a doctor in the world as dedicated. And she thought, He even forgets his wife and children! Otherwise, he would have agreed to come on this trip with me, after all my begging.

She never said these things to her daughter, though. She had not written to her daughter about her troubles. She didn't want to worry her. Her daughter had completed her studies; now she was working full time in a laboratory, but she wanted to spend all her time with her mother as long as she was there. It was not possible. It was only two months since she had started work. After lots of begging, the laboratory head had given her a week's vacation without pay, and the week had begun two days before her mother's arrival. Those two days were spent getting the house ready for the joyous occasion. The remaining days passed like a carefree dream. The five days during which she didn't have to wake up early, take a shower half asleep and get ready and rush through breakfast and go to work. Mother and daughter slept until ten, ten-thirty, and then ate a big breakfast, and then the daughter took her mother in her little car to show her the neighborhood. She took her to the little market and showed her the few villages in the area; once they went to the town of Swindon, about half an hour's drive from their house. That golden week had gone by like the wind.

When Sadaf woke up, she came out of her room very quietly, trying not to wake her mother, and when she saw her mother wide awake waiting for her at the breakfast table, surprised and embarrassed she said, "Mom, why did you wake up so early? The sun isn't even completely up yet. And you got everything ready. You shouldn't have. You should rest. Please, when I leave, go back to bed and don't do anything. There is fried chicken in the fridge for lunch. And for dinner we'll go to a restaurant. There is a beautiful Italian restaurant in our neighborhood. I want to have dinner with you there. Promise me you won't do the housework."

And to reassure her daughter, the mother said, "All right, Sadaf dear, I promise. And please don't worry about me. I'll take good care of myself and won't do a thing!"

About an hour later the daughter, like the first day she went to school, upset about leaving the house now filled with the scent of childhood, kissed her mother and left.

And now the woman was alone in front of the green farms that went on to the horizon and the large trees that, with their waves of colors, dark and light green, turquoise, silver and dark red, were emerging from the morning fog. And since autumn was coming, sometimes among these colorful waves, scattered trees with red and golden leaves rose like flames, and she watched them joyfully; just as during these few days she had watched her daughter walking, sitting, getting up, the light in her black eyes, her dimples when she laughed. During these days the daughter talked most of the time; she talked about her worries during the Iran–Iraq War and her separation from her parents, then about her present life and tranquility, her husband Farrokh and their love, and she regretted that her parents hadn't seen him. The mother had concluded that, contrary to her husband's expectation that one day Sadaf and her husband would return to Iran, her daughter and son-in-law were properly settled in England, and it would be wrong to endanger that. She thought, I should convince Javad to get our things together and move here so that we can spend our last days with our children.

Before the trip she had argued many times with her husband, "I just can't understand how you can be so indifferent. Sadaf got married, and you saw that I couldn't get the damned visa from England and be at their wedding. You didn't care. In no time she will have a kid, and once again I'll be here, useless, without seeing my grandchild. I don't want the same fate as my aunt. For years that poor woman cried because she wasn't with her children. Her room was full of photographs of her son and daughter; their pictures in their graduation gowns, pictures of their weddings, then pictures of her grandchildren. Do you remember, every time someone went to see her, she would take them to her bedroom first and pick up the photographs from the shelves one by one, and tears would flow and she would say, 'I know the pain of separation will kill me in the end.' And that's exactly what happened. She died surrounded by those photographs and never saw her children and grandchildren. It's every mother's natural right to see her children every once in a while, to touch them, to be present at the events of their lives, to see the births of her grandchildren. To be there for their first laugh, their first word, their first steps. How many years have I suffered. It's been ten years since Sadaf has gone and I've seen her only once; five years ago when I went to Italy to see Marjan. And my poor child had saved her money to come and see me and her sister. Back then it was impossible to get a visa for England, but now we can. If only you would agree, we could move there to live. I am miserable here."

And the husband, upset, would say, "There you go again, Mina! You have become like a broken record. You talk as if they weren't my children, as if I don't want to see them. Frankly, I'm the one who should be tired of this life. I really have had enough of it. You just close your eyes and say, 'Let's move.' You don't think about anything. You don't see the situation. There are a million problems. You know my degree is not from a European or American university, and it won't be easy at all for me to find a job there. Besides, here is where I am needed. Here I have my own identity; I am a doctor. What would I do over there? Beg? Besides, suppose we could sell what we have and decide to go to England as you wish. And suppose they give us residency permits without difficulty. All right, what will you do about Marjan? Can she simply leave her school and come and live with us in England right next door to us? You know, you are driving me crazy. I just don't know what else I should do. Sadaf said she wanted to go to England to study, and I said fine. Marjan said, 'I want to study painting and I have to go to Italy;' I said fine. I worked day and night to pay for their schooling and their lives over there. What more do you want from me?"

Every time they reached this point she got angry and said, "Whatever we have done was our duty. Besides, it's been a year now since Sadaf got married and we haven't sent her anything. Thank God her husband is educated and has a good job. My dear child is working, too, and doesn't need us. We really should thank our children for being so good and for having brought honor to us. Sadaf finished her studies, and God willing, Marjan will be done in couple of years and will start working and won't need us anymore."

Then the husband usually changed the subject and said, "That's enough. You're making me tired. You talk as if I were responsible for you being separated from your kids. As if I am in charge of the British Embassy and all the embassies in the world and specially ordered them not to give you a visa. In the six years since Marjan has gone to Italy you have traveled there twice at least. Where have I gone? Of course I have been traveling, too, but where? During the eight years of war I traveled back and forth to the front, and I had a lot of fun! Besides, this past spring, if you hadn't caught that damned pneumonia everything was ready for you to travel to England. You know what? The problem is that you decided for no reason to go on early retirement. If you had been busy these past five years, you would have been occupied with work and wouldn't have bothered me without reason. But then again I'm sure you would have found something else to accuse me of. The same way you treated your employees... "

And the woman would grow even angrier. "Please, Javad, don't say that! Back then you didn't understand my concerns as a human being, and you don't understand them now either. When you, a doctor, don't understand these pains, what can we expect from others? Oh my God... "

The couple continued to argue until the night before the woman's departure. But at the airport when they checked in the luggage, they realized that in about one hour they would be separated from each other. Then they went and sat down on chairs next to each other and the woman looked at her husband and said, "You don't know, Javad, how much I wanted you to be with me so we could see Sadaf and Marjan together. I will miss you a lot. Don't you understand? You will be alone here. Please take care of yourself."

And the husband said, "You have to be careful while you are there. Don't worry about me. You will have time. Think about our life. Stop dreaming. Encourage Sadaf and Farrokh to come back. Farrokh's roots are here. It's true he has lost his parents, but he has lots of family here. Be strong and patient, and all our children will return."

And now the woman, surprisingly calm, was sitting on the chair in front of the window and following her dreams. Suddenly the phone rang. Who could it be? Farrokh or Javad? It can't be Farrokh. He called last night.

It was Sadaf, calling to make sure she was all right. Javad had called twice in the past five days but she didn't know why she expected him to call. She looked at her watch: ten-thirty. In her mind she moved the time ahead three and a half hours and then realized that her expectation was unreasonable because during that time of day her husband would be quite busy in the hospital. She thought, What a wonderful dream. Now I am going to do the dishes and tidy up a bit. Then I'll do the laundry that Sadaf means to do when she's back. The poor child doesn't know what she's talking about. She says I shouldn't do a thing, just wait for her to come back from work and do everything. The idea!

When she picked up the sheets to put them in the washing machine she saw some patches on them and realized that Sadaf and her husband were being very careful with their finances, as was only right and proper. They were both young, and Farrokh had started working only three months ago. Her daughter had only been working for two months. Then she thought, These five days have added so much to their expenses. Then she felt a lump in her throat. And now she wants to take me to a restaurant tonight! Why? Only if she lets me pay for it. I know she won't. In the past five days she hasn't let me spend so much as a penny. This is not right. I have to plan ahead. I know she likes *khoresh-e fesenjan.*[2] And I have brought walnuts and pomegranate juice from Iran. Tonight we'll have rice and *fesenjan.* We will miss Javad. Sadaf and Javad love *fesenjan*; so does Marjan, but not as much as they do.

Then as she worked, the thought of her husband filled her mind. She remembered that a week before her trip, although she was busy buying souvenirs and every day she had to go to different places and stores in the city, she managed to find some time and buy a lot of food and prepare a few kinds of *khoresh* that she knew Javad liked, including *fesenjan*, and put them in plastic containers, one each for a meal, and put them in the freezer so her husband would have something to eat while she was not there. But when she told her husband proudly, "All you have to do is to take one of those containers and make a couple of cups of rice and you will have a delicious meal," her husband said, laughing, "What were you thinking of? You haven't yet arrived in England and you've already forgotten the situation here. Don't you see that most of the time we are without power? What am I to do with these cooked *khoreshes* that every day are thawed and then refrozen? Don't worry about my food. I am going to eat at the hospital while you're not here. Tomorrow when the cleaning lady comes you should give her all this. You know what, you can unplug the freezer and give her whatever is inside."

And the woman, annoyed, accepted the husband's logic. The next day when she put all the food in a bag and gave it to Fatemeh Khanom[3] and saw the light of happiness in her eyes, she forgot her fatigue and all the pains she had taken to prepare the food. Now she was thinking, What is Javad doing at night? With all those mosquitoes? I know when he is back from work he is so tired he doesn't have the patience to put up the mosquito net. I'm sure he sleeps inside. If he leaves the door and windows open the mosquitoes will drive him crazy. I'm sure he closes the door and windows and leaves the air conditioning on all night and puts up with the heavy, humid air. And still he wants me to encourage the children to go back. No, this is not right. I wish a miracle had happened and he was with me on this trip. Even this short time, this wonderful weather and so much calm would have taken away the fatigue and pollution and the pain of years of fear and war.

When she had tidied up a bit, she put the rice in water so she could cook it in the afternoon. Then she went to the large living-room window again and joyfully looked outside. The leaves of the trees and the petals of the colorful dahlias and geraniums around the garden were flashing under the sun, as if the ground and air had been washed with light a thousand times. She looked at her watch; it was eleven-thirty. She thought now that she had the time she would go and work a bit in the garden. She had seen a few dead branches that had to be removed. Some of the flowers were withered and looked unpleasant among the green branches. She put on her sweater, looked for the gardening scissors and finally found them in one of the drawers in the kitchen. She took some matches with her to burn the withered flowers and dead branches so everything would look tidy. Then she went through the hall door that opened onto the backyard and garden.

In the midst of white, orange, red, and pink roses she saw one rose with a light velvety color, the same color as the jasmine's gleanings, and once again she remembered how much her husband liked this color. Many times he had bought this flower and had planted it in the garden, and every time it had withered. How strange! Once more she wished a miracle had happened and her husband had come with her. She would have felt the pleasure of this trip much more deeply, without any guilt.

Very carefully she cut the dry branches and flowers. Patiently she picked a few branches of climbing passion flowers that had changed their direction and fallen onto the branches of the cypress, and put them back on the wall. Then she told herself, After I finish with the garden I'll make myself a coffee.

She remembered a few years ago, one afternoon in the month of Shahrivar, she had gone to see her husband at the hospital. Before entering the hospital she saw a peddler selling cigarettes. He also had a few small jars of Nescafé. She fancied having coffee. She went ahead and asked the middle-aged man the price of one of the medium-size jars. The man looked her up and down and in an almost offensive tone said, "Are you a doctor? An engineer?" And when she, startled, said, "Neither, and do we need a degree to ask the price of a jar of Nescafé?" the man objected insolently, "Then don't meddle with me and my business. You cannot afford Nescafé." And the feeling of being small, of being alienated, had hurt her so much that for two years she didn't touch coffee. Later, when she told the story to her friend Simin who liked coffee a lot, she realized that coffee was quite expensive, and that her friend who loved coffee hadn't been able to afford it for some time. One day three months ago Simin called her and said that her sister had asked a traveler coming from England to bring her two jars of Nescafé and invited her over for coffee and a chat. When she wanted to go back, Simin had insisted that she take one of the jars. Now she was feeling guilty that Simin wasn't here so they could have a coffee together without even thinking about whether it was cheap or expensive.

She was still busy gathering the dead branches when she realized that her back no longer felt the warmth of the sun. She looked up and saw there were scraps of clouds in the sky, and a gray one had covered the sun. All of a sudden a harsh wind came and she heard the sound of the building door closing. She rushed to the door and tried to open it and enter the building to get something warmer to wear. But it wouldn't open. She couldn't believe the door was locked. For a while she turned the handle vainly, in disbelief. Then she remembered detective movies and police and criminals who would use a pin or a card and open any lock with ease. She pulled a hairpin from her hair and tried to do likewise, but it was no use. Then she thought, I should find a strong, thin sheet of something. She looked everywhere, even under the flower bushes; finally she found a thin sheet of iron at the end of the garden. She was happy and came back to the door. She inserted it in the crack of the door. She bent and looked. She could see the lock's bolt, which touched the iron sheet. But no matter how much she pressed nothing happened; the bolt didn't move and the door didn't open. She thought about trying the front door.

She thought, It is a good thing the backyard is connected to the front of the building. There was a two-meter space between this building and the one next door. Through this alleyway she went to the front of the building and examined the lock. First she tried it with the hairpin. It didn't work. Then she tried with the iron sheet. She was busy moving the sheet up and down in the crack when she heard footsteps, along with the sound of a wheel on the street. She raised her head and turned toward the sound and saw a middle-aged woman with her shopping cart in front of the building next door. From her surprised look it was clear she had been watching her for a while. All of a sudden a weird feeling mixed with insecurity came over her. She lowered her head and rapidly went back to the yard. She told herself, It's no use. The door doesn't open. What should I do? What can I do until five-thirty when Sadaf gets back? There's nothing to do. For now I am going to finish my work in the garden. It's a good thing I have some matches. I'm going to burn the dried branches and flowers at the end of the garden; that should make me warm, too.

Then, as she was busy carrying the dried branches and leaves and flowers, she heard the voice of a woman who was standing on the path between the two buildings saying, "Hello... I say... Hello... I say... " She was saying other things in a loud voice; words that didn't make sense to her; she interpreted them as, "Hey, who are you? What are you doing over there? What have you come to this house for?"

Now she didn't just have the strange feeling of insecurity. A flood of fear and terror was pouring into her heart. Her mouth was dry. Her face, her forehead, under her hair, her ears and her whole neck were completely red. She tried not to make any noise so that the woman would think that she had made a mistake to consider her a stranger and go away. She was so terrified that even the sound of the beating of her heart, which was going round and round in her ears, made her shiver with fear.

She told herself, For sure she thinks I'm a thief. Well, why shouldn't she think so? She has seen with her own eyes that an odd-looking woman is playing with the lock. She thinks she's caught me.

The feeling of shame, of smallness, of crime, however uncommitted, hurt her. She thought, How hard it is not knowing the language. If I knew English I wouldn't be so miserable now. God bless my father. He loved the French language and literature so much, so instead of English I studied a little French at school. Although I don't remember much from what I studied back then, at least I could have made this woman understand that I am not a thief. And that this is my daughter's house and I've locked myself out. It would have been good enough.

The fear had so taken her that she thought her thoughts were being spoken out loud. She wished she could stop thinking. For a while she stood there motionless and quiet as a stone; finally after a few minutes, which lasted a few centuries for her, the woman's voice stopped; instead she heard the sound of the wheel and footsteps going away. Then she calmed down a little. Slowly she went to the end of the garden with the dried branches and leaves. She cut a few more dried branches from the trees at the end of the garden, placed them on the top of one another and tried to light a match. For a while she tried. There was a wind that prevented the flame from staying. A couple of times the branches caught fire, but the flame was so lifeless that even though she bent down and blew under the branches, nothing happened and the fire went out, and finally there were no matches left.

Now she was really cold. The wind was hitting her on the side; it seemed like it was going through her ribs; it made her shiver inside. She looked up. She could still see a bit of blue sky here and there, but that transparent, limpid, total blue was gone now. She looked everywhere but found no shelter to protect her from the cold. The problem with all these villas was that their structures were all straight without any outcroppings or incroppings. Although she was basically timid, she wished she had seen the neighbors once or twice before, or at least knew whether or not they were home, so that she could go there and knock, and tell them with body and sign language what had happened to her. But her daughter had mentioned that the neighbors on the left were a young couple who had gone on vacation to Greece for a week and the one on the right was an old woman whose nephew came to see her, but unfortunately she had been sick for ten days and was in the hospital. Her daughter didn't know any other neighbors because they hadn't been here for long.

Miserable, she began walking in the garden and cursing herself. How could a normal woman of her age be so stupid? Poor Sadaf had given her the key yesterday. But she was so immersed in the pleasure of seeing her daughter that she had carelessly left the house without the key! Then she justified herself by thinking, Who would have thought that that great weather and shining sun could change in less than an hour. Then she remembered that Sadaf had told her that on the north side their street turned directly onto a main avenue and at the corner there was a bus stop and it was less than three minutes away. She thought, I should go there. Then she remembered that she didn't have a single penny. She was disappointed. If she had two pounds she could at least take the bus and go to the town center and spend her time in the shops to be safe from the cold. Despite her despair, she concluded that going to the bus stop, which might have a shed, was better for her than her present situation.

She hurried. When she reached the street she saw the same woman with her cart. Luckily her back was toward her and she didn't see her; the same fear, even stronger, came upon her. She thought, For sure that woman is telling everyone in the neighborhood that she is a thief. There was no other way. She hurried up and reached the bus stop and sat on the bench. The bus stop had a roof, but it was open on both sides, and every time the wind rushed in she felt cold and her muscles tensed. Fortunately it was the middle of the day and there was nobody at the bus stop and there wasn't any bus. This was the only thing that made her happy: that there wasn't anyone to see her in this miserable situation with her slippers. She sat there for a while and busied herself with her thoughts.

She remembered her father, God bless his soul, and the day she was on her way back from visiting him at the hospital. Father was going through the last days of his life, in such pain. He had cancer. The war wasn't over yet. Her husband was working at the front and she was alone with the fear of him being far away, fear of bombing and missiles, fear of general chaos, fear of losing her father and of separation from her children. That day she was sadder and more anxious than any other day. When she got off the bus she tried to cross the street in the middle of the taxis, buses, and other traffic. She hadn't gone more than a few steps when she saw a young woman facing her from a distance who had covered herself head to toe with a black chador and scarf and was arguing with an imaginary interlocutor. She thought, What times; even young people have so many nervous problems. She was busy sympathizing with young people when another young woman exactly like the first one joined the scene and then the two of them came over to her. The first one said with a strange hatred and in an insulting tone, "Cover yourself, woman! How did you come out of doors like this!" Her hand involuntarily went up to her forehead and touched her scarf, and when she realized that not even one hair was out, she was frozen like someone who has suddenly received a blow to the head. She stood there, confused and surprised. The first one yelled again, "Why don't you listen? Didn't I tell you to cover yourself? Slut! Why do you think every day one of our *Umma*[4] is being martyred? So that you and people like you can go around like this? Have you no shame? You have reached this age and still don't give up such corruption? My God, look how shameless she is. She is staring at me! Don't you realize your neck is exposed?"

That was when she came to herself. The whole world turned upside down in her head. It was as if an earthquake, a storm, had scattered every part of her existence. She carried her hands toward her neck and brought back the two sides of her scarf, which had been blown back because of the wind and tucked them inside the collar of her manteau.[5] Then suddenly her face was covered with tears. Like a hunted animal looking innocently at the hunter, she gave the second woman a long look. The second one, who had probably understood the meaning of her look, with a touch of compassion yet also afraid of the first one, said, "Why are you so unhappy, mother? Why are you crying? You had to be guided, so you were. What are you waiting for? You can go wherever you wanted to go. Go on, mother." And then when the woman saw that she was about to fall down she took her arm and walked with her a few steps and leaned her against the wall of a shop.

Sobbing, she said, "That's it! I should go! Where can I go? I have no place to go anymore. I just want the ground to open up and swallow me. I am tired. Tired of being alive, of breathing. I am ashamed of being alive. I am not alive. This woman told me—I who am as old as her mother!—every single terrible thing, and as 'guidance' took every ounce of desire for life from me and walked over my dead body. What strange times! What children we have!"

This event was so bitter and catastrophic that she didn't want to remember it anymore. But now at this bus stop, in this strange land, in spite of herself she remembered it and told herself, Although I suffered that day, at least that was my own country; I could understand the language and the look of the people.

Then she remembered the day she went to the national retirement bureau to pick up the official letter of her employment status. She came back home at two-thirty in the afternoon, tired and hungry, with no success. When she arrived home she looked for the key in her purse but didn't find it. Very naturally and quite at ease she went to the neighbor's house and knocked. Behjat Khanom had welcomed her very amiably and happily, and had even joked, "Dear Mina, you don't know how happy I am that you have forgotten your key! I suppose such things happen so that you come to our house! You don't know how much I have missed you. Come in and call your husband first so if he calls home he won't be worried."

After talking to her husband over the phone, Mina realized that Bahjat Khanom had prepared a bowl of *ash-e reshteh*[6] with *kashk*[7] and hot mint, a dish of cutlets and one of vegetables, and a salad and had put them on the table. That afternoon Mina ate with a good appetite, and after that they sat and chatted. Mina talked about her children being away and Bahjat Khanom talked about her husband who was chasing other women; apparently, according to what she had heard, he had taken a *sigheh*[8] as well.

Then she remembered the war when her husband was away at the front; how every time they announced the possibility of air raids, this Bahjat Khanom, and sometimes other neighbors, with such compassion and sense of responsibility, would come to her house. If there was time, they would go to Bahjat Khanom's garage, and if there wasn't enough time they would stay with her, taking refuge under the staircase or under the dining table until the end of the raid, so she wouldn't be alone. Remembering all that compassion and friendship now, her heart was wrung and she felt guilty. Perhaps she had the same feelings that Adam and Eve had when they were driven out of Paradise after eating the forbidden fruit. In her heart she cursed and blamed herself: Oh, how wonderful are the honesty and friendship you find in your own homeland. You cannot forget these things. Over there, good and bad belong to you. But when you don't belong somewhere, you are small and without refuge. You have no security. By now that lady has probably reported me to the whole neighborhood, maybe even to the police. Maybe a policeman is even now waiting for me in front of the door. What a scandal! Oh, I have given my child a bad reputation. No, I won't wish Javad had come on this trip with me anymore!

A bus stopped in front of the station. A few ten- or eleven-year-old girls in school uniforms and an old couple got off. The driver didn't take off right away. He waited for a while so she would get on, but when he saw her hunched up in a corner of the bench, he drove off. The woman looked at her watch. It was four-fifteen in the afternoon. The wind was blowing faster now and was rapidly bringing black rain clouds over the horizon to her daughter's neighborhood. She was feeling very cold. She couldn't sit there anymore. She had to leave. She came out of the bus stop and started walking in the direction opposite the bus, which she knew was the way her daughter would come. She thought she could reach the intersection and the phone booth before the rain started. True, she had no money to call her daughter, nor did she know her work number, but she could stay in the booth and, with her weak lungs, be safe from pneumonia until her daughter's car passed the booth.

A few minutes after she entered the booth, the rain started. What a downpour! It was raining fiercely; the drops, big as marbles, hit the ground and scattered. Earth and sky were shaking with the roar of thunder, and the iron gratings of the sewers were pulling the flood inside along with the pleasure of the morning mist, the sunrise, the peace and quiet of the hills and all the magic of newly-regained paradise. In the midst of that misery she was happy only because she had found this shelter in time.

When Sadaf left the laboratory and set out for home she was filled with happiness once she remembered that when she arrived, the home would be full of her mother's warmth. Since the day her mother came, whenever she thought of Farrokh and missed him, she told herself, It's great that Mom is here and I'm not alone.

The one thing that bothered her was this downpour, which was not at all well-timed and prevented her from driving at her usual speed. She had to drive cautiously. The minutes were like hours. When she turned off the main avenue into the small street suddenly she saw from behind the windscreen and rain the silhouette of a woman the same age and figure of her mother who came out of the phone booth and waved her hand over and over and signaled her to stop. Hesitantly she put her foot on the brake and stopped the car. It took her a few seconds to believe that this middle-aged woman, pale and disheveled, tired and soaking wet, was her mother!

When they arrived home, Sadaf, after she had heard what her mother had gone through, was crying and thinking that all the years of living in fear and insecurity had made her mother weak and tired. She helped her change her clothes and then sleep on the sofa in the living room in front of the television. She brought her a hot water bottle and a blanket, wrapped the bottle in a towel and gave it to her mother. Then she began stroking her hair and kissing her. And the mother pressed the daughter to her bosom and said, "Sadaf, dear, don't worry. It's nothing. I'm just a bit cold. I'll be fine in half an hour."

The doorbell rang. Sadaf got up and went to the door. The mother heard her talking with a woman in English. If it weren't for the occasional laughter in the midst of their conversation, she would have become quite worried again. When they had finished talking and Sadaf shut the door and came back, before allowing the mother to ask a question she said, "You see, Mom? I was right. You imagined all those things for no reason. That was the same woman you thought took you for a thief and reported you to the neighbors and the police. She's in charge of delivering the local paper. She came by because she was worried about you. She said yesterday when we were getting in the car she saw us and waved to us but we were so busy talking we didn't notice. She said she could guess you were my mother because we look alike. She said she tried hard to help you. She was very unhappy she wasn't able to help you. She asked after you, and she says hello."

The mother, confused, looked at her daughter for a while. Then a teardrop rested in her eye; she sighed with satisfaction and said, "Sadaf, dear, don't forget to give her a box of pistachios and a box of nougat from me tomorrow."

Then, as she lay on the sofa she looked at the large window facing the garden. There was no trace of the paradise of those youthful days. It was drizzling, and the sky was completely gray.

Sylvia, Sylvia

Farideh Kheradmand

—Cool!

Sylvia had just arrived. She was tall and well built, with long wavy colored hair tied in back. Her jeans were worn-out, and on her T-shirt was written Los Angeles. She picked up the glass of tea and smiled at her cousin and her husband.

—So, kids, how's every little thing?

Farangis and Bizhan smiled.

Seven years had passed since her last trip. She was in her thirties, and her face had lost the old freshness.

The envelope of divinations was on the table.

As they were coming out of the airport, outside a young boy was selling Hafez divinations; he recognized the passenger and went toward her. Cheerfully Sylvia took the envelope.

Why should not I intend to return to my country
Why should not I be the dust of my beloved's home
Since I cannot endure the sorrow of estrangement
I shall return to my country and be my own king
I shall be admitted behind the veil of union
And be a slave of my Lord
Since the events of life are not revealed to us
It is better that on the day of resurrection I be with my beloved
My profession has always love and errancy
So I shall try and devote myself to them

Then she asked Farangis and Bizhan what they thought of the fortune.

—It's very good, Sylvie, very good.

—Excellent!

Silvie had smiled and handed a thousand-touman bill to the young boy.

—Cool!

Now the yellow envelope of divinations was on the table in front of Sylvie.

—I really missed you kids.

—Thank you; same here; you haven't told us; how was your trip? said Farangis.

—Excellent, but... I still haven't felt it!

And she broke into a boisterous laugh. Her laughter was long and abrupt; she threw her head back and laughed freely.

Bizhan kept his head down and smiled.

They were happy to see Sylvia after several years and were familiar with her character. They knew she had to enjoy her moments fully and fill her time with different activities such as traveling, museums, movies, concerts, theaters, photography; anything interesting to do.

—So, kids, what's the program for today? said Sylvia, and she set the glass of tea on the table.

Bizhan looked at his wife with downcast eyes.

—Are you kidding? Farangis said.

—Why kidding?

—But at this hour of the night everything is closed!

—You're right, cousin.

She went on laughing and teasing them.

She had been sixteen when she went to the States to continue her education. She was supposed to have come back when she completed her education. But she stayed there and started working at a company. It was a long time now since she had changed jobs; she is still working for the same insurance company.

She travels whenever she gets the chance. She has an adventurous nature, and she is more energetic than her years. She has traveled to many countries; tonight she came from Spain. She stayed in Spain for three months to learn flamenco.

Sylvie is also a musician. She plays Iranian instruments very well: *santur*, *setar*, *zarb*, and *tar*.

—So kids, tomorrow's program is set; we are going to the airline office to change my ticket.

—Our departure date? Farangis asked.

She had put off her departure date on her last trip as well.

—Well, to get a feeling, I need more than three weeks!

To get a feeling! To get a feeling! This was her own special expression.

While Sylvie was standing in front of their small bookcase looking at the books and pictures, Bizhan yawned secretly. It was a few minutes past three in the morning.

She had taken about 500 pictures during her last trip to Shiraz and Isfahan. She had enjoyed visiting the historical sights, mosques, and old buildings like a tourist and had gotten enough feeling, as she put it.

She saw a *setar* in the corner of the room.

—Who plays the *setar*?

—Bizhan; and sometimes I do, Farangis said.

—Wow, you're cool.

She smiled and picked up the instrument. As she was playing the *setar*, her head lowered she said, it's out of tune. And started tuning the instrument.

—But it's a good instrument.

She spent about half an hour tuning the instrument. Bizhan had fallen asleep on the couch with his head leaning to one side.

Farangis had put her right hand under her chin and was dozing off. When she saw Bizhan in that condition she called him softly:

—Bizhan? Bizhan? Get up and go to bed; get up!

Sylvie was so busy playing an old song she didn't hear Bizhan's good night. Farangis washed the glasses and sat down next to Sylvie. She had taken the week off, but she had to get up early in the morning to send Nazanin off to school. Farangis was waiting; she was waiting for Sylvie to finish playing to let her know about their travel plans together.

Sylvie would be so happy to hear this. Sylvie loved to travel.

Finally the last notes were struck on the instrument.

—By the way Sylvie, I've got great news!

Sylvia gazed at Farangis' mouth.

—The day after tomorrow we're all going to the north, until the end of the week, how about that?

—Really? Cool! Do you know how many years it's been since I saw northern Iran?

Farangis and Sylvie talked about the trip for half an hour or so. It was almost dawn before they went to sleep.

The next morning they all overslept, and Nazanin didn't go to school. She was standing there with disheveled hair, watching the newly arrived guest in amazement. Sylvie was eating breakfast with great appetite; then she brought out her suitcase and distributed the gifts. She had brought a blue summer dress, a pair of slippers, and some makeup for Farangis. Bizhan's gifts were three pairs of white sports socks and a short-sleeved shirt. And for Nazanin she had brought a white dress with small red flowers and a lace collar. They all thanked her. Bizhan said, Sylvie always embarrasses us with a lot of gifts. The special flamenco shoes and costume were in the suitcase. They were interesting shoes. Nazanin took them out and looked at them. Under the shoe soles there were some nails for making sounds.

Nazanin put them on and took a few steps. Tak, tak, tak... She looked at Sylvie and laughed.

They took off early on Wednesday morning.

On the way, wherever there was a nice view, Bizhan stopped the car and Sylvie took pictures. The slim cows, rural cottages, trees, plantations, brown, beige and black sheep grazing on the hills, were interesting views to Sylvie.

Oh my God! What beauty! I am really getting a feeling.

The road was not that long. About five hours later they

arrived at a small vacation house. They took their belongings inside. Bizhan was getting ready to go shopping for the things they needed. Sylvie took a deep breath and said: Amazing weather! I have to go out for a walk and take some pictures.

—You never know, maybe you can get some feeling, too, Farangis said.

Sylvie laughed.

Farangis stayed to clean the house and Nazanin went with Sylvie.

The rain had just stopped. The fragrance of rain and trees filled the air.

Sylvie had put the camera strap over her shoulder and was wearing a pair of sunglasses. She looked like a tourist. Nazanin was jumping up and down with childish joy.

It wasn't long until sunset. Sylvie stopped and took some pictures of the sky; some patches of clouds and long leaves. As they went further they reached some rustic dwellings. Water had filled the ditches in the alley. Three ducks ran behind a wall quacking as they went. A countrywoman in her local costume was standing in front of her house holding her child.

As soon as Sylvie saw them, she took her camera out of its case and took their picture. Then she went closer, took her glasses off and said hello. She was trying to be sincere and casual. The woman's answers were short.

—What is your name? Sylvie finally asked her.

The young woman paused and lowered her head. It was clear that she didn't want to tell her name.

— My name is Sylvia, but my friends call me Sylvie… Now you tell me, what is your name?

—Mahrokh, the young woman said shyly.

Then she said a quick goodbye, went into the yard and closed the door.

—Mahrokh, Mahrokh is a beautiful name!

Sylvia took the camera out of the case again and took a few

pictures of the house and the front door. A few steps away from Sylvie, Nazanin was playing with the ducks. Sylvie stayed there for a while and looked at the country dwelling; then she called Nazanin, put her sunglasses on and took the same road back.

When they got to the house, Bizhan and Farangis was busy preparing dinner. Sylvie told them the story of how she had met Mahrokh.

—She was very nice!

After dinner when Sylvie wanted to put a new roll of film in the camera she noticed there was no film in the camera. At first they all laughed at this, but then as Sylvie was putting the film in the camera she said that tomorrow morning she would go back there to take some pictures of Mahrokh and her kid again.

The door to Mahrokh's house was shut. Sylvie walked up and down the alley a few times and checked around to see if she could see anyone, but the alley was quiet and empty. There was no trace of the ducks either. She made up her mind. She pressed her finger on the doorbell.

Once, twice, three times… the door opened.

A middle-aged, heavyset woman in local costume opened the door; she put her hands on her hips.

Sylvia said hello and asked for Mahrokh.

The woman asked very gravely: What business have you with Mahrokh?

I am Sylvia, a friend of hers. I took some pictures of her yesterday, but… But unfortunately I had forgotten to put film in my camera. That's why I want to take a picture of Mahrokh and her child again.

—You want to do what?

—Picture; I want to take her picture, Sylvia repeated.

—What do you want her picture for?

Sylvie had a hard time understanding her.

—Well, we are friends; I want to have her picture as a souvenir…

—No, now, come on, lady, you go away! What business have you with Mahrokh?

—Look, Madam, tell her to come out for a few minutes; I've got to see her about something... just a few minutes! Sylvia insisted.

The woman stuck her head out and said angrily, What right have you to bother people? "I'm taking pictures! I'm taking pictures!" What are we, kissing cousins?

Sylvie paused. She didn't take her eyes off the lines on the woman's face, but she finally gave up.

—Okay, okay, I am going. Why did you get upset? I am going; goodbye. Say hello to... She didn't finish the sentence. She put her glasses on and took a few steps backward. The ducks came out of the woman's house. It was a good opportunity. Sylvie took a couple of pictures of ducks. Then she started back. As she was going out of sight, she heard the woman:

—Pictures... I'm taking pictures, I ask her, Why are you bothering people?, she says pictures... you go on now, lady; mind your own business!

With long strides, Sylvie returned along the same narrow road she had come; when she got a bit further she stopped and took a picture of the empty road. Then she took a few deep breaths. She drew the clean fresh air into her lungs and continued on her way.

When she got home, Farangis and Bizhan were having breakfast.

—Cool, guys!

Sylvia said hello cheerfully and sat down next to them.

—What happened? Did you take pictures? Farangis asked.

Sylvia paused a little and said: Yes I did, but...

She grew silent. Farangis and Bizhan looked at her.

—Mahrokh was not at home.

Farangis and Bizhan could sense that something had

happened. They didn't say a word. When breakfast was finished, Sylvia sat in the armchair and lit a cigarette. She took a long drag and puffed the smoke into the air.

Bizhan and Farangis were silent.

In the silence of the room, only the sound of the rain hitting the windows could be heard. Sylvia gazed at the window.

—It was sunny just now!

Farangis and Bizhan looked at each other.

—Should we go for a walk? Farangis said.

Sylvie paused for a moment and said: Yes… Yes… it's nice weather.

She went to the veranda faster than Farangis. The rain was coming down harder. She stood on the veranda and looked at the garden, then she went down the veranda's three steps; she held her face up to the sky.

Farangis, Bizhan, and Nazanin were looking at her through the window.

—Sylvia, Sylvia!

The Last Scripture[1]

Dariush Kargar

Rasul himself doesn't know what happened and why, but he left home fifteen minutes early; fifteen minutes earlier. And it is all about those fifteen minutes. Who reported them and how is of no importance. It is not at all important. They came, and Rasul was not home. Rasul had left home fifteen minutes earlier.

On Tuesday, Rasul went to the Kuwaitis' Bazaar. Rasul came back from the Kuwaitis' Bazaar. He sat in the hotel lobby; he talked about the exchange rate of the dollar with Kurosh Khan and delivered the dollars he had bought for him.

The Wednesday after, Rasul went to the Boyuk Bazaar.[2] Then he came back from the Boyuk Bazaar. He was standing in front of the hotel reception desk, and he was talking with Kurosh Khan about the price of Marlboro cigarettes. He gave him the carton of cigarettes he had bought for him.

The following week on Sunday, at three in the afternoon, Rasul went for a walk by the sea with Kurosh Khan.

Two weeks later, on Monday, Kurosh Khan went to Ankara and gave a notebook with somebody's address to Rasul with instructions to give it to that person in his absence.

Sunday, the day before yesterday, Kurosh Khan invited Rasul and his friends, including you (Do you remember?), to lunch in the hotel dining room.

In the middle of the square, there were two cranes. Between the crescents crossing Abasabad and Buali Avenues. The day or time is not important. What is important is Iraj, with that well-groomed look as always, and as always with a smile on his lips, and Yavar, as always with his head down, and perhaps agitated. The call of the salavat[3] *and* takbir[4] *was heard. What is important, they say, is that for all the calling of the salavat and*

the takbir and the crowd, the square was quiet. When the crowd gathered,
they dragged Iraj and Yavar forward. It is not important which of them
was brought forward to stand on the chair first. Iraj laughed and Yavar
was agitated. But it wasn't like that; it didn't happen like it is usually
described: "His body was dancing in the wind." It couldn't have been like
that. Because there wasn't a rope. There was a towing wire. But even
though it was a towing wire, the wind made Iraj's body, for all that heavy
build of his, shake for about an hour. It was jerking up there. Yavar's, too.
Though Yavar was small and skinny until that time you saw him. The
important thing is that they meant to bring three cranes. The important
thing is that though he himself didn't know how or why, Rasul had left
his home fifteen minutes earlier. And there were only two cranes.

Tuesday afternoon, you looked at Rasul. On Wednesday noon
that other week, too; and then the next Sunday you looked at
him again. And two weeks later on Monday evening as well.
The next week, Friday evening, you looked at Rasul. Rasul
didn't look at you. He saw you, but he didn't look at you. He
avoided your look. You weren't alone; Rasul was with you all
the time. But when you were left alone, he disappeared. He
didn't go with those others, but you don't know where he
went; it was impossible; you weren't able to have a word or two
with him. Rasul disappeared.

They go everywhere. Every place has its own appeal. Each one
picks a place and starts working on it. First they check the
conditions for seeking refugee status; checking means asking for
and getting information from those who came a couple of days
earlier. Later, it's asking about the costs: the cost of a visa, a fake
one or a real one; of a ticket, to a far or near place, cheap ones
and expensive ones, American and Russian lines. Some have
decided their destination from Iran. Some have complete
information; they are just waiting for their contacts to show up
one of these days. Some, according to the information, change

their destination and their smugglers every other day. Some have become fed up and want to go back and know they can't and then wonder what to do. There are few customers for America, because the costs are skyrocketing. Not many travelers to England. No one talks about Australia. Germany is the best known place. Not more popular, just better known. It is cheaper than anywhere else; you just get a visa for East Germany, then a few hours' train trip to the West and it's over. All the smugglers say the same thing. There are customers for almost every place; travelers going everywhere. The twin brothers are heading for Costa Rica. The fever for France and Canada is higher than for anywhere else.

Rasul is heading for Canada; his objective is Canada, it has always been Canada. Jimmy has pocketed Rasul's money; he says he hasn't and one of these days he will get some money and send Rasul on his way and until then, instead of 3,500 deutsche marks, he has given his suitcase to Rasul.

Rasul is calling you. With his eyes he indicates the empty seat opposite, between himself and Kurosh Khan.

You take the seat and Rasul gets straight to the point, he laughs and turns to Kurosh Khan:

—Where will you send our Khosrow, Kurosh Khan?

He said it laughing; very casually, sincerely, in a friendly way.

—Where does he want to go?

Kurosh Khan must have understood Rasul's tone. Had they talked about it before? You have a hunch they had.

Ashamed, you keep your head lowered. Rasul made you blush by what he just said. With these words, with what he said, he laughed at all the words in your heart, all the calculations in your mind, all your looks.

You search for his look and it is not there. He doesn't look at you. His laughter has subsided now.

—Wherever!

You wanted to say France but you didn't. You weren't able; you were too shy.

Rasul's tone said it, and your meekly-lowered head said it, too, and Kurosh Khan carries on with his generous act:

—I will send him somewhere sooner or later!

And he holds out his hand to you. Rasul nods, and out of the corner of his eye he indicates Kurosh Khan. You don't get it, and you shrug, and your look moves from one to the other, and Rasul rescues you:

—Give your notebook to Kurosh Khan!

A hand touches your shoulder. You turn. It's Rasul. He laughs:

—Kurosh said he'll send you to Sweden!

—Sweden?

His hand on the plane, Mr. Salimian stops moving his body back and forth. He takes the pencil from behind his ear. He shakes the wood shavings from his gray temples. He picks up his cigarette case and says:

—Sweden and Switzerland used to be one country, but the heavy hand of colonialism split them apart into two countries!

—Really?

Haji Anari says this in a questioning way, and Mr. Salimian, exhaling cigarette smoke from his ches, insists:

—Yes, sir, colonialism! Colonialism!

My tone shows my astonishment. Rasul asks arrogantly:

—Not satisfied?

And he regrets it immediately; his tone changes; his gestures, too:

—He says he'll buy your passport for fifteen hundred marks. Nine hundred goes for your plane ticket; for a hundred marks he will give you a passport—

—A hundred marks? A hundred marks? What is it that costs only one hundred marks?

—It is a passport, after all... he will also give you two

hundred marks to buy yourself clothes to wear for the airport... another two hundred for the police at the airport.

Laughing, the man asks:

—Where're you headed, Khosrow Khan?

The man is new at the hotel, but both he and his wife are so outgoing that they have made friends with everyone over the past few days.

—Me? Me... It looks like Kurosh Khan... It looks like I'm going to Sweden.

The man looks at his wife and frowns slightly. His wife was educated in Mexico. She said so herself; she has a shawl over her shoulders, like them; maybe from there. She toys with the fringes of her shawl and asks with a smile:

—But why Sweden?

The man says:

—You know, it's very cold in Sweden!

—That's not at all important. I come from a cold climate.

And the man continues as if he is not talking to you:

—It is not just Sweden; all Scandinavia is cold. They are all alike... Sweden, Denmark...

A thought strikes you, and you ask:

—Is Sweden like Denmark?

You see Dr. Eslami Nadushan.[5] Is it him? Yes, it is him. His very self, wearing a suit, in the magazine Negin. *He said he called his travel book* The Cry of the Phoenix. *He took the title from the martyred Sheykh Sohrevardi.[6]*

In the section concerning Denmark, the section concerning travel to Denmark, you underlined all the sentences. You read it; Mohammad read it as well. But you are describing it to Mohammad again:

—In the middle of Copenhagen, in the center of town, there is an avenue called "The Pedestrian Avenue." There the street vendors sell books, all kinds, books by Marx, Sartre, Che Guevara and Mao, and a man holding his book up on his chest: the Holy Bible. And another

*man a few steps away has porn magazines with thin transparent plastic
covers over them, hanging like the laundry on a clothesline.*

*—Mohammad, do you think it's gonna take a long time until the
day we get an avenue like that?*

*You stop Mohammad on the street. You point to the vendors and
with a smile, with enthusiasm, you say:*

—Do you remember The Cry of the Phoenix; *the Pedestrian
Avenue? It didn't take that long!*

*Mahmood the baker checks around and controls everything. Then
he raises a stick with wires on the end with his good hand and bangs
on the vendors' stuff. At every blow the apostles of Mahmood yell
behind him:*

—Oh…God…bless…Mohammad…and his family!

Again he asks:

—What do you mean? How do you mean it is like
Denmark? Of course, there are lots of similarities between
Sweden and Denmark…

Rasul gave your message to Kurosh Khan, and Kurosh
Khan said that under all the streets in Sweden is a heating
system and nobody feels the cold there.

—Didn't you tell him we're not that stupid?

—No, really, it's not just Kurosh who says this; all the
Iranians here say the same.

And to make sure, he asks again:

—Then you mean you won't go to Sweden?

There was an army truck. Standing in the middle of the
square. Scared and curious, the quarantined Iranians in Van[7]
walked around the truck and looked at its rear from a few steps
away. A man was handcuffed and sitting on a bench inside the
truck and leaning against the bars between two soldiers who
were holding their guns between their legs. At times he raised
his head and looked around at the crowd, as if he were waiting

for someone, looking for someone. The person next to you said, *They've brought him here on purpose to scare us.* Some people checked him out, looking at him from behind the shoulders of the people in front of them. Someone asked the soldier sitting up by the door of the truck something in Turkish. The soldier told him something, and the same voice said in Persian, *He's Iranian. They're taking him to Yuksokova[8] to hand him over!* The crowd moved back suddenly. *Do you want anything, brother?* Someone yelled from inside the crowd. You shake yourself, and answer:

—Why wouldn't I go to Sweden? I don't know what kind of place it is.

Rasul doesn't sound good; like his mood:

—In any case, whatever it's like, it's better than here, isn't it?

Mr. Dadgar, the English teacher, said, *I saw it myself, sir. I saw a gentleman holding a bag, shopping. I asked my friend, Who is that? He said, The king of Sweden! The king of the country, sir!*

You didn't believe it then, but later, when you read that the Shah, while in Cairo, had said, "I wish I had as much power as the king of Sweden," you think, maybe Mr. Dadgar was not far off the mark.

Rasul calls you, laughing. You remember his laughter that day in the hotel lobby.

Following him, you go to his room. In his room, without saying anything, he takes out a handful of passports from his pocket and puts them on the table in the middle of the room. He says:

—I told Kurosh Khan that our Khosrow's English handwriting is very good.

You were right; it is the same laughter from the other day when he was with Kurosh Khan. He opens the first passport and puts it in front of you. You don't know what it is, and he knows this. With the same laughter he says:

—It's the visa for Sweden. They all have it. You just have to fill them out. Put the name of the passport holder in the section for name and family name and then put a signature under it!

He doesn't ask, Will you write it or not? or Would you please do this for me?—he knows you know they are not for him. They are for Kurosh Khan's passengers, for you too, as well as for Rasul; Kurosh Khan has convinced him that conditions are not right for Canada.

You write the names and sign the name A. Martiny (a few years must pass until you realize that you should have signed a name like Martinson instead of Martiny for it to be closer to a Swedish name.)

You tell Fath-ollah about it, and to give you peace of mind, he tells you that one of the kids went to Sweden six months ago and upon his arrival the government gave him and his wife a pair of bicycles.

You throw cold water on him:

—God bless your father, what do I need a bicycle for? I don't even know how to ride one.

The kids talk about it and laugh; some of them have had a few drinks as well. Nevertheless, there is a feeling of anxiety in them all the time; in their restlessness, in their movements and their looks. A can of beer in his hand, Rasul comes and sits next to you. He holds the can out to you and laughs; as if talking to himself, he says:

—What a hard time I've had!

You take the beer from him. He puts his arms around your neck and kisses your cheek.

—Why are you still upset?

—My dear man, first of all we're still here and we don't know what will happen tomorrow; then...

—No, calm down! Kurosh has seen all the policemen at the airport.

You frown. Rasul opens another can of beer he had been hiding under his arm.

—Well, whether he's right or wrong, let it be, it won't be worse than this...

You remember again. You tried once but you weren't successful. You haven't said this to anyone; you haven't gotten the chance. You are reminded again, and you say abruptly, with no introduction:

—We ourselves are becoming like that, too, Rasul. Our destiny has become the same. You see?

—What? Rasul asks this in surprise.

You say it and you try not to let it bother him. You say it with a smile, in a friendly way:

—I am not talking about us, but many among us, do you remember what they used to say about the Afghanis? *You mustn't live it up at your neighbor's expense*—remember? In the old days, what did we call those who ran away after 1953?[9] Remember? We are becoming like them ourselves. Now we have ended up like them!

Rasul stretches his hand out and puts his beer can on the table. He looks around and gazes at each one of the kids. No, you didn't put it right. You realize that and try to change the subject:

—Are you checking them out, Rasul?

He picks up the beer can again. He taps the opening of the can with his fingertips, holds the can toward himself and lifts it up in front of his face, in front of his eyes. He looks in the opening. Then he stops and looks at you. He looks at the crowd again. Then he stands up. He turns his back without a glance or a word, and with his long stride goes toward the hotel door. He opens the door and disappears. You call him a few times. He doesn't hear you; he doesn't listen. You follow him.

He is not there; there is nothing but darkness outside; night and silence.

—Man, what do I need new clothes for? What's wrong with the ones I have? They're fine.

You have said that many times, but in the end you come home with a gray suit with white stripes.

—What—you don't want them? I'm not saying your clothes are no good, but if you're not well-dressed they'll catch you at the airport. Our papers are messed up; don't let our appearance add to the mess.

You look around and realize he is right. Every place you look, in front of every booth, you see chic suits and nice ties with fine knots. Rasul laughs:

—They're all Iranians, I swear. In this airport there are two kinds of well-dressed people: the flight attendants and pilots in their uniforms, or the ones wearing suits, who are all Iranians. I bet you!

You whisper "suit," and look around again. You miss Pooneh more than ever. They are all men; there is not one woman among them. *How could it be, how is it possible?* You ask yourself and don't find an answer. You think of asking someone, but then you say to yourself, *Who?*

You turn and go on. You say hello to the guys you've met in Istanbul these past few months and move along slowly.

He tells Mehdi he didn't know until last night. That very night. He had heard about it a lot, even more than a thousand times, "Some guy was deported from Belgrade!" "He is one of those deportees! He tried three different routes. But he is stuck with getting deported!" He has concluded, of course after much consideration, that that "experience" should have a meaning. To be a "deportee" means he has an experience. It means that he has the Belgrade experience. Although that doesn't make sense. That's why he asks Mehdi, because they said, they are saying: "If they don't deport you…" *They don't*—what does that mean? What kind of experience is this? Does it mean you have got it wrong so far? How can one give experience to another?

—Of course there is experience. Maybe that's its meaning.

But its real meaning is that he is fucked up. It means they've sent him back!

You greet everyone and move on. Something in your gut, in your mind, does not let you relax. You are restless. You go on. You look around and search for someone, though you know you are not looking for anyone. You go on. Further along, Reza holds your hand and says with a laugh:

—Where are you going in such a hurry?

And with the same laugh he adds:

—You know we are exactly 72 people!

Rasul is standing behind him and says:

—Like the plain of Karbala![10]

Reza's laughter grows louder:

—No, stupid! Like the office of the Islamic Republic Party![11] You look ahead and suddenly you notice, but it is already too late. You are standing ahead of Reza. There is just one person in front of you. And the passport control officer is sitting in his booth; he starts working.

You put the passport donated by Kurosh Khan on the counter. With the same entry stamp he has kindly put in it and the visa you have signed yourself.

You notice the officer's angry red face and hear him yelling and you turn to Reza. It is Reza's voice that says without laughter:

—He says why do you put fake stamps in your passport? Why don't you bring it to us to stamp it for you for free?

—Free?!

—Man, when you put your passport in front of the guy, put a 50-dollar or 50-mark bill in it. Don't forget!

You are stuck. You look at the officer and you don't know, you don't remember what you are supposed to say. You don't remember how, how you are supposed to read faces.

The officer reaches out and opens the low door next to him. He stands up. He grabs your hand, pulls you through the door, and takes you with him.

An officer—you are not familiar with the rank on his shoulder, you don't know—is walking with someone in the transit area. The passport control officer stands in front of him, saluting, showing him respect, and he points at you and shows him your passport; from that distance you see the hole in the first page of your passport.

The officer looks at you. You know a kind look when you see one. He checks you all over with his eyes. He smiles. He taps you on the shoulder and says:

—*Gelecek!*[12]

You raise your head to breathe and hold out your hand for your passport. Your passport, in the hands of the passport control officer, is hiding behind him. The officer's other hand goes into his pocket and comes out with money, and he shows you the duty-free booth:

—A carton of Winstons!

You laugh, take the money and go toward the booth.

He looks around at the crowd. Someone takes a risk and goes ahead and laughs in the face of the soldiers. He takes his hand out of his pocket with a pack of cigarettes and holds it out toward the truck. Toward him.

A voice, you don't see whose, calls:

—Do you want any money, brother?

A woman goes up and talks to the soldiers. The soldier shakes his head and waves his hands. And yells and says something in Turkish. You don't understand what he says, but his tone is not kind; you notice that.

—Man, I don't know what's wrong with them that they keep you two, three weeks in prison in Khoy;[13] of course it depends on your luck. I've seen people there waiting for three months to be sent to prison in Tehran to see what they will decide to do about them!

The plane gets caught in turbulence. It dives down; then suddenly, at the same speed, it comes up. Your guts churn. Reza, sitting next to you, translates the pilot's words for you without turning toward you:

—We are caught in a very bad storm. But don't worry. This is the natural Scandinavian weather, and besides, I have been through worse storms. Rest assured.

Your eyes are turned toward the flight attendants; both are sitting a few rows ahead and holding tight to the pole in the middle of the plane, one of them with closed eyes whispers something to herself. She must be praying, you think; you realize you don't believe the pilot.

The plane dives and you don't know how you came to slide under the seat and Reza lets out a yell and calls the flight attendant and nobody comes and Reza, his seat belt fastened, reaches down and grabs your hands. But it's impossible, you can't come back up. You turn halfway round and try to unfasten your seat belt, which has come loose and is now up under your arms; you turn to pull yourself up. You are coming back into your seat; at that point you notice a magazine; parts of a magazine in the pocket of the seat in front of you. A piece you think is in Arabic and then realize it's in Persian. You sit in your seat and open the magazine, and you realize it is not just one torn piece. There are many pieces, here and there, one after the other. Pieces and clippings from magazines published in Iran dated seven or eight years in the future. One is by the one you like a lot; you like the writer very much; for years you read his stories not with your eyes but with your heart. He has written that you, you and Rasul, have turned your country into a piece of gold; you have put it in your suitcase and are taking it with you. Another piece is by someone whose poems have a special place in your heart. He has written that you—Rasul, Mehdi, and Reza—you all belong to the country you have escaped to; the place the smuggler has chosen for you. There are many pieces of writing. Another one, a short note by someone whose writing and whose person you love, says, *I slipped and fell in a hole and damned all those who went to Sweden and all the other herd-raising countries.*

You notice Rasul is sitting far away from you; three or four rows ahead of you. You can't go show him. You must tear out all the writings in the magazine and put them in your pocket. You must save them for when you land. For the years that they will be published; to show him and tell him, *Didn't I tell you, Rasul?*

The Return

Azar Shahab

The knot is tight, and every time I move it scratches my skin and pierces my flesh. Around me are people who get firewood from nearby and put it around the stake to which I am tied and pour gasoline over it. My knees are numb and my privates are wet with a warm, thick liquid. I am out of breath; I can't scream. I am about to be burned. Someone screams, "That wicked woman should be set on fire!"

I see Hormoz coming toward me. But he is not wearing his shirt with its blue and white stripes lying next to each other, nor do his lips have the usual smile framing his white teeth. He is wearing a white robe and holding a torch in his hand. He has a wound on his forehead. As he approaches, the smell of blood and camphor fills the air. Uncertainly and sadly, he looks at me.

A cry makes him move. "Hurry up, Hormoz, what are you waiting for?" Hormoz thrusts the torch inside the firewood. The fire starts to blaze; then there is pain and burning. Think of it as eternal and everlasting. Moans tear my throat.

— Homa! Homa! Wake up, dear!

I sit up in my bed.

— Did you dream about Hormoz again?

—Yes; with the same torch.

Mother sighs. She stands up and goes to the kitchen to make me cowslip tea. She comes back with a glassful of the purple stuff.

— Get up and drink this tea; it will make you feel better.

— I can't; nothing goes down my throat.

— Force yourself; it's good for your nerves. And stop thinking so much. Don't cry over spilled milk.

— It's because of this spilled milk that I am suffering. Milk that could have been saved from being spilled, and which I could have stopped from spilling if I hadn't been so careless. Mother, if I had gone with Hormoz this would never have happened. What Hormoz went to take care of and never returned, we were supposed to do together. I didn't go. I got tied up and couldn't go. He went alone and got arrested. If I had known this would happen, I would have gone with him no matter what. No, no, I would never have let him go. I would have stopped him from going.

—I don't know what that poor unfortunate did that trapped him. Maybe it was God's will that you didn't go with him; otherwise you would have met the same fate. My dear, what's done is done. You didn't think through from the beginning how this would end. Such a pity, the youths who were executed. Each of them was like a bouquet of flowers. Such a pity, Hormoz. This is what we are left with! Your father has gone clean out of his mind; Hormoz's wife and children wandered off to a foreign land. Worst of all is the wound it has left on my heart. May God never let any mother and father suffer such a wound. My dear, it's not your fault; I don't know; maybe this was his destiny.

She says it wasn't my fault. But whenever the sound of her prayers rise, there are elements of reproach in them that follow me, and I run up the stairs, taking every other step until I reach the twilight in my room. When I light the candles, the darkness in my room grows thin; so thin that in the corner next to the window facing the street you can see a framed picture in which Hormoz and Sima are standing; young and beautiful. Sima is covered from head to toe in white lace with tiny white flowers resting on her chestnut hair; her long hands clasped under her bosom, shame at a hidden smile on her face, which bears no sign of the passage of time. Standing next to her, Hormoz is wearing a shirt, its blue and white stripes lying side by side, and blue pants. His right hand is on Sima's shoulder. Saddened, he is looking straight into my eyes. To block his gaze, I cover his eyes with my hands. I tell him, "Don't look at me like that!" I blow out the candles until darkness creeps in through the cracks like a ghost and spreads around my room, dense and weightless, to cover the picture frame and cast a shadow on the mirror that multiplies me; and I am left alone, once again, with no image of myself.

Mornings, Father sits in the room by the window facing the veranda and the courtyard, and the house becomes drowned in his hallucinations. He leans back on the cushion. His look passes through the fragrance of the jasmine. It crosses the narrow sand path, arrives at the round blue pool and turns around the moss-covered wooden stairs. Once it reaches the sunflowers, you can no longer follow the track of his look. It goes on. Ever so far away. Surely to times long past. It pauses somewhere. He stares, and when he turns his head we know Hormoz has come. But Hormoz is not wearing that blue-and-white-striped shirt, nor does he have a smile on his lips framing his straight white teeth. He is wearing a white robe and has a wound on his forehead that smells of blood. He walks so slowly that even silence cannot hear his footsteps.

He sits down. He talks to Father. We don't hear his voice; neither do we see his shadow. We do not even touch him. As if he is a feeling that is there and not there. Afterwards, Father tells us what he said and what he heard.

When Hormoz leaves, Father stoops like a bent bow. His eyes grow red. Sorrow shatters his look. He gets up and goes to the courtyard. The flapping sound of his slippers scares the fish in the pool.

Evenings, my mother wears a black headscarf as old as she is. She spreads her prayer cloth, a souvenir from Mecca blessed by circumambulating the Black Stone.[1] She slides the prayer beads between her gaunt fingers. She turns her head from side to side and whispers something rising and falling, which drowns the house in the scent of mourning. Prayer and weeping comfort her. Then she takes the prayer cloth away and puts it in its maroon velvet box and takes an old envelope out of the same place; she holds it under her *chador*² as if she wants to keep it away from the evil eye. She comes and sits on the veranda and opens the envelope. Hormoz's daughter slides out of it. Her hair has grown long; it is jet black, just like Hormoz's hair. With her fingertips she pushes the hair away from Nazli's face and says, "When her bangs are to one side, she looks more like Hormoz." I burst out crying. When Nazli's face grows wet, she draws her eyebrows together in a frown. Mother takes her handkerchief out from the pocket of her *val*³ dress and dries her face. She points at me to stop crying and forces herself to smile; when she sees the gleam of happiness in Nazli's eyes, she kisses the photo and puts it back in the envelope so that she will sleep peacefully. Then she spreads out their bedding on the rooftop. She puts my bedroll next to theirs so that when the fire burns my bones and I start to scream she can wake me up. And she does wake me up. I wake up drenched in sweat. I wrap the sheet around me and go down to the courtyard. It is twilight. They must have killed Hormoz at twilight.

I tell my mother, "I have to go, away from this city, this house, this country. I have to start my life somewhere else. I will go be with Sima and Nazli."

—Then your father will die of sorrow. He is not feeling well, as things are now. He keeps telling me you are wrong; they have not killed Hormoz; it's a case of mistaken identity. He says Hormoz comes to visit him every day.

—It's hard for me to leave you alone, too, but what else can I do? I have lost everything here. My friends, my brother, my hopes; I've lost them all. I am left with a handful of bitter memories and an unbearable nightmare. My hands are tied everywhere I turn. I am not allowed to work; to go to school; to have a house; not even to live.

—I know, my dear; I know you are having an awfully hard time.

—Well, talk to Father. Try to convince him. Show him Sima and Nazli's photos; tell him they are fine, they have a good life in Holland now. Tell him Homa wants to go be with them, too.

—But my dear, having a house and a good life is no substitute for a companion.

—I know Sima longs for Hormoz, but after all she has a right to live where she is. Her life there is better than in this godforsaken place.

—Go, my dear. God be with you.

Her voice breaks. She goes into the kitchen to turn on the samovar so I won't see her crying.

When I say goodbye to Father, he does not turn his head to bid me farewell with his look. He has leaned back on the cushion in the room facing the courtyard that is drowned in the fragrance of the jasmine. His look crosses the narrow sand path, arrives at the round blue pool and turns around the moss-covered wooden stairs. Once it reaches the sunflowers, you cannot follow the track of his look. It goes, ever so far away.

Tomorrow, with Hormoz, I will come to visit Father.

You're the Jackass!

Sirus Seif

The car stopped. The smuggler opened the door and said:

—We're here. Get out!

The man from Hell said:

—Where am I?

The smuggler said:

—Heaven!

The man from Hell said:

—Heaven?

The smuggler asked:

—Didn't you say you wanted to get away from Hell?

The man from Hell answered:

—Why, yes!

The smuggler said:

—Well! I got you out, now you're in Heaven. Get out, why don't you!

The man from Hell got out and the smuggler disappeared along with his car. The man from Hell looked around, wondering where he should go. A car stopped in front of him. A ghelman[1] got out of the car and walked toward him. From the appearance of the ghelman and his outfit, the man from Hell thought he must be one of the heavenly cupbearers. The ghelman, smiling, stopped the man from Hell and said something in heavenly language, the meaning of which the man from Hell couldn't understand. The man from Hell conveyed to the ghelman with gestures that he didn't understand him. Still smiling, the ghelman respectfully directed the man from Hell toward the car. The man from Hell got in. After driving around some avenues in Heaven, the car stopped. He and the ghelman got out of the car. Passing through some long and short hallways, they entered a room where the ghelman politely handed the man from Hell over to a houri; smiling at the man from Hell, he left the room. The man from Hell looked at the houri, who smiled at him in response. The houri's smile delighted the man from Hell. The houri said something the man from Hell couldn't understand again. This time the houri winked as she smiled and picked up the phone and dialed a number. She spoke on the phone and hung up. With some appetite, some fear, some love, some curiosity, some respect, some regret, some lust, and some... anyway, holding her hand under her chin, she stared at the man from Hell the way only someone from Heaven could stare at someone from Hell. At that moment, the door opened and someone who looked like he was also from Hell entered. First he greeted the houri in heavenly language and then put a folder he was holding under his arm in front of the man from Hell so that he could read the writing on the folder, which was written in the language from Hell. Then he shook hands with the man from Hell and greeted him in the language of Hell and sat on a chair. The writing on the folder read as follows:

> I have also come from the same place as you. I am a certified interpreter. In this room, our voices and images are being recorded with hidden cameras. I am here to translate this lady's questions and your answers. Be careful not to say anything private to me; it will be to your detriment.

After reading the writing, the man from Hell looked around the room out of the corner of his eye; having made sure of the existence of the cameras, he pulled himself together and in the language of Hell he said to the interpreter:

—I got it!

The interpreter responded in panic:

—Sorry. Did you say something?

The man from Hell, who realized his mistake, said:

—No! I just said I hope to be able to get a residency permit!

After a nervous cough, the interpreter turned to the houri and said something in the language of Heaven. Placing her heavenly fingers on the keyboard, the houri turned to the interpreter and said something. In the language of Hell, the interpreter asked the man from Hell:

—She is asking which part of your body is burned.

The man from Hell answered in astonishment:

—What do you mean?

The interpreter said:

—If you have come from Hell, then...

—From Hell?

—Didn't you say you came from Hell?

—Me?

After a couple of nervous coughs the interpreter said:

—This lady means that...

The man from Hell remembered what his smuggler had told him and said:

—Oh! Hell! Yes! I get it! From Hell!

The interpreter said:

—Well, if you have come from Hell, you should prove it. That's why she is asking you which part of your body is burned.

The man from Hell laughed and said:

—It looks like this houri is joking. What does she mean, Where am I burned?

After a few more nervous coughs, the interpreter said:

—No, this is not the place for jokes; where are you burned?

Offended, the man from Hell answered:

—My soul is burned. Tell her my soul is burned!

The interpreter asked:

—Your soul?

The man from Hell said angrily:

—Looks like you didn't understand what I meant! My soul! My soul!

—I understood you perfectly, but... here...

—Then please translate!

—Very well!

The interpreter said that to the houri. The houri typed it and said something to the interpreter. The interpreter said to the man from Hell:

—She says you have to show it. You have to show where you are burned.

—Show the burn on my soul?

—Yes.

The man from Hell got up in frustration and said:

—What kind of question and answer is this?

The interpreter, who was trying to control his coughing, said:

—I said! I mean you said it yourself that your soul! Well! I said I understood... but here... well that's why... well... calm down and... well... not much can be done... well...

The man from Hell said:

—You don't need to keep saying "well, well." I know what you mean!

—Well this is what this lady means: she wants to know where on your soul is it burned.

The man from Hell sat on the chair, grumbled in anger and frustration, and said:

—I can't show you!

The interpreter, who had given up on helping the man from Hell, told that to the houri, and the houri typed it as she looked at the man from Hell with a smile and said something to the interpreter in Heavenly language. The interpreter said:

—She says, do you have any questions? If you have any questions for her, you may ask them!

Suddenly, the man from Hell leaped to his feet and...

Until a few years ago, as long as the color of your eyes and hair was black and the color of your skin was brown or dark, it would be enough. But ever since the people of the world started coming to Heaven in large groups, due to the excessive supply of the people in their markets, the different parts of Heaven have gotten together to close all the air, sea, ground, and underground routes of Heaven to the people from Hell. They have revised their laws for accepting people from Hell. According to the new laws, despite the pressure from the "Dis-United Nations" to accept a few people from Hell, the black or brown color of skin and hair and eye is no longer a decisive factor. The criteria now are the burns on people's body by the fire of their Hell. The higher the degree of burns, the greater the chance of being accepted for residency in Heaven. There has been a rumor that lately only those people from Hell whose degree of burn is one hundred percent have a chance to stay in Heaven. That is probably why some of the people from Hell living in camps have started setting themselves on fire.

Accused of assault on the houri, in one of the prisons of Heaven, our man from Hell, is now awaiting his trial. The reporter who returned from the prison after conducting an interview with the prisoners has said that our man from Hell is suffering from a very dangerous mental illness and will be transferred to a mental institution. It appears that the dangerous mental illness of our man from Hell became evident to the agents of Heaven when, in response to a compassionate agent of Heaven who suggested he set himself on fire to obtain residency and freedom, he said:

—You're the jackass!

Postcards Side by Side

Ghodsi Ghazinour

When I told the doctor something was wriggling in my head like a creature, moving around in its sleep, he laughed. He said, "Sometimes one tends to have such thoughts. A while ago I had a patient who insisted he had a tumor as big as an apple in his head; he would even show its size with his hands; do you think the matter was solved after a few X-rays I took of his head?" He laughed again.

I told myself this ridiculous laughter would fade from his lips once he saw everything with his own eyes, but when he showed me the X-rays he had taken of my head, the smile was still there. He said, "You see! One does tend to have such thoughts."

It didn't make any difference to me whether I saw the X-ray of that sleeping creature or not, because I could still feel it as clearly as I feel my heart or my kidneys although I don't see them.

Yet for a few days there was no sign of any movement from that ill-natured creature. I thought, perhaps it slipped out of my ear while I was asleep, and not being able to find me, it got lost. Behrooz had gone on a trip for a few days, and I had left the house early in the morning.

When Behrooz returned and I gave him the good news on the doorstep that I didn't feel lightheaded any more, he said, "Did you feel lightheaded before?" I didn't get mad; it's been a long time since anything about him has made me mad; I have come to realize that his ears function only when he hears something related to himself; as far as he's concerned, everything else is a lot of rubbish he doesn't want to waste time over.

I asked him how the weather was over there. It was great here. He said, "I didn't even have time to scratch my head; I went straight from this room to a friend's house and stayed there until I returned. It was a very important meeting." I asked, What about on the way? Didn't you enjoy the scenery? The road to Switzerland is very beautiful. He said, "I was working on my notes all the way." I asked, All the way? He looked at me.

All of a sudden I felt that strange creature rolling about in my head; so it hadn't got lost. I burst out laughing. Behrooz said, "What's so funny?" I said, I didn't laugh at what you said; I've been happy ever since I found out that there is no tumor as big as an apple or a coiled snake in my head, I found the cure for my dizziness. He said, "I didn't know you get dizzy." I said, I don't anymore!

As I looked at him, I felt sorry for him. During these few years we have been living in Brussels, he has not even seen a street or two; he has been spending all his time with his old friends ruminating about the years of the Revolution.

As it's a long time since he left Iran, whatever he has in his baggage belongs to those years, and because he has turned his back on everything here, he belongs neither here nor there. His words have grown moldy, and their foul smell fills the room.

A while ago on TV, I saw a film called *Twenty Square Meters of German Soil* about a Turkish laborer who had come to Germany with his wife to work. Every day on leaving the house, he locks his wife in; until his return the woman can only move around within the twenty square meters. Only after the man dies does the woman get to leave the house and see the light of day. Her husband left her in that room; Behrooz, though, has imprisoned himself, and no one can liberate someone who has imprisoned himself; he has no jailor by whose death he can be freed; there is no freedom for Behrooz.

I decided to liberate myself; to find out about the things I had read about in books; to visit the places I had only seen in pictures; and I set out.

A few days later I sent Behrooz a postcard; I wrote: The

saying, "The sky is the same color everywhere" is a big lie; the sky here is bluer.

I don't know what his response was; since he doesn't know where I am, he cannot answer me; but I can imagine the reaction on his face; he has raised his left eyebrow, his nostrils have flared, and, shaking his head in disapproval, he has said to himself, "I had noticed the signs of such petit-bourgeois fantasies in her;" and to feel better he has started playing "Dayeh Dayeh Vaghte Janga"[1] and started to make notes on the anti-revolutionary nature of the petty bourgeoisie; I wished he could see the smile on my lips resembling the doctor's smile.

One day I saw an unfamiliar suitcase among the stuff I had brought with me; I wondered, To whom might it belong? What could be inside it? And what is it doing here? I decided to open it and find out.

It contained a lot of bitter memories of bygone years; as soon as these memories started to spring out and fill everything around me again, I closed the suitcase and dumped it in the garbage can at the end of the street; but when I returned home I noticed that it was still sitting there. I realized there was no escape from this baggage for me; whether I wanted it to or not, it would follow me everywhere. I put a heavy lock on it and left it somewhere out of sight and threw the key into the big river in the city.

I sent Behrooz another card; I wrote, There is a girl here who can tell the difference between the fragrance of cherry and almond blossoms, and I envy her.

It would be interesting to see the look on Behrooz's face after he reads this card.

One day Behrooz was talking about some subject; all the time pointing at me, he would say, "In our opinion... " When I protested, he said, "We are one, aren't we?" I said, Yes we are, because I have been dissolved in you; I have no opinions of my own; but from now on I want to be my own self. He looked at me in amazement. I said, Why do you think you are the Ka'aba? And whoever turns his back on you is an unbeliever? He was going crazy.

The next card I sent him, I wrote, There is a woman here who used to hear a scream that others couldn't; she thought the other people were deaf, but now she has found out that she has been hearing her own scream. A scream she had never let out and should have; now she is screaming and no longer hears the sound. I have met someone here who has made a collection of the names of strange people with a detailed biography for each one, like a story; the collection is called a human menagerie; when I asked if these are the people who were not supposed to be born, I was told that these are the only people who should have been born. This person says she hates the people who want to save the world, because they will shoot the ones who do not want to be saved; she says dictatorship started from this point.

I think after reading this, Behrooz's mind must have been swelling up like a mushroom. He must have thought it was referring to him, but the one who wrote these words does not know him.

In my last postcard to him I wrote that I met a man here who says the sky anywhere nearer to the beloved is bluer; I am learning the meaning of love from him; by the way, why didn't we know what the meaning of love is? I have realized that I like fresh air; I like the sky, the snow, the rain, and the sunshine. I watch the rainbow after the rain, and I grow. I wrote to him that I am growing and growing, and that whatever mold he makes for me would become too tight after a while.

If he puts the cards I have sent him in order, side by side, he will realize how much I have grown. Like the pictures of a child at different periods of her growth; if you look at them, the first one looks like a picture of a frog with its eyes shut; the second one with open eyes but crawling; and in the third picture she is upright.

Where she will go, and for how long, will be shown in the next pictures; the pictures that haven't yet been taken. I don't know where I am going and how far I will go, but I know that I am standing on my own two feet.

Hourglass

Mahasti Shahrokhi

Once I wrote something before I went to sleep; a few days later when I was looking for something among my notes I came across the piece again: "Oh, man, what's this? How come...? Hmm... how could it be?"

Apparently it could be! I had written these few lines:

> My life has become just like an hourglass; the moments fall one by one and pile up until the night arrives. At night you have to turn this hourglass over so you can measure the time. Then once again, the sands fall, in the darkness, grain by grain, moment by moment. It seems a balance has been found between this sleeping, these nightmares, and the nightly trips of my soul, and that I can no longer continue my days without them. As if I am leading a double life.

I was thinking, Is it because of rereading *The Blind Owl*[1] or because of this dog's life in Paris? But if this situation continues... I hope I don't... I hope it doesn't happen to me that one day I am compelled, in his style, to get rid of the story's only heroine, the only worthwhile woman, and without rhyme or reason... but no! There is nothing to worry about! In any case, my feminine language and my independent way of looking at things will prevent me from catching this malignant illness and that contagious virus... but it seems I knew this delirious piece of writing... Once, just as an experiment, I read it to a friend.

—Who wrote this? Can you tell?

—It is Hedayat, isn't it? Why are you laughing? I am right, aren't I?

—How did you know?

—Told you, didn't I? It was absolutely obvious!

Maupassant once wrote: *La solitude est dangereuse pour les intelligences qui travaillent... Quand nous sommes seuls longtemps, nous peuplons le vide de fantômes.*[2]

Maupassant was right; otherwise what could have been the meaning behind writing that half-finished paragraph, with no beginning or end, without any preamble, on a blank piece of paper? After that, for a long time, there was no sign of wandering ghosts in the middle of the night... Some time later, I took another look at those few lines. I was thinking that one day, if they leave me, a member of the post-suicide generation, alone, I would write a few lines describing the life of this international writer and what was going on with him in the winter of 1936, when he was sitting behind a pitiful mimeograph in Bombay and, to get in the faces of governmental and non-governmental publishers, making fifty copies of his handwritten novel with his own money; but this was just an idea. It came and went. It came, but it didn't settle on the paper. It came, but for reasons other than lack of paper, rather because of the ordinary mundane problems of living in exile, the writing of these few lines was postponed.

Last spring, on a cold and rainy day, the sound of the thunder and pouring rain made me spring up from sleep. I had heard a sound. It seemed that someone was pounding on the door and trying somehow to find a way in. Then they were banging on the window. It was dark. I wasn't sure whether they were knocking at the door or the window! I sat in bed until morning, eyes wide open, and gave myself over to the assault of feelings of loneliness, terror, and fear of the supernatural, which were changing places with one another regularly.

In the morning the thunder and lightning stopped. The downpour was over. The sky was clear. The intermittent sound of blows stopped. Then I was able to close my eyes and sleep a while. The following day I was telling myself: "Three or four days living like this and you will go out of your mind!" I was arguing with myself: "Why are you fussing and carrying on? Do you want to go out of your mind? Fine, go crazy! Why are you looking for an excuse? One needn't have a reason to go crazy!" And then I was giving myself moral support: "Believe me, there are so many people who have gone crazy for no reason, with no motive! Why do you take everything so hard?" But during the following nights I kept waking up suddenly. One night I woke up to the sound of tapping. It was the heater. Another night I heard another sound; it was the drain in the bathroom. Another night it was as if someone were scratching at the door. Another night it was as if someone were knocking at the window. Another night the wind was swirling under the eaves and a small window had been left open and kept on banging. The last time I was wakened abruptly by a noise that sounded vaguely like a child crying or howling far away, and from the edge of the curtain I saw the glittering of two bright eyes on the opposite balcony. I was telling myself: "Oh poor you! It's all up with you! You're done for!"

"Tomorrow morning birds will sing!"

Charlie Chaplin said this in *City Lights*, I still remember it. The following day when I woke to the singing of the birds, I thought of Charlie and slowly opened the window to the spring. Outside the window a large black cat was sleeping on a large, round flowerpot.

"Ah, so it was you!"

Finally, after years and years, having so often said "I might come," "In any case, I think I will come," toward the end of autumn, Siyavash came from Tehran to Paris. In those days, some of the Iranians residing abroad held conferences and lectures so that famous people and unknowns would express their views about Iran and its future problems. By the way, what would happen to the "Motherland" in the twenty-first century?

That autumn Sunday morning, "we all," that is Siyavash and

I, like all necrolatrous Iranians, instead of thinking about what we could do about our poor motherland, went to the Père Lachaise Cemetery, to the graves of Hedayat and Saedi.[3] Before going to the cemetery, I went to the florist to buy flowers, but suddenly all flowers seemed to me faded and artificial, decayed and banal. Fearing that I might get lost among the graves, I bought a map of the cemetery and left the florist.

Like a well-kept garden, neatly laid out, orderly and tranquil, the cemetery awaited us. Throughout the previous night it had rained. Everything was washed and sopping wet. Stone statues with pained, suffering faces were silently standing guard among the graves. I was looking at the statue of a winged angel kneeling on a grave as if reading the writing on the stone: "By the way, why should we, during our holidays, disturb the sleep and comfort of the dead?" I was walking slowly so I wouldn't disturb the sleep and repose of their Sunday morning. Some of the graves were covered with flowers or wreaths. By the way, would this rain of flowers on the graves heal any pain?

I wanted to tell Siyavash, "Saedi, too, was greatly influenced by Hedayat." But I didn't say it. In fact, which of them hadn't been influenced by Hedayat and, imitating him, hadn't examined the darkness of existence? I looked at the stone statue of two weeping women standing on either side of a family mausoleum.

—You know, instead of a bouquet of flowers, some friends come to his grave with a bottle and a glass!

He wasn't at all surprised. Whenever he was surprised he would shake his head and say, "That's amazing!"

He said, "I might have guessed." So he probably had guessed. For a moment I stood in front of a statue whose two hands had taken hold of the bars of the tomb from inside the mausoleum. One might say that these two stone hands belonged to someone who was trying to uproot those bars and save himself from the black hole of death.

—Siya, they seem to have forgotten that despair and alcohol killed him; he might still be alive otherwise.

I hadn't yet finished my sentence before I regretted saying it. We hadn't reached his grave yet. I wanted to explain something to Siyavash, who had just come from Iran. "One cannot experience it in a short trip. It is exactly like an hourglass... grain by grain... moment by moment... until one's patience is exhausted and finally one day one reaches a point where one can no longer tolerate this kind of life... no longer wants to turn over the hourglass of this repetitive, routine, unchangeable life... That's when one puts the final period to one's life... or drowns himself like Gholamhosein... in a small bottle."

An angel with broken wings was sitting on a grave. Was it death that had broken the wings of the angel? But angels didn't die, did they? I didn't say anything. I waved to Siyavash:

—Move away! I want to take a picture!

We walked in complete silence until we reached his grave. Still in silence, we set the wet flowers on the grave aside and took pictures. Siyavash smoked a cigarette in silence; then, as if he had finished a conversation with himself, he said, "That's amazing!"

Now he was definitely surprised by something; but his voice was choked; it discouraged me from saying a great deal. I couldn't let him sit, in his mind, next to his "immortals" and like all Iranians, go willingly and in a "spiritual" way toward mourning and be drowned in a world full of sighs and moans and regrets. I wanted desperately to dispel that atmosphere.

—He was so alive that he cannot be dead and people cannot cry for his death. Every time I come to his grave I think he is asleep under this gravestone... because he is tired. I don't know why I feel he needs a long rest and we shouldn't wake him up... sometimes I think he is coughing inside his grave...

See!... Now!... Right here!... he has just lain down!

I pointed to the white stone on his grave and said:

—He has pulled this white stone over himself like a heavy blanket; he's pretending to be asleep... but I am sure that under the ground he is quietly listening to us and laughing at us.

—You've all changed a lot.

It was Siyavash who was speaking to me.

—All of you have become like stone!

I had pulled him out of the world of the dead but I had gone too far joking. It was tasteless. "You have changed!" "You have become like stone!" Why don't you say it, "You are dead!" It was pretty difficult for me to say "Believe me, by God, I am not dead yet!" By the way, why did he say "You all" and not just "You?" Which group of people did he include me in? With these dead people? Or in which group of living people? We reached Hedayat's grave. Did he think "all of us" were dead? That "all of us" had become stone? That was certainly it! Had "I" changed so much and turned into a stone? Was I just a ghost in his mind who belonged to the past in the cemetery of old memories? Once more, a mistake... it was my fault; I had brought him to the cemetery. Of course I knew him well enough to know that if I had taken him to a discotheque or a dancehall he would have said, "So, is this what you mean by freedom?" If I had taken him to a library or museum or exhibition he would have said, "So, with all this cultural freedom and abundance, why are you complaining all the time?" Of all the rotten luck! Now that we have come to the cemetery he thinks "all of us" are buried alive.

We removed the flowerpots and flowers from Hedayat's tombstone. The black marble cone-shaped rock with the design of an owl carved on it was revealed. We took pictures of the tombstone and moved a little away from it.

—Saedi said that this is not a tombstone, this is a desk on which to work.

He took a deep breath and said impatiently:

—Yeah, yeah!

While I wasn't at all sure whether he was listening to me or not, I continued:

—A year before his death, he said, "This is not Hedayat's grave, this is his cradle."

He glanced at the conical black tombstone:

—So he said!

I kept telling myself, "Listen, dear lady, sometimes it is better, I mean, more respectable, if you don't talk at all rather than ruminate over these trivialities!" Finally I kept quiet. We had moved a few steps away from Hedayat's grave and were standing next to the grave of Marcel Proust, Hedayat's current neighbor. A tall, thin woman who was not at all beautiful came and placed a spray of red flowers on Proust's grave. For a little while, she stood there in silence; then she left and we watched her as she was walked away in silence. Proust had written, *Laissons les jolies femmes aux hommes sans imaginations!*[4]

The tall, thin woman moved away slowly until she was out of sight and we couldn't see her any longer. Our eyes returned to Hedayat's grave and that large tree that shades it and reminds me of my grandfather's grave in Zahir al-Doleh[5] under the shade of a huge eglantine, and, as my mother would say, "How fortunate!"

—Do you see the tree?

—Yes!

—How fortunate!

As if it were yesterday that we had gone to the cemetery together. But no, it wasn't yesterday; it was many years ago. We were both ten years old. Grandfather had just died and we, carefree, were running among the graves. We had not felt the greatness of death yet and we were very surprised that the grownups were crying so much. As if it were yesterday. But no, it wasn't yesterday. It was a few years ago. We were both twenty years old. We were wearing black, head to toe, and crying like grownups over the death of Siyavash's father. He had died too soon. When it comes to dying, it is always too soon! The summer of that same year we were sitting on the veranda of their house. It was midnight. The sky was a plain of stars. Everyone was asleep. "All of us" were hearing only the sound of crickets at the end of the garden and the singing of the flies around the fluorescent light on the veranda. Suddenly Siyavash broke the silence, "My life is finished!"

Since childhood, I mean, as far back as I can remember, ever since I learned how to think, Siyavash would say strange things. When he saw my surprised face he continued, "I have gone through the most important stages of my life: infancy, childhood, adolescence, youth."

—Well, that's just the beginning!

—Ah no! From this point on it is the continuation of youth and then old age and death. And I don't like the idea of dying of old age at all.

I can't remember what my answer was, because many years have passed. Certainly like Charlie Chaplin in *City Lights* I said a bunch of clichés in praise of life. Certainly.

—How fortunate!

As if it were yesterday. How far we had come from yesterday to today, from Zahir al-Doleh to the cemetery of Père Lachaise. The voice of my mother watching the branch of eglantine over grandfather's grave and saying "How fortunate!" was still in my ears.

I wanted to explain to Siyavash, like a tourist guide, "There are furnaces near here where they burn the corpses!" My eyes fell on a black cat sitting on Hedayat's tombstone, and I remembered the cat that had come behind my window.

That spring morning as soon as I opened the window I saw a black cat outside the window. It was completely black. That was it! The cause of that scratching on the window and the door; and the glittering of those bright eyes from the other side of the window, and that untimely nightly knocking. Yes, that was it. The black cat woke up to the sound of the opening of the window and opened his eyes and glanced at me. It seemed as if he had been waiting for a long time for me to open the window. He was looking at me with a dispassionate, yet wrathful expression, as if he wanted to say, "Well, so you finally opened the window?" I was standing there looking at him. But before I could think of something or show a reaction, he drifted slowly away. He was gazing at me insolently. Slowly he rose from the dirt of the flowerpot, shook his body and went away. He was moving off in such a way as if all this time he had been waiting for me to open the window and then look at him so that he could leave me and I could see him leaving; because leaving someone without them seeing it is useless. When someone leaves us we suddenly feel their presence, exactly like this cat. All his supernatural signs, the glitter of his eyes, that nightly scratching on the door and the window had not given him the presence that his leaving did. His back was still toward me and he was passing heavily on the edges of the windows of the fourth floor. I could see him from the window; his tail was so short... no, it was cut off! Why? In a fight with other cats... or because of the mischief of bums? The black cat was not looking at me anymore. I wanted to call him but he was walking with such dignity that I couldn't find any suitable name. I remembered Nazi, the cat from "Three Drops of Blood."[6] But the severed tail reminded me of the scar on the face of Dash Akol;[7] the same scar which gave him character and dignity and made him different from other men. We were still in the cemetery standing next to Marcel Proust's grave. Proust had written, *On ne connait pas son bonheur, on n'est jamais aussi malheureux qu'on croit.*[8]

I pointed to the black cat on the grave:

—This is one of those who like his work.

Hearing our voice the black one turned and glanced at me. Siyavash was looking at the cat.

—That's him!

The black cat turned his face and shook himself as he was rising from the tombstone.

—What do you mean?

—Maybe his soul has been reincarnated in the body of these trees and pigeons and other birds here!

Now the black cat was going toward the box trees. I wanted to ask, "Are you joking or are you serious?"

Before I could say anything he said emphatically:

—It could be him!

The black cat had stuck his head in the box trees. We were not talking seriously, or as seriously as anyone can be while uttering such statements. I said:

—I wish this poor beast could tell us... I wish I could know...

The cat had run off into the box trees and could not be seen anymore. Laughing, Siyavash said:

—What is it that you want to know?

—For example... for example, is suicide much more painful than ordinary death, or are they not that different?

I was looking at the grave. The black cat was not visible anymore. Siyavash followed my look:

—The one who doesn't stay is actually escaping!

After that, we walked along the paths of the cemetery, in silence, aimlessly. Siyavash was on a roll and he was walking one step ahead of me and as always when he was on a roll he was talking continuously and lecturing:

—Suicide and alcohol and narcotics... or madness and exile are inseparable pieces of a writer's destiny...

I was looking at that crowd of tombstones and stone

statues. Logically, by now we should be at the northeastern end of the Père Lachaise cemetery. As I was looking at the tombstones and statues to figure out where we were, I wanted to say, "Some writers, maybe because of bad luck, carry the weigh of all the side effects of writing." But I didn't say anything. I was confused. I thought we weren't where I thought we were. Paying no attention to me, Siyavash was continuing his lecture. He was walking straight in front of me and was somewhere else. As always, he was busy with his speech:

—For example, from Naser Khosro to Molavi, from Hedayat to Ferdosi, from Masud-e Sa'd-e Salman to Khaqani...!

I took out the map. I was trying to find out where exactly we were standing:

—Oh, man! As usual, we are lost in the vast realm of cemeteries and death!

At the moment when I was looking at the map to find a way to get out of the cemetery I wanted to tell him the story of the black cat, "I am sure he won't believe it! He would think as he always does that I have 'imagined' things!" I changed my mind. According to the map we were at the southeastern end of the cemetery. What a big mistake!

On our way there was the memorial for the Jews who had been killed during the Second World War... the same Jews who had been lost in the crematoria or the gas chambers. For a moment I thought I would show the memorial to Siyavash, but I knew this would spoil his short trip. I let it go. Without my wanting it, the black cat and those few drops of blood at the foot of the pine tree[9] and those scars were on my mind. For a moment I wanted to just tell him, "In the building where I live there is a black cat that I have named Dash Akol." But I realized that then I would also have to tell him about the scratching and the knockings, and so on. I knew that after half an hour he would bring up some subject so that he could show off his sympathy, "Take good care of yourself! I mean the cold weather!" I was afraid he would say, "Don't work so hard!" or that he would start performing in order to display his pity, "Take better care of yourself," or try to be compassionate, "With the kind of demanding schedule that you have and all the energy you are putting into your work one cannot expect anything more from you." Or he could, in his own mind, become nice and kind and order me, "You should rest a bit!" Or in the end, he would think for a while in silence and then ask suddenly, "Don't you want to return? What have you stayed here for?" I was afraid of all this. I didn't say anything so I wouldn't hear an answer. But a thought was gnawing at me inside. Words such as "all of you," "all of us," "the motherland" were going round and round in my head and even the thought of "the motherland" entering the twenty-first century brought tears to my eyes. For a moment I just looked up from the map:

—Siya, sometimes I feel that every step we take we get one step closer to death.

He was walking ahead; he turned:

—What? Did you say something?

—I said, if we keep walking like this... we will get to the exit gate right in front of us.

We were out of the cemetery now and were walking in the world of the living. His head was up and his eyes were exploring the architecture of the Parisian buildings. Then they came down to the ground and watched the people hurrying past us. On the other side of the street a minibus distributed hot soup among the homeless and vagabonds. They had lined up in front of the minibus with their raggedy clothes and dirty faces for a bowl of cabbage soup. I looked at my watch; it was noon:

—Remind me to show you something before you leave.

—What is it?

—I can't tell you in words. You have to see it!

—Don't tell me you too have started to draw on the penholder?[10]

He knew better than that. It has been many years since I gave up painting. For simple reasons: first, I didn't have the talent. Second, I didn't have the wherewithal. Third, I didn't have the time; finally because from the time I was a child nobody had encouraged me to paint. On the other hand, though, the numerous aunties of the family had sincerely encouraged me to learn to sew, to knit, to crochet, to cook *qeymeh* and *qormeh* stews. Of course I didn't tell him those things. Not even later. First, because he didn't remind me. Second, I was distracted. Third, I forgot. Fourth, we were so busy with all the things we had to do for his trip; visits to the Eiffel tower, the Louvre and Montmartre and to dead and living Iranian friends and acquaintances, that the sacred word escaped my memory.[11]

The day he was going to return, we were sitting in the airport coffee shop. Outside, it was cloudy, as always, and far away a smoke-colored cloud lay on the silky blue sky.

—Have I worn you out these few days?

"All of you" and "the motherland!" I had taken a week's leave without pay. During his stay I had followed him around from seven A.M. to one A.M. During this time I had rearranged all my plans so that I could spend more time with him. My personal life was at a complete standstill. My nerves were so shot that after he left I needed at least two or three days of complete rest just to return to normal. Would he understand this? Something like a thick gray cloud was pushing on my heart and taking the desire to talk away from me. Still, in a choked voice, I said

—Not really.

—You know, in these few days, I think a few years have been added to my life!

—You haven't seen anything yet!

—Oh, yes. I feel it. Now I know why all of you have changed so much!

Again he said "all of you!" This time I wanted to say something. I didn't know exactly what, but whatever it was, it seemed that my teeth were locked, and I let it pass. Just then the speakers announced his flight and I remembered that he was about to leave. I told myself, "Wait these few minutes and let it go! Who knows when 'all of us' are going to see each other again?"

—What is it? Why are you glum?

Once again I preferred to stay quiet and bite my tongue. But that gray cloud was growing heavier and darker; it was going to rain. They were still announcing his flight over the speakers, "Oh, this is serious. He is leaving, right now!"

Of course his departure didn't keep me from being glum because of his "all of you." "All of you" come, "all of you" stay a few days and then "all of you" return. But even these few days are enough for us to get used to your presence, like a pet, or that cat outside the window. Then all of a sudden I felt sad. "How long is it going to take all of you for 'all of us' to see 'all of you' in who knows which cemetery?" While I was listening to the loudspeakers, "There isn't much time left before he leaves... in a few minutes... " Suddenly the thought made me sad and I shut up. I just pointed to the speakers and then, in a quiet voice, so quietly that he wouldn't know I had a lump in my throat because of his departure, so quietly that it would get lost in the commotion of the airport and the speakers, I said:

—Do you hear that?... It's getting late!... The plane is waiting for you!

It is now a few minutes since he has left. And I, in the middle of this huge airport, which is as big as the Père Lachaise, without a black cat outside a closed window, lonelier than before, am sitting perplexed in the airport's coffee shop. I should get moving, get myself home before it starts to rain. I should return now; I should turn over my hourglass so the sands start to fall, grain by grain... moment by moment....

PIR

Farkhondeh Hajizadeh

When the newspapers reported the increase in the number of Afghans leaving Iranian soil due to the flight of Mullah Omar and the establishment of the Karzai government, her heart began to pound. The figure of Atef in his light blue shirt and black pants, with his straight hair, slender form, black eyes; and his mouth... the mouth that if it hadn't opened to say, "If you need help, give me a yell," she would not have known he was Afghan, appeared before her. Even if the Afghan nationals had not been leaving Iran she didn't have much hope of seeing Atef, unless she was able to check every queue of day laborers, or go search city by city and ask, "Have you any word of an Afghan named Atef?" All this in addition to her troubles and for no reason other than the fact that a few years ago, every morning at 7:45 AM, Atef, with his slim hands and a piece of beige-colored cloth and Right glass cleaner, gave the glass on her desk such a sparkle that she could see the reflection of her bright eyes in the glass; after which he would clean the legs of her desk and the bookshelves around her. And whenever the library supervisor with his thinning hair, elegant outfit, and straight teeth would call him, Atef would answer nonchalantly, "Sir, let me clean Ms. Sabahi's desk first." The supervisor would say, "Atef, be careful; Ms Sabahi's desk is very important." Then he would turn to Ms. Sabahi and give her a sweet, meaningful smile, which meant, People get what they deserve.

Paying no attention to the supervisor's meaningful smile, Ms. Sabahi would listen to Atef's sad humming; he would gradually move away from her, and she knew that once he got to the last bookshelf he would turn and take the tray and the cup of tea from her desk and she would give him the cheese and walnut sandwich wrapped in a napkin so that when Zahra

Khanom was serving the tea at her desk she would tell her, "Of course your tea is special." And Farideh from the other end of the hall with her Yazdi[1] accent would say, "Well, well, Parvaneh, do tell your Alain Delon to help me clean up around my area one of these days."

The first day Atef had arrived at the library with a few Afghanis to move the bookshelves, Farideh said, "Parvaneh, check out the Alain Delon!"

Parvaneh's look turned on the Afghanis, but she didn't see any Alain Delon. Atef's clean outfit and appearance caught her attention. He was wearing a beige shirt with black pants that day.

Parvaneh suggested to the supervisor that he keep Atef on as the cleaner in the library.

The supervisor thanked her for her attention, and Atef stayed.

Those first days, she didn't know anything about Atef's life other than that he owned a blue shirt, a pair of black pants, and a beige shirt. She didn't even know that Atef straightened them on the cord when he washed his clothes or that he ironed them so much with an old iron to take out the wrinkles.

When the decision was made to transfer the storehouse for the books from the first floor of the library to the second floor, the employees were forbidden to take any leave. A few people from the service staff of the university, all Afghanis, were dispatched to the library. The tasks were divided according to a very efficient plan. Some were packing the books downstairs and writing the call numbers with a thick marker on the boxes; another group upstairs was shelving the books.

She was assigned to work on the *PIR* series; as always, no one was willing to take on the task of shelving these series, both because of the heavy volume and the complicated numbers; but she, who had not yet learned the ins and outs of the office, accepted the job. Colleagues were also obliging her by saying,

"Parvaneh, you like literature, you can have the *PIR*."

The silence of the library had been disrupted; once in a while someone from upstairs would yell, "Either write on the cardboard boxes or tell them the serial numbers!" The banging of the boxes could be heard on the ceiling of the first floor, and at times an accented voice would call out *QA* or *DS*. Holding her nose, Farideh would say, "Pew, I can smell the Afghans. Do you smell that, Parvaneh? Is it the smell of their feet or their bodies?" and she would gag.

Atef came up; he checked through the shelves and when he saw Parvaneh he looked up the shelf and said, *PIR,* and after a few minutes he tossed the first *PIR* box onto the floor next to Parvaneh. Bending, he quickly opened the box; he picked up the books in batches, set them on the shelf vertically and said, "It's easier this way." And he went to take care of the other box. Farideh said with laughter, "Good to be lucky."

"What do you mean?"

"At least he doesn't smell."

As soon as Atef tossed the box on the floor, he said, "Done," and noticed Parvaneh's bare feet; she had taken her socks and shoes off and rolled up the legs of her Lee pants. He blushed, "If you teach me I will help you finish quickly."

When Atef looked at the top of the shelf he said "PIR," and Parvaneh realized that he could read; she asked, "Atef, how many years of schooling have you had?"

"I have studied."

"I know; how many years? What was your profession in Afghanistan?"

"I was a high school teacher."

"A high school teacher! What subject?"

"Literature."

In the midst of work on the *PIR* series Parvaneh and Atef carried on their conversation. Parvaneh found out that Atef worked as the concierge of a private apartment complex at night and worked at houses on Fridays and sent his income to Afghanistan. She felt embarrassed to discover that Atef worked so hard. So much so that she couldn't say, Why don't you come to our house some Friday?

The retired General Shaham, who had become the head of Human Services at the university, in accordance with the law that called for the prohibition of all Afghan labor from working in public institutions, ordered all the Afghans to leave the different departments in the university. The efforts of the library supervisor, Parvaneh, and Zahra Khanom to keep Atef on got nowhere. Atef left without saying goodbye; Shaham had forbidden them to be in the university for even a few minutes.

Parvaneh was hopeful that in her country the laws and orders had no permanence. Then the ban on Afghans working in public institutions could be lifted, and Atef could come back.

With the kind, motherly sparkle she always had in her eye, Zahra Khanom, who always held her hand in front of her mouth whenever she laughed to hide her broken front tooth, pointed to the back door of the library with her left hand. When Parvaneh got closer, she whispered in her ear, "Be careful no one finds out; Atef has come to the back door; he says he wants to see you for a moment."

As the key in Zahra Khanom's hand was turning in the lock of the glass door, Parvaneh stared at Atef's eyes through the glass. In Atef's eyes she wanted to find the reasons for his affection. Was Atef, who was only a few years older than her sons, thinking of her as his mother? Did Parvaneh resemble his sister, fiancée, cousin, the girl in the neighborhood...

whomever Atef was attached to for no reason, or did he just like her without any reason? Zahra Khanom put the keys in her pocket and pointed to Atef, saying she would be back soon; she turned to Parvaneh and said, "I got so panicky, the rascal, how did he dare."

There was no traces of hatred in Zahra Khanom's saying rascal, nor in the pupils of Atef's eyes could she find anything but a simple friendship, the kind of friendship that has no particular color and is everlasting.

Zahra Khanom was coming back with another set of keys, Parvaneh was remembering Atef's voice when he was putting the Divan of Hafez[2] in its place on the shelf—*I am liberated from any confining colors.* Atef would take a step, and as he was putting Hafez, Moulavi,[3] Ferdowsi,[4] Attar[5]… on the shelf, he would recite a line of their poems and Parvaneh would follow with the other lines. The day after Parvaneh had finished in one day the *PIR* series that had the most number of books and was the most difficult job, as a bonus the supervisor gave her a three-day leave. Farideh in a naughty yet friendly way said to her, "Good to be lucky." And it was agreed that Atef would help Farideh the next day. After that day Parvaneh would see Atef once in a while in the storehouse of books sitting in a torn leather armchair with his back to the library facing the university under the sunlight reading a book.

Atef disappeared with a piece of paper in his hand. They had agreed that he would work at Parvaneh's house next Friday. Parvaneh was embarrassed; it was Zahra Khanom's suggestion; with a blush on her face Parvaneh asked Atef and he accepted very comfortably.

By that Friday evening Atef had cleaned and polished all over the house; he had even cleaned the keyholes in the cabinets with a pin around which he had wrapped a scrap of cloth. Parvaneh was embarrassed to put money in Atef's hand, so she asked her husband to take care of it. Her husband, who would never involve himself in these matters, told her, "You pay him yourself."

When her son saw Atef, he asked her, "Mom, do you think Atef was in the cleaning profession in Afghanistan?" Parvaneh discreetly told him of Atef's profession and his level of knowledge. Her son's eyes filled with tears, "Then why did you ask him to come and work at our house?" And he went to his room and closed the door behind him. And at lunchtime he said, "I am not hungry." Why had she asked Atef?

She held her wallet in front of Atef. Atef blushed again. He kept his head down and said, "I didn't come for money."

"This way I would feel very bad; I won't be able to ask you next time I need your help."

Atef stretched his hand toward the wallet and picked a thousand-toman bill as if he were holding a mouse by its tail. Parvaneh added another four thousand to the one thousand-toman bill in Atef's hand, and after that Atef would come once in a while on Fridays and would polish Parvaneh's house by the evening, until the day he disappeared.

Parvaneh had no address for Atef; from time to time he would call and they would arrange for a Friday that Parvaneh needed him, or even for some times when she didn't have much work to be done at home.

Zahra Khanom said, "Don't be sad, he has probably gone to his country to visit his family; or maybe he got married; he will turn up."

Whenever there was news on TV about the events in Afghanistan and a report on the casualties among the Afghans, Atef's blushing face and the sparkle in his eyes would appear before Parvaneh's eyes, until the time that, in the midst of her troubles and illness, the memory of Atef got lost.

It was the last session of her chemotherapy; she was coming back home from the hospital; in the hallway Mr. Suleymani, her first-floor neighbor, told her laughing, "Ms. Sabahi, congratulations! I got rid of a pest for you. I thought to myself, poor Parvaneh Khanom has enough burdens on her shoulders to be disturbed with visitors from the provinces and Tehran who drop in on her every hour. Considering the condition you are in. The fellow didn't look like an Afghan; he wasn't dressed like them either; he said, 'I have heard the lady is not well, I have come to visit her.' I said to myself, What does Ms. Sabahi have to do with Afghans? At least if he had said he was American, that would be something else. That's why I told him you left Tehran a while ago."

In front of Ms. Sabahi, her son said, "You don't know, Mr. Suleymani; my mother has a lot of these friends like that; bus drivers, Afghan workers... "

Ms. Sabahi, who was taking the steps up the stairs leaning on the railings on the way, asked, "Didn't he say what his name was?"

Just as her son was saying, "Mom maybe it was... " Mr. Suleimani said, "Atef." Parvaneh's eyes filled with tears. When she blinked, the tears rolled down. She decided to travel back in history, to the time when Afghanistan was part of Iranian soil, and then she could imagine herself breathing under the same sky as Atef.

PART TWO

Another dream, in another marsh!

The Road To Arizona

Nasim Khaksar

When I saw a black fellow standing on the corner of the canal near our neighborhood staring at his surroundings with a strange look on his face so early in the morning, I wondered what he could be looking for. I had seen many of them around here before. I mean, strangers like myself. But until now I had not seen anyone coming out of their house so early except for the drowsy Dutch people who usually come out very early on Sunday mornings to walk their dogs.

Behind, where the black fellow was standing, at the other side of the avenue crossing the canal, you could see a large meadow. The avenue divided the canal in two. One part, on the right, was connected to the meadow; then it curved along a bicycle path to a country road linking the big towns with the road along which the whores had their houses. The left side, where the black fellow was standing, was great for walking; if the Dutch and their dogs gave you a break.

When I first saw the black fellow and observed his manner, to figure out what he was after, I watched him from far off so he wouldn't know. It seemed he was looking for someone he could ask some questions. Because every minute he would turn to look around or to look at the crossroads not far from there to see if another bus or car would appear and drop off a passenger. That early in the morning it was unlikely a bus would come, but it wasn't unthinkable a cab or a bicycle rider would turn up. When two cars quickly passed the black fellow and I saw him rubbing the back of his hands in disappointment as he watched the car slowly disappear, I moved within range. Once I made sure he was waiting for me, I went toward him. I had guessed right, I was a few paces away from him when he bounded toward me and in a deep voice, with that heavy black accent that never fades away even if they stay somewhere else for thirty years, he asked me in Dutch, "Sir, do you know how to get to the road to Arizona?"

I said, "Do you want Arizona or the road that heads there?"

He said, "No! I just want the road, I'll find the rest."

The streets and avenues in the neighborhood where I lived were all named after American cities and states. But I didn't know exactly where Arizona was. I said, "Wait, maybe I can remember!"

He came so close it was as if he had been my friend for years; his curly white hair was only inches away from my chin. Then he raised his head and, with his eyes that like other blacks had a shine to their whites, stared at my face. When I took a good look at his face, I saw he was about 70 or 75 years old. Though it is very hard for me to guess the age of blacks correctly.

I said, "Look!" I pointed to the left, to where I usually took a walk, and went on, "The neighborhood behind here is called Washington, and behind that is California. Next to it is Boston, and that's connected to Salinas. As far as I can remember, I think if you take the road we are on and go straight ahead, you'll find the place you're looking for!"

He clapped his hands in delight and said, "Fabulous! I love your last sentence. Can you repeat that?"

I said, "Which sentence?"

He said, "The one that started with I think!"

To make him happy, I said it again in the same tone of voice. He said, "It's fabulous. I love that sentence!"

Hastily he rummaged through his pockets and took out his cigarettes and lighter. He held it up to me.

"Do you smoke?"

I said, "No. Though if it were a few years ago I wouldn't have passed it up! I loved getting on the road early in the morning when not a creature is awake, and leaning against a fence somewhere to smoke a cigarette. But I haven't been able to do that for a long time!"

He said, "Oh, why is that?"

I said, "My lungs are in a bad shape. I've got asthma. The truth is that's why I came outside. I can hardly breathe at home. I thought I might feel better outdoors."

He leaned on the railing of the iron bridge over the canal and, as if his mind was anywhere but on his surroundings, lit a cigarette and started puffing.

He said, "The air here is no good for anybody's lungs. I'm no better off than you. But I smoke."

I said, "If you like, I can come with you."

Again he said, "Fabulous!"

I couldn't see why he thought my words were fabulous. I was dying to know what had brought him out so early in the morning. I kept looking at the sky, then at the sparkling water of the canal; small waves rippled because of the cool June morning breeze. I was looking at the willow trees with their branches bending over the water and their upside- down reflections and shadows clear in the water.

I said, "I'm ready. Let me know when you want to go."

He said, "Let me take a puff or two. Don't you know how much fun it is not to know the way to the road to Arizona?"

I said, "You'll find it eventually. When you find it, it will stop being fun."

He said, "No!" and puffed on his cigarette. "It's not clear whether we'll find it or not. We might get confused and go another way. We might even give up halfway there and not go on to the end. I could mention hundreds of these if's. Only one of them could be what you're guessing!"

He tossed his cigarette through the railing into the canal. A few ducks that had been watching us flew toward the cigarette, thinking he had thrown food into the water. The water started to make waves. The sound of their wings and their shadows over the rippling water made a fabulous scene from where I was standing watching them.

The black fellow came closer to me again and, his curly hair under my chin, said, "Let's go!"

As we set off, I noticed his head barely reached my shoulder. He was walking very fast.

I asked, "Do you have any kin in Arizona?"

He said, "Do you want to know the truth?"

I said, "Of course."

He said, "No!" and slowed down. "Look, I told you earlier, for me the fun part is to ask and for someone else to say just what you said."

Then he walked a little faster. I hastened my steps so as not to be left behind.

He said, "Look! I've been here 41 years." He counted on his fingers and said, "Yes—41 years. I mean, in one more month it'll be exactly 41 years."

Then all at once he went silent and looked around. And said, "I wanted to make sure you were here! I suddenly felt I had lost you."

I said, "What would you like me to do so you don't think you've lost me?"

He said, "Do you know how to whistle?"

I said, "Yes, But my lungs won't let me."

He said, "What a pity."

I said, "If these damned lungs had let me I certainly would have whistled for you."

He said, "I know."

I said, "But I can do something else for you so you know I'm here."

He said, "What?"

I said, "I can put my hand on your shoulder and be careful we don't lose our way. And I'll tell you if I see anything interesting or something occurs to me."

It seemed as if he wasn't listening to me at all, since he went on talking without giving me an answer, "As I was saying it's 41 years I have been here. Right here in Holland. To tell you the truth, I didn't want to come. It just happened. I'm sure the same thing happened to you. I was fifteen years old when I had to leave the real Arizona. You know what I mean. The real Arizona is the name of a village where my parents and I were born. Over there, too, there are little places with the same names as big cities and states. I think ours was because a big company from Arizona had a hold on the land and so it had gotten the same name. My mother gave birth to me in a barn in the middle of a cotton field. To tell you the truth, a fistful of cotton and straw went into my throat, with my first cry, and it hasn't come out yet. All the life and love of life in me goes back to those years when I was a child. Most of the time my father worked the land and I held on to my mother's skirt. Whenever my mother wanted to go to the town I cried so hard she was forced to put up with me. In the beginning it was hard for her to take me along with her in the heat and the sun. But by the time I was about five or six years old she had gotten used to me. She would never go to town without me. We usually went in a cart. The kind of cart that was pulled by a horse or a mule or a donkey. In the back of that same cart I would see the world very well with these eyes of mine. I have been around a lot of places these 40 years, but I haven't seen as much as I used to see during those trips back and forth from the village to the town. If I got distracted for a single moment I would miss a lot of interesting things. A bird hopping around in the dirt. The hoopoes walking straight ahead. As though they wanted to show off their crowns to you. A goat standing and staring at you. A sky like a sheet of blue paper that moved along with you. I watched the horizon so long under the sun that all night a bright yellow color danced behind my eyelids. The movement of the color would eventually put me to sleep. On the way home the driver would always get lost. As soon as the mule would stop, my mother would slide me off the cart and say, 'That old man has gone the wrong way again, and he's all mixed up. Run, my boy; I want to know if you can ask for directions to the road to Arizona from the people around here.' I would fly. I would really fly. If I saw someone as far away as 40 miles, I would run toward him to ask the same thing, 'Hey, sir, do you know the way to the road to Arizona?' I would say the very same words my mother had ordered me to say."

All at once he fell silent. I was so caught up in his words that I turned my head as if I heard the sound of the cartwheels.

He said, "I couldn't stay there. I had a fight with someone when I was fifteen. I struck him on the temple with my fist. The man collapsed and died. I ran away. I ran away because I knew if I were jailed I would cause my mother a lot of pain. And then imagine, that poor wretched woman would have to take the same cart every week to come to town to visit me in jail. To tell you the truth, the thought of them getting lost on the way home and my mother being reminded of what she used to tell me would have killed me. I went to Canada first. But I couldn't stay there. It felt as though now that I couldn't be in Arizona I might as well go far away. So far that I couldn't even smell it. When I was told they needed workers in Holland, I came here."

He was walking two steps ahead of me; I stopped pretending I was watching the canal water. To be honest, I didn't have the heart to take him to Arizona Street. He wasn't paying any attention to me; he kept talking to himself and moving ahead. As soon as I crossed a wooden bridge over the canal I went behind the trees thick with leaves and branches and the wild plants that had grown there in plenty, whose names no one knew. When I saw him from that same corner turning back without going to the end of the road, I grew happy. To get really far away from him I took roads that ended in the wooded parks a few neighborhoods further away from the canal.

As I was walking by myself, all at once I remembered his request. I remembered a pretty tune I know. A tune that, if my asthma allowed me, and if it wasn't that early in the morning when I had a hard time breathing, I could whistle wonderfully. Of all the tunes I could whistle this one was the best. It was unique. One of those pure rustic tunes that I couldn't remember which black American or African had made based on an old song. The song was about a southern boy searching for a sad-eyed girl in Memphis and finding her later in Boston. After whistling the tune a few times I was tempted to find the black fellow and sing it for him. I didn't know why I thought I could find him in the same place where I saw him first. I strode quickly along. When I arrived near the canal I felt very hot. When I saw him from far away leaning on the railing I became very happy. I kept my head down and walked toward him slowly, not giving him the impression that I had anything to do with him. I had wanted to whistle before when I was standing beside him so he wouldn't feel he'd lost me. But when I got near the bridge I didn't see him. I was surprised. I looked around and there was no sign of him. I thought perhaps with the neighborhood waking up and the people and dogs coming out into the streets he would not have been interested in standing there watching the others. He was right. When I stood on the same spot where he had been standing I felt the iron railing was still warm with his body heat. Looking at where he had thrown his cigarette butt and the ducks that were eagerly watching me, I really craved a cigarette. But I knew my pockets were empty. As soon as a man passed me with a cigarette between his lips, like the smokers who haven't had a cigarette all day and feel pain all over their bodies out of their longing to smoke, I felt a pain in the roots of my teeth and the flesh of my gums. As soon as I wanted to ask the man for a cigarette I burst out coughing.

Realizing from my expression and the way I behaved that I wanted something from him, the man waited for me to stop coughing, then he asked, "Did you want something, sir?"

I felt embarrassed to ask him for a cigarette. Something in his voice made me afraid he would refuse. While I was thinking how to answer him, without knowing why, I said, "Sir, do you know the way to the road to Arizona?"

The man thought for a bit. Since he wasn't familiar with the neighborhood, he thought either that I was making fun of him or that he was dealing with a lunatic. Without answering me he went on walking. I didn't say anything either. I took a deep breath or two and headed home. The day had already begun.

Without Roots

Mehri Yalfani

Mother says it's all my fault.

But, I don't agree. Everyone likes to put the blame on somebody else. Well, I do. Maybe I'm wrong, but if Mother and Father put themselves in my place and were fair, they would see I'm not to blame. They think it's easy for us to adjust to a new society and culture. Father, especially, always talks about his roots in Iran, says he is going to die here like a plant without roots.

What about us children? How can we have roots here? If we stay locked inside our homes, we'll never put down roots anywhere! And even if we do, they won't be firm. Father doesn't want to understand, and doesn't want to think about it. He and Mother are stuck in their Iranian culture and customs. "We have to preserve."

No one is going to ask them, "When you were planning to escape from Iran, why didn't you think about these things then?"

Father's reasons are clear and, in his opinion, very sound. Firstly, it was on account of Behzad and me. Secondly, for himself, when his career ended. He was a colonel in the Iranian army and was afraid that if he appeared to be against the revolution, his property would be taken by the government.

Well, he had no choice but to leave the country. Or, as he says, "I had to." For two years he couldn't find a job here. He didn't want to learn English. He went to ESL classes reluctantly and found out how hard it is to learn. He left after one year.

Poor Mother was working day and night in a donut shop in those days. Father's nerves were in such a state we always had to keep voices low at home. He hated Behzad's long hair. One day he grabbed the scissors and cut it. We laughed at him; how funny it looked. Then Mother cut it again, properly, all the while cursing and groaning. At first she couldn't do hairdressing. Now she's an expert. The haircuts she gives me are so beautiful, no one believes me when I say that my mother did it.

I suggested to her, "Open a hairdressing business."

"Who will come?" she asked. "And if they do, won't they expect me to do it for free?" She didn't go into business, she just does her friends' hair for free.

When Father is angry he always says, "In a foreign land, if you close one eye, the other one won't give up its light. Why are you devoting your free time to others?" But he is just like her. When Mrs. Soraya was moving, he lent her his cab for the day and switched to the night shift. Mother was angry and thought that there was something between them. Poor Mrs. Soraya. Her husband was an army officer executed during the revolution, leaving her with two small children. Father respects her and says, "She is the only woman who has not changed here. Most are no longer themselves. They take one whiff of freedom and become unbridled." My father talks about women as if they are sheep. Whenever Mother says something, he sneers at her, and then laughs. This makes Mother very angry.

Once when he ridiculed me, I cursed him with dirty words in English. Lucky for me that he didn't understand. Behzad giggled. Mother didn't understand either. Father screamed, "What did she say?" Mother looked innocent and said, "How do I know? I didn't grow up in Canada."

But Behzad continued laughing. Father finally understood that I'd cursed him. If we'd been in Iran, and I said such things, he would have punished me, sent me to the basement, and perhaps hit me too. Who would have dared say anything rude to my father over there? When he became a colonel, he would stand in front of the mirror in his uniform and ask Mother, "Ashraf, how is this?" And Mother had to admire him and smooth any wrinkles from the shoulders of his jacket.

Father would sometimes talk about the soldiers and officers under his command. He would send for his army servant at home and scold him for no reason. I didn't know what was going on. I remember going to Aunt Nasrin's house and Father would make fun of her husband. He'd say, "Yoosef is his wife's servant. He serves the guests, he does the dishes." He especially targeted Yoosef's dishwashing. At home Father never lifted a finger. Aunt Nasrin thought Mother was lucky having a servant.

I sometimes wish Aunt Nasrin was here to see Father wash the dishes. When Mother was working and he was staying at home. And, especially the time Mother was in the hospital with appendicitis.

I would come home late on purpose and mumble an excuse. "I had... class." Mother blamed me for Father having to wash dishes. Mother seemed to think that Father belonged to a special species whose masculinity would be lost if he washed some dishes. Since he began working as a taxi driver, he has touched nothing at home. If he came home and found Mother out, if she'd gone shopping, for example, he'd blame me. But I didn't care about him. I heard what he said with one ear and it went right out the other. He thought I was like her, that he could bully me.

One day when he grabbed my ear, I warned him, "You be careful, or I'll call the Children's Aid."

His eyes opened wide, "What did you say?"

Behzad was laughing, but controlled himself when he saw Father about to slap him. Behzad seized his hand, "You know what Children's Aid means?"

Father was stupefied. "What does it mean?"

"If she calls and tells them you hit her," Behzad replied coldly, "they will come and take her away and give her to a family who does a better job with her."

Father was about to slap Behzad again, but suddenly he sat down, put his head between his hands and sobbed like a child. Mother came in and asked, "What happened?"

He shouted at her. Behzad continued, "Father, Mother can complain about you too. So stop shouting so loudly!" Then Behzad said that wife assault is a criminal offense here, but I'm sure neither of them believed him. Father was cross for a few days. He didn't talk to any of us. Mother had to treat him gently. She grumbled at Behzad and me, "Why were you bothering him?"

We told her, "Father should change his behavior."

She didn't agree, "Poor man! In Iran he was such a remarkable person, an army unit under his command. If they saw his shadow, they wouldn't dare breath; they might be slapped or spat upon. Now his children curse him."

"Here it's different," Behzad said. "I mean everybody has value, even the animals are protected."

Mother didn't want to listen to us. "That has nothing to do with us," she replied. "We have our own culture and our own traditions. In our culture, children must obey their parents. They should respect their elders. They should not complain when they are hit or punished."

Mother never stopped giving advice. If Father was in a good mood, he would join in with his favorite poems and proverbs. He would recite them for us in order to hammer Iranian culture into our heads. The longer we live in Canada, the more Mother and Father mention the value of Iranian culture and Iranian tradition. At first they ignored Chelleh Night[1] and Noruz.[2] Later on, however, for Chelleh Night Mother invited friends in and served the watermelon and pomegranate that father had searched for all over the city. Mother also cooked her own special *fesenjan* and *qormeh sabzi*.[3] Father told fortunes, using Hafez's poetry, reading the poems aloud. When we asked,

"What does it mean?" he wouldn't answer exactly. Just that it was good or it was bad. Then he wanted us to tell him what our wishes were. I didn't wish for anything.

When we arrived Father was only interested in assimilating quickly into Canadian society. He used to tell us to make friends with Canadian children. I brought Salima home with me one time. After she left, Father and Mother made fun of her and said, "Why do you make friends with colored children?"

Father sneered, "The pot always looks for its own lid."

I asked, "What does that mean?" His explanation was meant to show me that I'm colored too.

When I was older, kids would ask, "Are you Hindu or Pakistani?" I answered, "I'm Irani."

"Where is Iran?" they would ask. I wished Father and Mother could have heard those questions, so they wouldn't force us to be proud of our country. Maybe one day we will be proud of our homeland, but first we have to know who we are.

In those early days, Father used to say, "If you don't want people to look at you, you'd better blend in." I was so young then—just ten. Behazad was thirteen. Father wanted us to learn English and make Canadian friends. After a few years he found out that for him to be Canadian was not easy to do. But it was for us. We spoke English without an accent, and if we hadn't had such black hair, it would have been hard to tell that we had only been in Canada five years. But for Mother and Father it was different. They stayed home more and socialized with Iranian friends. As our time in Canada grew longer, they tried to discourage us from making friends with our Canadian classmates. "You won't be nice anymore," Mother used to say.

The day Behzad pierced his ear, Father almost brought the house down. But he didn't dare hit him. I'm sure he was afraid of the Children's Aid. He threatened to throw himself over the balcony. An Irani man of the same age had killed himself about the same time. I didn't take his threats seriously. In my view they were just to frighten us. But poor Mother was always anxious. Sometimes she fainted or grabbed her hair and pulled it.

Another time when Behzad shouted at Father, "Why are you bothering us so much?" Father cried. What a mess. Behzad said to father, "I spit on that army you commanded." Father stared at him, wanting to hit him. Mother led him away to the bedroom and gave him a glass of cold beer. Things were calm for a couple of weeks. Behzad removed his earring and cut his hair. But one day I saw him in the street on the way to school and he was wearing an earring. He said he only put it away at home.

I pierced my right ear a second time. I'm lucky that my hair is long and covers my ears. Otherwise there would have been another row at home.

Mrs. Shokri, who comes to school sometimes to help Iranian students, told my parents about Allen. I don't know how she found out about us. I'm sixteen years old, in grade eleven, and didn't have a boyfriend till now. In fact, kids teased me, and called me "Virginia." I can't believe they all sleep with their boyfriends—most of them are Pakistani, Hindu or Chinese, with their own cultures, traditions. At least their parents have strong beliefs. I didn't know why they made fun of me! I was scared to have a boyfriend. Mother always used to tell me, "You should keep your virginity. You should be such and such, for your first night of your marriage. No man should touch you before marriage."

She used to tell me many things about boys, and I believed them. That to have a boyfriend would happen naturally. I tried to be the girl Mother would like me to be. But it didn't work. First, because the kids teased me. Secondly, I liked Allen. He was tall and blond. He was the most handsome boy in our class. When Salima heard that Allen and I were friends, she almost died of jealousy. She knew how my parents thought. I mean, I had talked to her about everything. She was crazy about Allen. I went home from school with him, but I didn't sleep with him. He never mentioned this. We were just friends.

When Father and Mother found out about us they made my life miserable. Father hit me hard. I wanted to call the Children's Aid, but didn't. In fact, I felt sorry for them, especially for Mother. She was always crying as if I had died. Father said, "It would be better for us to go back to Iran. Even if they arrest me and put me in jail, it will be better than here."

Mother objected, "We can't go. Don't you know how expensive life is over there? We have nothing left. We have spent all the money we had." Mother's reasons convinced Father.

The day he saw me with Allen in the street there was another big scene. It was Allen's fault—he hugged me and kissed me just as Father's cab passed by. I turned and saw him stop. He stopped in the middle of street. I was sure he had seen me. That night he didn't come home. Mother came to my room very upset. Behzad was studying in the living room. He was in his first year of university and had to work hard. We all felt anxious. Mother called Father's workplace. They said they hadn't heard from him since afternoon.

We didn't hear from Father for a week. Mother called everywhere he was supposed to be, even the airport, but couldn't find out anything. Then he called home. Mother came back to life. "Where are you calling from?" she asked.

Behzad and I were listening as Mother talked. When she finished her telephone conversation, she smiled and said, "He's nearby, he'll be coming home soon."

Now, months later, some nights he still calls her. When she puts down the receiver, she always says, "He's going to come back home, soon."

Close Encounter in New York

Reza Baraheni

When the cops arrived, drew their pistols, and arrested the driver of a getaway truck and two looters, shoving them into two police cars, Rahmat saw two familiar faces in the tunnel of light the cars made while turning. Seyyed stood next to the concierge in front of the building, a bottle of whisky in one hand, and something resembling an oil container in the other. Rahmat had asked the concierge earlier, after repeatedly going around the skyscraper, whether he had seen Seyyed. He and his friend Seyyed were going to meet in front of that building. Rahmat was so excited to see Seyyed that he started running toward him. He had had a tough time finding him. Seyyed spoke no English, and if he got lost on a dark night like this in New York, Rahmat would have found it difficult to explain the situation to his family and friends. In the midst of the swarms of people and looters on this unusual night in New York, he had gone around the building several times, but every time he passed by the concierge, he seemed to be seeing him for the first time. And the concierge's behavior confused him. He stood in the same spot—as if he were a huge statue or a picture of himself—and looked beyond the cars and the people, with a strange blindness on that Middle Eastern face of his, more like Sinbad the Sailor. All he had to do was lift a hand to his brows to turn into the sailor, contemplating the horizon to find a trace of the shore on the other side.

Rahmat ran up to him in such a rush, that when he arrived in-between the two of them, if the crowd had not snatched him up in midair, he would have lost control and taken a nosedive into the asphalt. Seyyed asked the concierge in Farsi, "Who shot out like that?" Rahmat freed himself from the people and walked up to Seyyed, "How did you find this place?"

The concierge opened his mouth to speak—as if he spoke Farsi and had seen Rahmat zoom by—but instead he turned around and went back into the building. Seyyed watched Rahmat, bewildered.

"How come you didn't come out of the building?" asked Seyyed.

"How did you find this place?"

"I called your house and got the address from your wife."

"How did you get here?"

"Easy. I gave the piece of paper with your address to the cab driver, and said very politely, 'Here.' He was a sensible fellow and brought me here."

"You mean you had no trouble getting here? We did have a blackout you know!"

"The blackout happened as soon as I got here. It's my luck. Wherever I go, there's a blackout. What about you? Where were you? And why are you breathing so hard?"

"I kept thinking you were lost. You weren't in your room. Then everything went dark. Believe me, I've gone around this damned building more than twenty times. What a building! As if the architect copied it out of Nizami's *Seven Domes*.[1]

"You are drinking whisky! Where did it come from?"

"You think I'm gonna be stuck with no booze on a night like this?"

"The sky ripped open and a bottle of whisky dropped on my lap. Now take a sip!"

"No, I can't drink on an empty stomach. Let's go."

They got going and turned into one of the side streets. But they didn't know where they were going. Finally, Rahmat said, "Why don't we catch a cab and go to my place?"

"For God's sake, don't drag your wife and kids into this. I'm alone. You should be alone too," Seyyed said.

Rahmat turned and stood in front of Seyyed, "What's that in your hand?"

"I'm surprised a rascal like you wouldn't know what it is."

"No, I don't. How the hell should I know? It looks real heavy. You're breathing hard. Do you want me to carry it for you?"

"No. I've never given this to anyone. It's my whole inheritance. It's been with me for more than 24 years or so. Wherever I go, I carry it with me."

"It looks like an oilcan. Like a barrel of Kermanshahi cooking oil."

"It's even greasier than that. Kermanshahi cooking oil, my foot! On this night of utter darkness and turmoil, you want me to cook a good pot of rice and chicken for you?"

"Don't talk about food, because I'm starving."

"Well, have some of this whisky."

"Whisky won't do. But I'll have some anyway. To your ill health!"

Seyyed placed the oilcan on the ground. He did not give the bottle of whisky to Rahmat. He lifted it in the air.

He said, "Close your eyes, like a good old boy, and open your mouth." Rahmat shut his eyes and opened his mouth. Seyyed poured a few sips of whisky into the other's mouth. Then he lowered the bottle. Rahmat swallowed the whisky. Then knelt and sat down. Seyyed put the top of the bottle in his mouth and he took a few swigs. Rahmat got up. It seemed as though the whisky had been absorbed right through his mouth and throat, and his stomach hurt. He felt better, in spite of that. Suddenly he noticed the oilcan. He bent down to pick it up. He could not. It was really heavy. Seyyed saw what he was doing, but he pretended he was not looking. Rahmat bent once more and tried to lift it. Again he failed. When he got up, he was panting. Seyyed bent down and easily lifted the oilcan. He said, "This inheritance is too heavy for you, friend. It's my inheritance. You can't lift what belongs to me, and I can't lift what belongs to you."

"What's in it?"

"Take a guess!"

"It must either be gold or iron. Or shit. I would have lifted it, even if it were filled with rocks."

"You don't need physical strength to lift it. You have to be the right person for it. That's all. The right person. You have to own it. This is heavy for you. This is my burden. I've carried it around all these years. What do you think it is? Huh? A father's heirloom? A mother's womb? God? The Old Testament? The head of Gilgamesh? Judas Iscariot's ass? Achilles' heel or Esfandiar's eyes?[2] The head of Tieresias? Huh? Is it Rustam's two-horned beard? Tell me, why can't you lift it? Do you think it's Adam's head stuck under the earth for seven or eight thousand years, and has been swelling all these years? Huh?"

"Let me try one more time."

Seyyed put the oilcan down and said, "Bend down, kneel, and try again."

Rahmat bent down. He gathered all his strength and placed both his hands around the oilcan. He could not lift it. Seyyed bent and lifted the oilcan, and took off. It was dark. They did not know where they were going, but they left the main street behind. Sometimes a car would go by and light the way for a few minutes. In the silent darkness of the buildings the world seemed to be dying for a piece of light. The light disappeared momentarily, as if in fear of the darkness inside the buildings and behind the windows. And once a police car stopped by. One of the cops got out and placed his hands on his waist and called out to them. Rahmat turned around and said, "Yes!"[3]

"Where are you going?" the cop asked.

"Home," Rahmat said.

"Be careful, anything might happen," the cop warned them.

Rahmat said, "Something has already happened. Don't you think? Something heavy."

"Ya, it's a heavy night!" the cop said.

Rahmat said, "You say 'heavy.' I know what you mean."

Seyyed said in Farsi, "Tell these scoundrels to leave us alone! I don't know why they won't even leave us alone here!"

"Your friend, he doesn't know English?" the cop asked.

"No, he doesn't. And he's a bit drunk!"

"Take him home and keep him there!" the cop said.

Seyyed said, "Yes Mr. Police. Light, no here tonight. Iran, no light day and night. Night and night. It is Iran." And then he said in Farsi, "Wow, what a poem! I just composed a good poem in English. It even rhymes!"

"You people come from Iran?" the policeman asked, "Did he say Iran? Where is Iran, Africa?"

Rahmat laughed. Seyyed asked him in Farsi, "What is he saying about Africa?"

"He thinks Iran is in Africa," Rahmat said, in Farsi.

Seyyed said, "How strange, the fucking Iranian cop at least knows the difference between Africa and America!"

"What is your friend saying?" the cop asked. "He's talking a lot. Why don't you give me an idea of what he's saying?"

"I told him you told me that you thought Iran was in Africa, and he was surprised you didn't know where Iran was," Rahmat answered.

"You tell me where Iran is," the cop said.

Rahmat said, "Iran is in the Middle East. Two things from Iran are famous, oil and the Shah."

The walkie-talkie inside the police car blurted out. The cop sitting inside answered it, and then shouted, "Come on Fred. Let them go to their fucking hell! We've got work to do."

The cop still stood with one hand on his waist. He flashed his light onto their faces. As if he wanted to keep the images of the two men's faces in his mind. Then he turned off his flashlight and went back and sat in his car. The cop at the wheel started the car and they left. Seyyed said, "We have no luck.

Wherever we go, they think we are criminals." And then he took huge steps as if he wanted to get as far away from the police as possible. Rahmat shouted, "Where are you headed in such a rush? Watch your feet."

"Anywhere but here," Seyyed answered. "Don't you see? They're suspicious of us!"

They started to walk. They could hear the sirens far away. And that was to be expected on such a night. Sometimes it came from miles away and at other times it was just around the corner. And at times the sounds from near and far combined. But the street was empty. It was clear that the looting was still going on. The river glowed in the distance.

Seyyed said, "I wish somewhere were open, so we could get a bite."

Rahmat said, "Maybe by the water."

And he lifted his head. The starry sky seemed to have swollen, with the skin bulging out and hanging down from the walls of the endlessly tall buildings. Rahmat had never thought that New York had such a scary and starry sky. Like a crooked sieve with its edges neatly cut out by scissors, the sky seemed to be coming down with its heavy burden. The homes were still dark. And the windowpanes of the buildings were opaque. And people had gone to sleep for sure. But nowhere was safe. Anyone seeing them from behind the windows, would have been terrified. And where was this place? All these sirens! The sirens came closer and closer, and suddenly Seyyed said, "We're trapped, Rahmat! They're coming for us!"

The police cars were breaking and stopping around them. Their lights lit the street. Windows of buildings were opening and closing. Someone shouted from one of the windows, "What's going on down there?" Three or four cops rushed out of their cars. One of the cops suddenly pointed his pistol at Seyyed and shouted, "Put that thing down and move away from it. Do it now!"

"What is he saying?" Seyyed asked.

Rahmat said, "Put the oilcan down. They want that."

"They've lost their mind. They think I've stolen an atomic bomb!"

The cop shouted, "Put that thing down! You are surrounded! There is no way you can carry that!"

Rahmat told Seyyed, "Put that oilcan down. He wants to shoot!"

Seyyed put the oilcan down and stood beside it. An agent shouted, "Now move away from it!"

Rahmat interpreted, "Seyyed, move away from it! He doesn't want you to stand by it."

Seyyed said, "What a trap! Tell him I inherited this from my father. What is he gonna do with it?"

The cop shouted, "Move away! Otherwise we'll shoot!"

Rahmat grabbed Seyyed's hand and moved him away from the oilcan. The agent aimed the pistol at them and the other cops followed. Then the agent waved his hand. Someone came out of the car and pulled a strange machine out of one of the cars and drove it on its wheels toward the oilcan. It looked like something designed to trap a mouse or catch a lost cat and throw it into a sack. He pulled some wires from around the machine, separated them, and placed two of the wires in his ears and walked toward the oilcan and knelt down. And he listened as if he were waiting for a message to come from inside it. He moved a bit closer and knelt again. Then he raised his head, and motioned Rahmat to move forward. The cop who was holding the pistol was closer to it than anyone else. He came closer. The person in charge of the machine ordered Rahmat to pick it up. Rahmat said, "It's too heavy. I cannot." The man ordered, "Pick it up!"

Rahmat bent down, and gathered all his strength, but he could not lift it. This time the man tried. He could not lift it either. Seyyed said from the distance, "Tell them they won't be able to pick it up even with a forklift." One or two cops surrounded the oilcan and tried to pick it up. But it seemed to have been glued to the ground, and if they lifted it they would have to lift the ground with it.

Rahmat said, "I know it's crazy, but my friend is the only one who can lift it."

The man said, "Then tell him to come and lift it. We have to take it to the office for observation."

Rahmat told Seyyed, "Come and pick up your masterpiece. They want to take it to the lab to find out what's in it."

Seyyed came forward, knelt and picked up the oilcan with great ease and stood up straight. He said, "Do they want me to bring it or do they want to put it in the car? Rahmat asked the man. The man said, "We'll take it in the car."

"Wishful thinking," Seyyed said, "If they put this in the car, the car won't budge!"

Rahmat translated. The man said they should give it a try and ordered Seyyed to put it in the car. Seyyed obeyed like a good little boy and took the oilcan and put it in one of the police cars. The man ordered the driver to start the car and get going. The driver started the car but the car did not move. The man got angry, "What the hell is in it?"

Rahmat asked Seyyed, "Wants to know what's inside."

"Heirloom." Rahmat translated.

The man said, "What the fuck is he talking about?"

Rahmat asked Seyyed. He said, "I'm the only one who can carry this around. No kidding. One person's burden cannot be carried by someone else."

"Could he put it on his lap and sit in the car?" The man said, "Then we can go to the station."

Rahmat translated. Seyyed asked, "Is he an FBI agent?"

Rahmat asked. The man answered, "Yes."

"It's not necessary to translate 'Yes.' Tell him to take the trouble himself," Seyyed said.

The FBI agent did not wait for the translation. He walked quickly to his car. He stood there and started to speak to his machine; and he constantly kept an eye on Rahmat and Seyyed, especially Seyyed. It seemed to be clear in his mind that something fishy was going on. But he did not know what. Rahmat did not know either. Seyyed did not feel like explaining. Suddenly, Rahmat felt like he hardly knew Seyyed. Perhaps he did not know him at all.

He turned to Seyyed and said, "Fuck you, Seyyed!"

"Curse me all you want," Seyyed said, "I know I got you involved in this shit. But even if we stand here until doomsday, no one but I, can lift this. This is my Atlantis. Understand? They can't lift it even with nuclear power! Especially tonight, when all their technology has gone down the drain. You see these skyscrapers in the dark, hoisted to the sky? Someday, they won't even see them. Just like those ancient domes in Iran, which don't exist anymore. Whatever gets built slowly over time, slowly disappears over time too. Same thing with anything that goes up in a blink. It goes down in a blink. Yes this is heavy. As heavy as history's testicles. Let them come and try to lift it now."

Rahmat said, "Whatever this history ate, it sure didn't poop out the waste."

Seyyed laughed. In the light of the cars his face looked strange. As if it weren't the face of a human being. It was a painting or a picture. His eyes were yellow. His mustache was crooked; and his hairline had been messed up. He looked lonely and desperate. Didn't even fit the New York blackout. Someone shouted from one of the windows,

"What is happening down there? Is that guy responsible for the electricity!"

"Hey, you better close that window and get back to sleep," one of the cops shouted back.

"No harm watching you catch them bastards!" a woman shouted from a window.

"Now, what the hell are those guys saying?" Seyyed asked. Then he walked toward the sidewalk, turned his back to the others, stood against a wall, unzipped his pants and started to piss.

Rahmat saw the FBI agent walking toward them. "He's coming," he told Seyyed, "It's against the law to pee on a wall in this country."

"Where the hell am I gonna find a modern toilet in this hell?" Seyyed asked.

By the time the agent could reach the other side, Seyyed had pulled up his zipper and turned around. He looked at the cop with his strange expression. The agent walked straight up to Seyyed. He gestured to Rahmat to come closer too. Then he placed his hand on Seyyed's shoulder. Seyyed was staring straight into the agent's eyes.

The agent said, "Look, I don't want any trouble for you. And I don't want any trouble for my country and myself either. We don't know what happened tonight. We are trying to find out. It may have nothing to do with what you are carrying. I have informed my supervisors, and they in turn have reported this to their higher-ups. Please help us solve this problem. My government would appreciate your cooperation."

Rahmat translated the agent's sentences one by one. Seyyed was listening as if the invincible enemy was announcing his surrender.

The agent continued, "You see, we cannot wait here forever. We have to do this in the best friendly manner possible. You seem to have at your disposal a very precious thing. We have no right to take it away from you. As you see for yourself, we couldn't take it away from you even if we wanted to. So please cooperate with us. I give you my word that my government will not hurt you."

Rahmat translated again. Seyyed said, "Now he's trying to be reasonable. What does he want now?"

Rahmat translated.

The agent said, "Since I am not allowed to solve the case here, I am asking him to kindly carry it to my car, and come with me to our office so that my supervisors can discuss the matter with him."

Rahmat translated. Seyyed said, "Coming from the old Iran, and dying for affection, these words of his should make me cry." Then he raised his hand and with the tip of his fingers he took the agent's cheek, pulled it toward him, and kissed the side of his mouth. The agent silently gave in to Seyyed's move. He didn't laugh or say anything. "Tell him," Scyyed said, "to get in the car. I'll take care of the can myself." Rahmat translated these last few words too. The agent said, "Thank you." And then he turned around and went to the car. Seyyed lifted the oilcan. The agent opened the door for them, telling Rahmat to get in first, then he told Seyyed to sit in the middle, and then he got in and sat next to Seyyed. He shut the door. In addition to a driver, there was another officer sitting in the passenger seat in the front. As soon as the police car took off, Seyyed leaned onto the agent's shoulder, the oilcan on his lap, fell asleep and started to snore.

It wasn't clear what trap they had fallen into. The streets were deserted, and it was still dark everywhere. The car was moving fast. Rahmat hadn't eaten a thing, and the whisky was still burning his stomach. He closed his eyes. The speed of the cars was unbearable. New York seemed to have been cursed. It was as if they weren't in New York anymore. Sometimes, with the lights of the cars cast on the windows of the buildings, strange figures could be seen behind them. People had several heads and tens of eyes and mouths. Children with monster heads stared at the long train of speeding police cars, in the direction of God knows where. No one was sleeping in New York on this night, except for one man, the one who had placed his head on the FBI agent's shoulder. But a few moments later,

Rahmat was astonished to see that the agent too had fallen asleep, and soon his snoring knit into that of Seyyed's. They still sped on, to where, it was not clear. They seemed to be circling Manhattan. He felt that they had passed by the same building called Elijaic Khazars, in front of which he had seen Seyyed. Perhaps the plan had been this from the start, to circle the building as many times as possible. When he woke up at the sharp turns of the road, a couple of times he felt that he was around his own apartment complex in the Bronx, and a strange feeling held him in its grips. His son had probably just jolted in his sleep and unconsciously grasped one of his mother's breasts. And Marziyeh was probably so down with fatigue and anxiety, that she had fallen into a deep sleep, her legs spread out, her head to one side, her lips half open, and her eyes shut. Rahmat started to curse himself, Seyyed, the darkness of New York, and especially himself and his life in exile, with those time-old itchings and scratchings, and those distressing obsessions haunting him and leaving him no respite. The images flashed through his mind once again. These past few days when he got home from work late at night, his bedroom was like a painting of the mutual love of a sleeping mother and a child. As if Marziyeh and Siyavash had thrust these dismembered pieces of their bodies out of their sleep. Marziyeh's long leg had moved to one side, her right or left arm to another side and the nipple of her right breast was still between Siyavash's two fingers. He wanted to say again, "Fuck you, Seyyed." Then he thought to himself, what had poor Seyyed done to create this situation? And now, Seyyed's snoring had stopped; but the agent's continued.

Seyyed complained, "This guy's snorts woke me up."

"You were snoring too. It was like a real barnyard in here."

"Shit! We forgot to bring along the whisky bottle," Seyyed said.

"There wasn't much left anyway. You chugged it all down!" Rahmat said.

Seyyed said, "Where are they taking us?"
Rahmat answered, "How the hell should I know?"
Suddenly Seyyed started to sing:

Her mom pretty, herself pretty.
If they have any kids, their kids pretty too.
Eyyyyy!
Sit on my knees, let beauty sit on this dark world.
Burn me like fire, burn my heart,
Let me die, ey, heyyyyy!
Then let me open my eyes,
To see that darkness is gone,
Freshness has come, freedom has come,
it has taken you in its arms, taking you to other tribes,
The wind carrying it to other places, other places
Look now, blowing that hair, that hair blowing and blowing.
Heyyyyy, Oh my pretty one heyyyyy, Oh my little one.....eh!

The agent's snoring had stopped. His eyes were wide open
and he stared at Seyyed in shock. Rahmat said, "Seyyed, what's
wrong with you? Have you lost your mind?" But Seyyed did
not care. He went on singing.

Went along with the King of China
Forty nights through forty rooms
Then stayed alone a thousand and one years,
I stayed alone a thousand and one nights
I saw you and I went blind
But you were there between my eyes and my eyelids
Then the storyteller Shirin kissed me one night
I rose from the ghettos against the world
With Khosro Parviz's crown on my head
Barefooted, Eyyyyy!
Barefooted, Eyyyyy!
Crown on my head, barefooted Eyyyyy
Oh my little one Eyyyyy, Heyyyyy,
Oh my little one, little.....eh![4]

The agent interrupted Seyyed, "Please don't sing any more.

We will be there any minute now."

Rahmat interpreted. Seyyed stopped singing. The agent sitting in the front turned around and looked at Seyyed in shock. His blue eyes were sleepy and tired in the light of the cars behind them. But it seemed that Seyyed's singing had stopped him from thinking of his mission. He thought that this must be a really strange specimen of a man to have suddenly broken into singing in such a strange language. The agent suddenly burst into laughter. Seyyed, who had stopped singing, started laughing too, as if imitating the agent. But a moment later they were both quiet. Now the car turned right. The destination seemed to be close. The car quickly crossed a wide road and turned right and left two or three times, and entered and exited through one or two big gates, then went through another one and slowed down and came to a halt. The cars following them stopped too. The agent got out and motioned to Seyyed to get out of the car. It was bright as day in the light of all the police cars. Everything could be seen clearly in the light of the cars. Rahmat got out of the car after Seyyed. The cops surrounded them. They did not know where they were being taken. The agent said, "Follow me!" And started to walk. It was dark in front of them. But the agent seemed to know where they were going. The sirens could still be heard in the distance. It must have been a few hours past midnight. The sound of birds, awakened before dawn, could be heard, as if coming from a park nearby.

Seyyed said, "Rahmat, tell him that I need to pee again. I have to pee or I'm gonna wet my pants."

The agent said, "What did he say?"

Rahmat translated. The agent said, "He'll have to wait."

Rahmat said, "Seyyed, hold yourself for a few minutes!"

Seyyed said, "I'll be more than happy to oblige, but peeing doesn't understand human language." He waited no longer. He put the oilcan down, pulled down his zipper and peed into the dark. Everybody waited until he was done. He pulled his zipper up again, knelt down, picked up his oilcan, and gave the agent a raw and tough, "Go!" The agent set out again, Seyyed and Rahmat following behind and the rest following them. They could hear birds busily chirping away, as though from the depths of the endless park. They went through a gate. They seemed to be walking toward the singing birds. Candles could be seen lit in the distance. Otherwise, it was pitch black. Now, they could see a short flight of stairs in the light. That was all they could see. The light seemed to be there to light up the staircase. The agent went forward. Only his feet were visible. Seyyed and Rahmat followed from behind. The others did not come up, as if they had been instructed not to. The agent went forward and the light went with him and Seyyed and Rahmat followed. They entered a large place, perhaps a hall. It had an open feel to it, with no chairs or anything blocking their way. And then in the distance, they saw the silhouette of a man, who grew clearer, larger, and taller, as they got closer. He was about 60 years old, with neatly groomed salt-and-pepper hair, parted at the edge of his head. He had a long face, blue eyes, thin eyebrows that seemed to have been trimmed only a minute ago. The man instructed the agent to leave them alone. The agent walked backwards and then left. Seyyed with his oilcan, and Rahmat empty-handed, stood there. The man kept staring at Rahmat. After a minute he said, "So you are that worm?"

With this sentence Rahmat started translating for the two sides.

"But you are not that very Solomon who put his hand under his chin and leaned on his cane so that I could chew the cane underneath and inside the wood, with you and the cane finally pouring down as dust. Solomon was only around for a few hundred years. I am that worm that chews wood, a hundred millennia old. Neither the worm is a figment of the imagination, nor is Solomon a myth. I chew. And that's it."

"That is the past. You have no idea of your future. Interpreting the past has no meaning for the future. We have passed the past. This heavy thing you have brought for us from the other end of the world, means nothing to us. We can feel its weight. We cannot lift it up. But its meaning is only for you. What does it mean that you carry this heavy thing around with you? Its heaviness or lightness is meaningless. Fossils are heavy too. What's the point of your showing off its heaviness to us?"

"Its use is in its difference. This is different from what you are. You can send messages to the future. But you cannot enter into a dialogue with the past. You can kill the past. Just as you're killing it now. But you cannot take it on your shoulders. If I put this down, try as you may, you cannot lift it. You can destroy it, but you cannot lift it. You are destroying it today. Tomorrow you will destroy it even more. But you cannot understand heaviness, and you cannot carry its weight."

"We leave the carrying to you. As for us, we stand and watch you. We won't even come to watch you. Did you ever ask yourself what happened to the worm?"

"The worm repeated itself in every century. It suffered the torments of being a worm. It still suffers. When a worm was crushed under feet, another grew from under the earth. As long as there is a cane, there is a worm. And this is not opposing Solomon. It is opposing standing death rather than standing life. We have no crown to place on anyone's head. We chew that cane slowly and silently. Believe me, the worms will chew you too. You are a piece of wood, a cane. You see far away, in the distance, but you cannot see under your feet. Do you know where that worm is? That worm has gnawed into the world. The worm has grown so heavy that you cannot carry it. What I have in my hand is the world's decay, the indestructible heaviness of the world's decay. It is the heavy burden of someone who has grown up with it. He has experienced humiliation, torture, betrayal, loneliness, homelessness, the wandering of the body and spirit, and above all, degradation, so that he can lay down its heavy burden here and leave. Because he has his work cut out for him. In reality there is no laying it down on the ground either. There is no going away either. My inheritance is the world's decay, heavier than anything else in the world: death. I will not put this down before you. No one can lift it. I will stand here, to the end of time, with the heaviness of the world in my hands. In a few days, you will think of future elections, and your winning or losing will have no affect on the death of the world. I stand here, the heaviness of the world in my hands. I stand forever. You speed off before you became deep. The understanding of slow and heavy things is impossible for you. You give birth before you got pregnant. What I hold is the slowly-impregnated mother of time. It gathers onto itself moment by moment, all the heavy fruits of the world. I stand here, with the world's greatest dream in my hand, the most uninterpretable dream of all. More mother than any mother. With a different language, so that the world will be brightened, in a new way."

The words came to an end. Neither one said anything else. Rahmat turned and went back down the stairs. Seyyed stayed up there. In front of that man. Rahmat got into the agent's car. It was daylight. They left.

An hour later, when the car was passing by the Elijaic Khazars Building, Rahmat, upon seeing the concierge with his hand above his eyes and looking far away, he told the agent to stop the car so that he could get out. He stopped the car. Rahmat got out and walked toward the building. Remnants of the lootings of the night before were still there. The power was still out in New York. Rahmat did not go inside the building. He passed by the concierge, turned into one of the side streets by the building, and under the watchful eyes of the agent, disappeared.

Translated from the Persian by Aleca Baraheni

Farrokh-Laqa, Daughter of Petros, King of Farang[1]

Mehrnoush Mazarei

It was all like a dream. I couldn't believe that I was in Tehran. I had gone through the time tunnel and returned to years gone by. I wanted to go and see all the places where I had lived sometime and all the people of whom I had a memory. At the airport, and then at home, many people were waiting for me; relatives and friends I had waited to see for a long time; and they were now strangers to me. In the days that followed I was to see faces and places that were unfamiliar to me; wives and husbands of friends who had married, and children who were not children anymore, and a Tehran that I didn't know well anymore, so I was getting lost in its streets.

A few days later I flew to Shiraz where most of my memories of my childhood and youth were.

But Shiraz was no longer happy, beautiful, and carefree.

I was dying to see the old streets and acquaintances, but anyone I asked my mother about had either migrated or had died, or she had lost their address.

Baqer was my last hope. Mother promised to take me to the place where he worked. He had to be about fifty by now, but in my mind he was still a fourteen- or fifteen-year-old boy with narrow Mongolian eyes and delicate cheeks and a beard that had just sprouted.

The first time I saw him, he was a ten- or twelve-year-old boy my father brought home. Baqer had gone up to him in a coffeehouse and told him he was willing to work as a servant in exchange for food and a place to live. He had come all alone to Shiraz from his birthplace, a town near the Persian Gulf, to make a living and to discover the wonders of life; or maybe just for the adventure. He told us about the strange and bizarre events and people he had encountered on his way, and we believed it all. In those days, to me, my sister, and brother, who were eight, six, and ten, Baqer was a respectable and astounding character. We looked on him as a hero. He always had a story to tell us. Stories of *The Thousand and One Nights, Hosein-e Kord-e Shabestari, Samak-e Ayyar, Jamshid Shah*, and *Amir-Arsalan-e Namdar*, stories that he knew from before or had read from the books he would buy with his meager wages. Every chance he found between the household chores, when he was free for a few minutes from my parents' errands, or at night, when we were all asleep, Baqer used to go to the basement where he had a place to sleep and read. We would wait for him to finish the book and tell us the story. When he was washing the dishes or when mother sent him to buy bread and he had to wait on line, the three of us would gather around him and listen to his stories.

When after a long wait he bought *Amir-Arsalan-e Namdar*, Baqer was so excited he couldn't wait to finish the book:

> But the narrators of news and the relaters of stories and the sweet-speaking parrots and the harvesters of the field of eloquence and the head money-changer in the bazaar of matter have thus brought to parade the goodly steed of words that once in the land of Egypt... They named him Amir-Arsalan... When he had learned to read and write Arabic and Persian, they entrusted him to a foreign tutor... until he attained perfection in all the sciences and could debate Egyptian scholars... and when he spoke, nobody could tell whether he was from Rome or Farang, and... he was well-versed in seven languages... and within two years he had become such a horseman that he could confront a hundred swordsmen... he had become most strong, firm and brave... all the men and women of Egypt were taken captive in the net of his hair...

In the months that followed, Baqer's attention was completely taken up with Amir-Arsalan. Along with him, we entered the world of Amir-Arsalan's battles and his courage, of his love and of his falling in love, of his defeats and victories; and the secret-filled world of demons and fairies, demonesses and sorcerers, and war between good and evil.

When Amir-Arsalan, went into battle for the first time, Baqer, too, made a wooden sword and entered the combat with him:

> Arsalan took hold of his wrist... and dealt a blow to the crown of his head in such wise that... man and mount fell to the ground...

The climax of the story, and of Amir-Arsalan and Baqer's confrontation, began when Amir-Arsalan, after his victory over the forces of the land of Farang, won the kingship of Rome and then saw in a church a portrait of Farrokh-Laqa, the daughter of Petros, King of Farang:

> Behind the curtain his eyes fell upon a maiden of fifteen summers who shone on the earth like the moon in the sky. Her beauty of form, her loveliness and charm, her stature and her manner had no peer upon this earth. As soon as Amir-Arsalan's eyes fell on this portrait, he was robbed of heart, life, mind and wisdom. For two hours he stared dumbfounded at the picture...

Once, when I went to the dimly lit, humid storeroom in our house where Baqer used to sleep in the corner, to call him, I saw him standing in front of a picture staring at a beautiful girl with long wavy hair.

> He set the painting on the ground before him. Gradually the thrill of love penetrated his head. Suddenly he cried, O cruel beloved,
>
> Oh fresh flower which hath no scent of loyalty
> And knoweth not the sting of the thorn of unkindness
> And hath no pity on the hapless nightingale...

O merciless one, thou art passing thy time in all joyance in the apartments of thy father's ladies and art unaware of the heartache of the poor lover and his cares, who will die in loneliness, O my kind friend…

Two or three days later when Mother was less occupied with paying and repaying calls, she carried out her promise and set off with me to find Baqer.

Baqer had become the custodian of an Emamzadeh[2] next to the Shahcheragh.[3] We asked many people there but nobody had any news of him. Finally an old prayer reader who was his colleague said that he had heart trouble and hadn't come to work for while. Then he sent us to another one, and the next one to another one, until we finally got his address from a blind Quran reciter.

Ever since Baqer began reading Amir-Arsalan, our affection for him had grown even greater. We had constantly followed him and asked him to tell us more. When we went to the bakery, when it was our turn we would beg him to give his place to the next one in line. When he got to crucial parts in the story he would get quite excited; he would come out of the bakery line into the middle of the street to play Amir-Arsalan's part or to tell us the adventures in the book by imitating the voice of Vizier Shams or Vizier Qamar and the mother of the demon Fulad-Zereh.

The best days were those when my parents left the house and Baqer was left to watch over us. Our roles would change immediately. My sister and I would wash the dishes and clean the vegetables. My brother would sweep the house, and Baqer would become Amir-Arsalan. On his head he would set a crown he had made from cardboard and small pieces of colored glass; he would draw a moustache with charcoal and hang the wooden sword from his waist. A real Amir-Arsalan!

> Arsalan, covered in a sea of pearls and gems, a crown upon his head and an emerald-hilted dagger at his waist entered the court...

When Amir-Arsalan went to see the Fortress of Sangsar, Baqer made a bow and arrow using wood and rubber, and when Amir-Arsalan took the emerald-hilted sword from the demon Fulad-Zereh, we helped him stick pieces of green glass on his wooden sword.

Sometimes in exchange for this help he would give us small parts to perform, but he always played the important roles. Sometimes he became the deceitful Vizier Qamar who was in love with Farrokh-Laqa and deceived Amir-Arsalan to get her:

> He came forward and pressed Arsalan's hand slightly. He took the dagger from his hand and struck him so hard that fire sprang from his eyes...

And sometimes he turned into the kind Vizier Shams who had converted to Islam but wouldn't reveal it because he was afraid of the king of Farang and was trying to help Arsalan:

> Vizier Shams laid Arsalan's head on his breast and wiped the tears from his eyes and said: Child, beware the ruses of Vizier Qamar who beguiles even seventy-year-olds, let alone you who are young and inexperienced and ignorant. It was your fair fortune that he did not kill you...

When it was about the passages on the demon Fulad-Zereh and his mother who were the accomplices of Vizier Qamar and who had captured Farrokh-Laqa, Baqer's excitement and hatred would reach its height.

> The demoness told of the coming of Arsalan, his bravery and the killing of Fulad-Zereh and how he took the emerald-hilted sword from Fulad-Zereh's hand and defeated his army and then stole Fulad-Zereh's corpse and, hiding behind the corpse came to the Garden of Fazahr and killed Vizier Qamar until I deceived him and took the emerald-hilted sword from him...

He had drawn a picture of Amir-Arsalan that had Mongolian eyes and delicate cheeks.

In form and stature like the redoubtable Sohrab, in beauty like Hazrat⁴-e Yusef, tall as a cypress, broad chest, strong arms, small waist, a face like a ruby, eyebrows like Rostam's bow, eyes like two beautiful narcissi, and his upper lip newly bedewed with the green of eternal youth.

Farrokh-Laqa's role however, was always given to that beautiful picture, which was next to Amir-Arsalan's:

As soon as their eyes fell on each other two steps apart, a thousand heart-piercing arrows from the eyelashes of each sprang and landed on the other's breast. The queen's knees weakened and her legs trembled; she was about to fall...

The story of Amir-Arsalan was a secret between Baqer and us that we didn't speak about in front of my father and mother. My father once caught him by surprise while he was performing the role of Amir-Arsalan and beat him pretty hard. After that, my father called him Amir-Arsalan, "Amir-Arsalan, bring the water pipe," "Amir-Arsalan, your mind went to Farrokh-Laqa again and you didn't wash the dishes properly," "Amir-Arsalan, run and make a snack for our vodka." Baqer would blush and look down and would not answer. Whenever the annoyances became too great, especially when Father took the picture of Farrokh-Laqa from the storeroom and showed it, mockingly, to his friends, Baqer didn't talk to us for a few days, and for a long time he didn't tell us any story no matter how much we begged.

Mother couldn't figure out why I insisted on seeing Baqer, but she finally gave in to my pressure and the following day she set out with me to find his house.

Baqer's house was somewhere far from town, outside the city limits. The taxi driver took us to the end of the main street and said he couldn't go any further. In front of us was a dirt field with small houses here and there.

He entrusted himself to God and went forth into the desert. As far as he could see it was a dry and barren desert with nothing except quicksand and deadly thorn bushes. He relied on God's charity and chose a direction in the desert and set out and he traveled five parasangs[5] before sunset, he sat himself down beside a rock...

It took a while until we found someone who knew where Baqer's house was, but since he couldn't give us the address he came along to show us the way. The sun was about to set when we found the house.

Suddenly a garden appeared in the distance. He went closer and saw such a pleasant garden. Cold-weather trees and tropical juniper, poplar, box, and pine rose to the heavens. Green, fresh earth, flowers of diverse colors...

A ten- or twelve-year-old girl with a nursing baby in her arms opened the door. Water from the child's nose was hanging over her lip and she was looking at us with curiosity. They were two of Baqer's daughters. His wife had gone to help the third daughter, who had just given birth, and Baqer was at the house of one of their neighbors. The girl invited us inside. Then she sent one of the boys, who was seven or eight years old, after the father, and the other, who was a bit older, after the mother. In the corner of the house there were two rooms; the floor of one was covered with a carpet and the other with a rug. She took us to the carpeted room. We removed our shoes and sat on the floor in a corner. The room was small, clean, and bright. On the mantel they had put a few pieces of crochet-work. On top of one of them was a framed picture of Emam Khomeini and on top of the other a portrait of Hazrat-e Ali. Above the mantel hung a painting of the desolate plain of Karbala and Emam Hosein's battle with Shemr.[6] In the center of the painting, Shemr had raised Emam Hosein's head on a spear. Brothers and sisters and the household of Emam Hosein, in black chadors and veils, were gathered around Shemr and the severed head. In a corner of the painting was Hazrat-e Abbas with two severed hands who had carried a skin of water in his teeth. In another corner of the painting, Moslem's children were gazing off at some unseen spot with their innocent eyes and sad look.

Five or six minutes later, Baqer's wife arrived.

> Arsalan thought they had changed Farrokh-Laqa. Her moon-like face was like a crescent and her ruby hue was now like saffron and her body was like a thin sugar cane... Without wishing to, Arsalan began to weep . . .

She had a small figure with a black chador on, and she covered her face tightly. When she saw there was no man with us she tossed her chador into a corner. She was extremely thin and pale. Her two front teeth were of gold, and a few others were missing. Her eyes were somewhat crossed, her hair was disheveled and her movements were quick. She kissed us both as if she had known us for a long time.

Baqer arrived a little later.

> The queen opened the curtain and her eyes fell upon the sun of beauty and youth... and the ringlets and beauty-spot of Amir-Arsalan. She knew that ever since the sky has covered the earth the eye of heaven which sees the whole world has not seen one like him...

His figure was bent, his hair was white, his teeth were yellow and decayed. He had a worn suit on and a skull-cap on his head. There was a rosary in his hand and he turned it over continuously.

We were there for about an hour. We had tea and recalled bygone mementos, many of which had not remained in Baqer's mind; and before it became too dark we returned to our home.

Original Position

Tahereh Alavi

But the basic problem lies in these few hours of flight, which makes what was good up until last night turn bad, and also makes what was bad become good and praiseworthy. Especially the efforts of most of the girls on board Flight Number 733 to preserve their chastity. Those efforts will turn into smoke and vanish into thin air at one in the afternoon Paris time.

However things get more complicated if you have a Greek classmate who is about 22 years old (exactly six years younger than you). For your sake he is trying to learn Persian. But the only sentence he has learned is, "What time do you have?" As if your time is different from other people's time. And he wears a watch with a metal band and a large face. Many times you have wanted to tell him in response, "My watch shows the same time as yours." But you have never said anything. Because with him you are always shyer and more apt to blush, and certainly embarrassed and ill at ease. The Greek guy sits to your right and on the slightest pretext turns his head to the left, so that once the professor said to him harshly, "It seems you are particularly interested in the left side of the room. Perhaps, for your sake, we should move the blackboard and put it by the entrance door. How about that?"

Little by little his attentions attract your attention; so that, pretending to look at the greenery on your right, you turn your head in that direction every now and then.

But since it's just your intention to establish a simple friendship with someone of the opposite sex, you see no problem in starting a clearly defined friendship with that young Greek man. One benefit of this is proving to all the mothers and grandmothers of the cotton and fire persuasion[1] that a healthy friendship between a man and a woman is possible.

Feeling a responsibility toward this commitment, you try to justify your words or actions. You interpret his actions as being unintentional. But you expect more of yourself. Then you blame yourself and promise yourself that this time will be your last time. But this is not your last time, and this is what you have been afraid of. Then you enter into another phase and warn yourself that if you continue like this it will mean your efforts have been in vain and the relationship has gone beyond its limits and you may have to break up with him.

Although this phase arrives sooner than expected, again you try to find a solution; maybe there is no need to sever the relationship; that is, it might be enough to limit it. Under the circumstances, for a long time you continue in the same cautious way. But in a few weeks you are back in the same situation. In addition, you have grown tired of blaming yourself and feel you can't go on any longer. And since you can't satisfy your own expectations of yourself, you keep finding fault with him and criticizing the way he walks, the way he speaks, and... It is impossible for you to have him in your home, but when he invites you to his house, you accept. In response to his desires, you keep saying, "No, don't even mention it." And when he insists in a different way you try to divert his attention by talking to him. You tell him about the wedding night and the problems arising from the lack of many things.

And you constantly try to raise the level of your mutual understanding. But he has no interest in understanding your culture, especially not that particular aspect of your culture, and he sees no connection between what is about to happen between the two of you in that small apartment, in a city famous for being the bride of Europe, in that hexagon whose south borders Spain, and whose north... anyway, he can't see any connection between this event and what is going on in another part of the world. However, he puts up with you; it's clear that he still loves you; although he doesn't call you as he did before, and doesn't invite you to his house. Still, from time to time he accompanies you to a museum or a painting exhibit, and sometimes more patiently, sometimes less patiently he analyzes the news from Asia and the Middle East but when you are relaxing at one of the big bright cafés on the Place Charles De Gaulle, while he orders *une bière* and you insist on ordering your good old ancestral tea, if you want to carry on your discussion there, you notice he is not paying any attention to you at all, and when you follow his look you notice he is concentrating on a young couple with their arms wrapped around each other, whispering and laughing together. Less than a week after this he sets all the formalities aside and points out a young woman who in a dark corner without any inhibition is satisfying all the desires of her man. But you consider all this immoral and want by all means to introduce him to grander, more beautiful values. The young Greek man, though, does not understand your values, no matter how much he tries. At this point, you have no choice but to end this relationship. And even though you have certain desires, since you are a human being after all, you convince yourself that a decent and good man is not to be found in this world.

Then you decide to turn your back on the world and live like a nun. Following this decision, you stay home for a while, and when this situation becomes unbearable, you borrow a few tranquilizers from your next-door neighbor.

But contrary to expectations, your Greek friend, who could not understand your behavior before and is a total stranger to the concept of "Pushing away with one's hand and pulling toward by one's legs,"[2] far from being angry at you and treating you harshly, grows more polite toward you day by day. But of course he no longer makes any dates with you, and if you offer to visit an art exhibit or a museum with him, although he thanks you sincerely, half an hour before leaving, he calls in haste and tells you something important has come up and he can't make it and he promises to get in touch with you next week or at most the week after for a get-together. Or sometimes he ends the conversation with a simple *à bientôt*. But if you are just a little intelligent you realize that with this behavior he is playing games with your head. He won't be calling you anymore, and you will gradually turn into a very good person, marginalized, whose presence is not a cause for happiness and whose absence is not a reason for anyone to miss you.

Although you are very sweet, warm, kind and friendly, your remoteness from other people grows greater as the days go by. It seems as if there is a divide between you and the others; when you enter into a crowd, no matter large or small, the crowd suddenly grows silent. As if they have been asked to observe a minute of silence to honor someone dead. But then they pull themselves together and, rolling their eyes, they tap their temples with their fingers. These few taps are full of significance. Then your existence becomes like an insecticide that scatters a crowd at the point of contact.

Your neighbor, who has been living abroad longer than you, the same person who takes tranquilizers for other reasons, tells you are overdoing it, and she is thinking of taking you to a gynecologist as a step toward solving your problem. The doctor only focuses on giving you an hour-long lecture on the harmful effects of this kind of lifestyle. And speaks of what you are still safeguarding as a heavy weight hanging from you. That is why when you come out of the doctor's office you waddle as you walk, so that a kind man on the subway takes you for a pregnant woman and offers you his seat. But as you take the seat you remember the cold, dry face of your doctor who shook her forefinger in warning and said, "Next time you come to me, you should have recovered from this problem, you understand?" and just as you are shaking hands with her to say goodbye, she adds, "Otherwise, you are not to come here again; I won't see you," and shuts the door firmly behind you.

Quite some time after this visit, you are still hoping for a change in yourself, but your neighbor disappoints you by saying, "No one knows how to waste Dian better than you."

As if none of this is enough for you, one day you hear your kind Greek has found a girlfriend. Of course before this you had noticed that he no longer looked toward his left or had any more interest in learning Persian. And of course it's a long time since he asked you for the time, and instead of that metal watch with a large face he wears a small watch with a leather band, and to anyone who looks at his watch he says, "It was a gift," and you understand completely what he means by this. You think you only have to change your seat to once again give all your attention to your studies. But when the Greek only thinks about his watch with the leather band, how can you think of studying?

Finally, one of those Sundays that are great for suicide, the Greek guy calls you again and wants to see you. You make plans to see each other that very night. You haven't hung up yet when you think of three reasons:

—He regrets his behavior.

—He hasn't been able to forget you.

—He wants to make up with you.

You see him with his sweet smile at one of the nice cafes on the Place Charles de Gaulle. He gets up and shakes hands with you politely and kindly. So far everything seems all right. To start with, you talk about the weather, and you keep waiting for the more serious talk, but you never reach that point; instead a woman arrives and sits at your table. Your friend, who has been waiting for her, briefly introduces you, and taking a quick look at his watch, picks up his newspaper in hurry and leaves. Everything happens so quickly you don't even have time to be shocked.

The woman is about forty and heavy-set; she smokes constantly. She wears a denim shirt and pants and has a short haircut. A particular forcefulness is apparent in her manner. She gives you meaningful looks from the instant she arrives. But you show no reaction and continue to smoke inexpertly. The woman is now comfortably leaning on the chair watching you, and freely, without restraint, she asks you about your private life and your plans. She even goes so far as to ask you if you have a friend. Well of course you do, what does she mean? You have a lot of friends; it would take you a whole night to name them: Shayesteh, Simin... but she waves her hand in the air and you grow silent immediately. When you mention a list of friends, it's clear that you don't have a significant friend. At last she suggests you take a walk. When you start walking by her side, she boldly holds your hand in her large hands. You just hope no one sees the way she looks at you or notices the pressure of her fingers on your hand. In her hands yours is sweaty, and it feels as if your whole body is on fire. You want to pull your hand out of her hands. But you think this would be very impolite. You still haven't realized why she is acting like this. Until you get home at night, you keep wondering why she was behaving like that, but you still can't come up with an answer. The Greek calls you late at night and wants to know what you thought of Christian. Was the woman's name Christian? But that's a man's name. But she was a woman. You saw her. But you start to have doubts. Does that mean she wasn't?

Years go by since the story of the young Greek, and you turn into a good and kind person whose life story can be summed up just in a few lines.

This time you fly Flight Number 732. The flight attendant announces that in a few moments you will land at Mehrabad Airport and that she wants the passengers to fasten their seatbelts. A kind hand is placed on your shoulder; it's the young flight attendant, who wants you to return your seat to its original position.

The Wolf Lady

Goli Taraghi

All of us, my children and I and the friends who come to see me from time to time, were terrified of my downstairs neighbor. In exile, in Paris, life is accompanied by hidden anxieties and guilt for being a foreigner who has come from beyond the borders to cramp the space of those who belong here. And with this comes a kind of apology, and a forced retreat, and a silent anger that dares not express itself, and a stinging sense of inferiority that waits for revenge, and a pride rooted in 2,500 years of history, and a dubious, mocking looking down on the symptoms of civilization and modernity, and a belief that we, descendants of Cyrus and Darius, even in our defeat, misery, and wretchedness, are superior to others. (Why? God only knows.) A belief that if we are in this miserable state and nothing remains of our vain glory and grandiloquence, you are to blame; you, the materialist, money-loving, colonialist Westerner.

If not one of these accusations is true, one thing is clear; all my present misfortune is caused by the woman who lives on the floor below, who, like a menacing ghost, is an everlasting presence in our chaotic life. We don't dare walk around, laugh, talk; and since we have just arrived here and don't know the ways and where of life in *Farang*,[1] and since we have been thrown to this part of the world away from a large house with a courtyard full of trees, away from family and friends, we act like moonstruck people and don't know how to walk around without bumping into each other, or how to live without being a nuisance to others. The children have turned into wild animals. My first child is five, and the second is four. They are confused and frightened, and they express their feelings through loud screams and kicking and banging on the door and the wall. My son hits my daughter, and I hit my son, and the neighbor woman bangs on my door. Sometimes she bangs on her ceiling with a broomstick, or she yells, "Shut up!" out the window. Or she yells over the phone so that I hear her voice not only through the receiver but also from the end of the hallway. And this angry, never-ending tune that seems to be coming from the four corners of the earth and sounds like Israfil's trumpet[2] turns my stomach and troubles my naïve backward logic.

I open the door; my glance bashfully lowered, my quivering voice uttering broken and incomplete words, my hand unceremoniously hanging in the air, my feet ready to give up and retreat, my body defeated, defenseless, nailed to the spot, and I express remorse and confess guilt. I promise the neighbor lady that this inhuman noise will not be heard again, and the children who haven't had dinner (the hell with it) will now go to bed with kicks and smacks on the head, and I will move like a weightless mosquito to the end of the hall and remain under my blanket, or under my bed if necessary, for three days and nights in deadly silence, and will try my best to abide by the laws of this land and the rules set by the people of this city.

The lady on the floor below does not believe me. She attacks me again, raises her voice, looks straight into my eyes, twitches her nostrils, huffs and puffs as she speaks, and in a voice like thunder informs me that the situation is worse than ever and the war still continues.

Our cramped apartment, which is so small that even the street vendor of Mahmoodiyeh[3] wouldn't want to rent it, is very expensive since it is in the center of Paris and has a hallway and closets. It is on the fifth floor of a building overlooking a church, and, thanks be to God there are some trees in the churchyard, and a few sparrows and some fat pigeons hang around under the gable roof, and all this reminds me and the children of Tehran and Shemiran⁴ and the Gardens of Darband⁵ and brings us joy. Besides this blessing, the other advantages of this mouse hole are that there is a two-meter balcony in front of the living-room window where we entertain, rest, and have fun. In this garden of delights, we've put as many pots of geraniums and petunias as will fit, and in the evening, weather permitting, we sit peacefully in this tiny spot in the midst of flowers with no fragrance, to munch on the seedy cucumbers and tasteless peaches of *Farang*. If a friend happens to visit us, we invite the guest to this place where there is no room to move and share our good fortune, and he forgets the pain of homesickness. The lady on the floor below, called by the children the Wolf Lady, objects to our get-togethers on the balcony and makes her objections known all the time. She yells, "Quiet!" and this command is so absolute that it chokes us and takes the smiles from our lips. We give up sitting in the garden, I shut the window quickly and tell myself I should be a model of patience and suppress ancient pride with painful humility; especially I, the Iranian, accused of an unknown, already adjudged crime, have absolutely no right to protest. And that in this city people don't sit on their balcony in order to chat and laugh and don't waste their precious time on meaningless chatter and giggling; and if they need to meet with a friend, no doubt in order to discuss world politics, philosophy and literature, they invite her to a café and finish their business while hastily drinking thick coffee, trying to convince each other. But the children don't understand. They have been exiled to a cold, sad, unkind place from the bosom of their grandmother, their aunts, from an abundance of love and affection, charming airs and caresses, and they don't understand the reason for this great injustice. They love the sound of the phone ringing and the doorbell; they even prefer the coming of the Wolf Lady to the deadly silence and isolation in our home.

The French don't open their doors that easily. First they check through the small peephole in the door to see who's outside. Then they ask who you are and what you want. When they're completely reassured, they open the inside latch, then the first lock and then the second one; at which time, they check again; then they cautiously open the door. If you're there without advance notice, they immediately excuse themselves and ask you to leave; if you're there for something important, they take care of it right at the door. Our home has no locks and peepholes. We open the door quickly, without checking; we're happy when unexpected guests drop by. The children invite everyone in, even the Wolf Lady. I turn the light on under the kettle and greet the person at the door with a smile. I don't like to talk with people in the hallway, I like it when we sit down, take our time, drink tea, and even if there is a problem between us, to solve it peaceably. The lady on the floor below has no time for such things. She comes up. Knocks at the door. Yells. Leaves. The concierge is the same; she comes, she knocks, she gives us packages from the postman, she leaves. The agent from the power company is just like them; comes, knocks, checks the meter and leaves. Saying hello or goodbye is not the fashion here. The next-door neighbor is a middle-aged woman. She is not ill tempered. She has no complaints about us. She doesn't bang on our door. But it seems as if she is not there; that neither she nor we exist at all. I sometimes run into her in the hallway, or we take the elevator at the same time. She doesn't say a word; neither do I. If I say hello, she responds; if I don't, she says nothing. She leaves early in the morning and comes back late at night. Her loneliness troubles me; the thought of someone being so isolated and lonely in her own city turns my stomach. The lady on the floor below is very much alive. She is insane. We have a quarrel with her, which is a kind of bond in itself. Not a moment goes by when we are not aware of her existence, and nothing in our lives is unconnected.

I have enrolled the children in the neighborhood kindergarten, and I'm glad they look after them all day; from eight in the morning to five in the afternoon. I am happy above all because the Wolf Lady is pleased. I wish the kindergarten were open on Sundays as well and classes were held until late at night. Taking the children to school is not easy. They don't want to go; they're afraid of teachers whose language they don't understand. The mornings are dark and it's usually raining. We don't have a car; we have to walk down one avenue and three streets. They both cry. As soon as we get to the second street my son's morning tummy ache starts; he turns around and clings to my legs and wants us to go back home. I feel sorry for him, but when I think of home, the neighbor's face appears before my eyes and overwhelms maternal pity. My daughter is barely awake; she keeps dozing off all the way to school; she sits on the steps of every house on the way and yawns; if I leave her she falls asleep right there. The only way to get her to walk is with the help of chocolates and sweets. As soon as she sits down, I tempt her with a sweet in a colorful wrapper. She jumps up and runs after the candy a little, as soon as she puts it in her mouth she wants to go back to sleep. Then I grab her by her collar and drag her along to the kindergarten. Rain is also a great nuisance. I don't know whose head to hold the umbrella over. I know they face sneezing and fever and shivering and coughing at night, and all that noise is going to pass through the window seals to reach the sensitive ears of the lady on the floor below.

If it were not for the war, I'd go back. If it were not for fear of the bombs and missiles, I wouldn't stay here a single day. The truth is, though, the battlefield is right here, and the real enemy is lying in wait on the lower floor. There was a good chance we wouldn't have been hit if we had stayed on, while here we are constantly on the run and getting hit by an invisible machine gun aiming straight at us. Saddam Hussein is beyond the frontiers, and the Wolf Lady is only a few steps away. We have put our hands on our heads like prisoners of war and yielded in humiliation. Our crime and the cause of our problems is not knowing the language and not understanding the words. No weapon is more lethal than words; our lips are sealed and the enemy's victory is complete: she has power over words. The lady on the floor below has come up with a new stratagem: she has sent us a long formal letter resembling a formal indictment. In it she has issued several important regulations; firstly is to cover our wood floor with a thick carpet to muffle the noise of our footsteps. We were to avoid wearing shoes (especially ones with high heels) and wooden clogs; we were not to sit on the balcony; we were not to talk in the bathroom and kitchen because the vent carried our voices; neither were we to take a bath early in the morning or after nine at night, nor were we to flush the toilet during these hours. We were not to slam the cabinet doors, nor were we to emit any loud noise, such as laughing, sneezing, coughing, or farting. The final directive, underlined in red ink, emphatically recommends that we stay home less and try to spend as much time as possible outside.

We have no choice but to obey; immediately we cover the floors with padding. We walk around; we speak in murmurs. Friends who drop by leave their shoes at the door. Our fear is communicated to them as well. We have accepted being circumspect and quiet and suppressing our desires. Little by little we have forgotten that we are human beings, and that people have freedom within their own four walls. Very soon, and without question, we have agreed to the regulations as issued. We have submitted easily and naturally to the Wolf Lady's dictatorship. We are not used to defending our rights; we don't know our own rights in this country. We didn't know our rights in the past either; we thought what we had was enough for us, that it was the remainder of our heritage. The Wolf Lady is conscious of her own superiority; her fangs grow sharper every day. Of all her regulations, the last is the hardest to obey: "Spend most of your time outside." Where can we go? Most of my friends are artists and writers; they don't have wives and children. They don't have a lot of money and big houses; they can't possibly entertain. They live in small rooms filled with books and papers or paints and brushes and easels. Their apartments are no place for a child. Those who do have families have enough trouble with their own children; they have no patience with other people's kids. The only place to escape to is the park. In front of our home is a shabby park where the old women of the neighborhood and Arab housemaids hang around. At dusk the drunken beggars gather there and count their money. I hate this park; it fills me with melancholy. The only amusements for children in this park are playing in the sandbox and on the wretched slide. The Luxembourg Garden is beautiful; but it's far away, and going anywhere far away in the unpredictable Parisian weather is a risky business. As soon as you get there it starts to rain, and as we're not used to umbrellas and hats we're utterly unprotected and have to take shelter for hours under the cover of a shop awning; we return home disappointed and soaking wet. Unfortunately, it always rains on Sunday and we are condemned to stay at home. We seek refuge on our small balcony, but our neighbor's protest is taking this last place of refuge away from us. The happiest time in our lives is when the children are asleep and the lights on the lower floor are out and I have received a few letters from wayfaring vagrant friends and relatives scattered around the four corners of the earth. I don't read the letters immediately; I save them for the nighttime, when I'm in bed with a cup of hot coffee and a perfectly lovely cigarette. The first letter is from Leyli; she lives in Tehran and is happy and content; her children are going to school and she has thousands of friends, and they roam around in the gardens and side streets and the public squares of the quarter and they are not afraid of the war and the bombs. She has a job and is not afraid of the Islamic dress code; she goes to parties or has scads of guests over. The second letter is from Dariush "A;" it is so bitter and sad it makes me cry. He is unemployed and penniless. His son is a fugitive. His friends are in hiding, and he paints such a bleak picture of the future it scares me. The third letter is from Mr. K; it is a minute, and concise report of the bad news; his nephew has been shot by a firing squad and his mother has tried to commit suicide twice. The high cost of living is iniquitous; soon everyone will die of hunger. The Afghan construction workers raid houses every night and cut the throats of women and children, old and young, from ear to ear. The Russians are hand in glove with the Americans, the disintegration of Iran is a certainty. The sons of Mashd Akbar, the gardener, have joined the Komiteh[6] of Mahmoodiyeh and are planning to confiscate his property. The last letter is from my mother; it's several pages long; it's like an Iranian film script; action and adventure and contradictions. The characters in this letter are both extremely fortunate and extremely unfortunate. There is no end to the parties, the excursions, the fun and good cheer; they get together all the time; they eat and drink and they are eternally grateful to the Islamic Republic. Suddenly the page turns; the letter's next lines tell of deprivations: there's no electricity, there's no water, you can't find meat, there's a cholera epidemic, there are no doctors and no medicine, there's no security, there are no police or watchmen, the high cost of living and the scarcity of goods are tyrannical, iniquitous, and protection, inflation and scarcity are oppressive, there are two feet of snow on the ground, you can't find fuel oil, the cold weather is deadly, and the hardest to bear is the loneliness and separation from the children. The letter ends with the renewed abuse of Farangestan[7] and Paris and says we have all we need here, we are respected in our own city and we are not under obligation to foreigners and everyone who has left has made a mistake, and again she talks about parties and eating and having fun, and in conclusion, in a motherly way, she suddenly announces that she has decided to sell the house and everything she owns to provide herself with a hole abroad where she can spend the remainder of her days in peace.

It's late. I can't sleep. My daughter has the chickenpox; she's burning up with fever. I am worried; and I don't know who to ask for help. I want to write, but my brain isn't working. I turn the pages of the book I have in my hand; I read a page and realize I haven't understood a word. It's been raining nonstop for two days. I wish someone would come visit me. In spite of the winter, it's sunny in Tehran, and Leyli talks about the Friday morning walks. They all go to the mountains and have breakfast at a coffeehouse on the way. Dariush "A" makes fun of all that; he writes that even the mountains are in mourning and black snow has fallen from the sky on people's heads. The children are asleep. They both have a fever. I am worried. I wish someone would come see me. I tell myself I will go back. In my own city at least my aunt, my uncle, and my mother are there to help me. There isn't anyone living above and below me. I'm not scared of my neighbors, and I can yell in my own house. I can jump up and down. I can cry. I can dance. I will go back tomorrow. Dariush "A" is the only person who encourages me to stay; he tells me, "My dear, just where do you have freedom in your own home? You are not allowed to breathe, talk, think, wear clothes, eat without observing rules and regulations; there are even guidelines for going to the toilet. Even your sexual intercourse, your lovemaking, your dying are not free; and every second, every moment of your life is ordained." What should I do? Should I stay or should I go back?

Someone is knocking at the door. I listen. I get up. Who could it be? The doorbell isn't working; they are banging on the door. My heart starts pounding. It's bad news; I'm sure it is. Something must have happened to my mother. My brother has been arrested. It's the police. A friend is homeless. The book drops from my hand. My foot gets tangled in the wire of the bedside lamp. Quickly, I put something on my nightgown. The children are asleep. Who could that be? "I'm coming," I say in Persian; and then in French, hastily, "Coming." I open the door. What? It's the lady from the lower floor. I wasn't expecting her because she is usually asleep this late at night; besides, there's no reason for her to come here. I am dumbfounded; I feel I have turned pale. My heart beats fast and I am frustrated because of my helplessness and mumbling. The Wolf Lady notices my stuttering and shakiness and attacks. She raises her voice; she says:

—What is going on? What are you doing?

—Who?

She asks, "What is all this noise?"

—What noise?

I am used to thinking she is in the right; that the children are up jumping up and down. I take a few steps toward their room. I stand. I listen; there is complete silence. She is talking nonsense; there is no reason for her to come here. This time I am right. It is obvious. It doesn't require knowledge of the French language or of Western and Eastern cultures. It is simple human logic. There is no sound in our home; the lady from the lower floor is wrong. This time I don't give in to force, and since I am right, and my being in the "right" is a great advantage which gives me energy and courage, I raise my head, my voice comes out and I ask:

—What noise?

The lady does not expect a reprimand; she is taken aback. She stretches her neck out and takes a quick look inside. I ask in a louder voice:

—What noise?

The Wolf Lady's hesitation makes me bolder. An old anger buried in my gut suddenly erupts and fills my body like fever. I get hot. I perspire and yell. The downstairs neighbor does not expect me to yell; she is dumbfounded. I grow brazen. My stomach starts to growl. I take a step forward. This time I look straight into the Wolf Lady's face and see her for the first time as she is. I had a different image of her; I thought she was an old hag, that she even had horns and beard; I thought she looked like Dracula and had fangs. She isn't anything like that. She's as old as I am; the same size as me. She has short brown hair, which is oily and unwashed, and her dress, unlike the usual French woman, is not chic and tidy. She has two deep lines around her mouth, which give her face a bitter look. She is tired and angry. She is pregnant. She looks like all the sad women who go to work early in the morning, and at night, tired and hopeless, collapse in front of the TV.

In broken French I explain to her that the children are sleeping; that I was in bed. I suddenly think of speaking to her in my own language or in English; that's easier for me. The French are scared of the English language and, with childish pride and backward stubbornness, refuse to learn English, but their dislike of English is very superficial; deep in their hearts they are fascinated by America and Americans.

My mouth is open in amazement; it seems as if I have wings. Nobody is able to stop me anymore. I chirp like a nightingale and swim in the ocean of words. My thoughts are the same as my language. I don't have to control myself, to simplify and shorten my sentences. I want to give a speech; I am drunk with the power of my ability to speak. I can curse in this language over which I have control; I do just that. I don't know if the Wolf Lady understands the meaning of my words or not; but I don't care. The vibration of my voice, the flash of my eyes, and my aggression are telling the woman from the lower floor to get the hell out. If she shows up here again she'll be cut into pieces. "Shitty, stupid bitch!" I yell. I shake my fist in the air and stomp my foot. As I reach the apex of my power she grows smaller; she looks like a lamb about to be slaughtered. I, on the other hand, have grown taller, and my teeth have grown like those of Dracula's. I've grown horns and a beard; I look like a dragon and I love it. If they let me, I will swallow the poor Wolf Lady. Ha ha! I whirl, Ha ha ha! I attack. The lady lets out a feeble shriek and runs toward the elevator. I don't want to let go. God only knows what I say. I am enjoying my power; I want to go to the upper floor and knock at the door and complain; to lay down the law that they don't have the right to talk and walk and scratch their faces.

As soon as the door opens, the lower-floor lady jumps into the elevator and disappears, panting; she disappears for real. The next day, that month and the following months there is no sign of her; she seems to have melted into the floor. A while later, we see each other accidentally in the hallway next to the entrance of the building, we turn away our faces and go on quickly. The only thing I remember of her is her big belly and tired eyes; she is in the last days of her pregnancy.

With the grand absence of the Wolf Lady, life takes on its normal shape. We walk around the rooms with our shoes on, speak comfortably without fear; we even sit in our balcony when it is sunny and are not afraid to laugh. The children are calmer and don't feel Dracula's heavy shadow over their shoulders. We go out as we like and we don't have to stay out.

Summer comes; it is around dawn when I wake to an infant's cry. Listening carefully, I realize the sound is coming from the lower floor, I laugh to myself. The Wolf Lady is tied up; it's her turn to care for the baby and go without sleep.

Years pass; we still think of going back. The children have grown and don't create any difficulties about going to school. They go and come back by themselves. They have fewer anxieties and they have forgotten about the lower-floor lady.

It is the beginning of autumn, and one of those Sundays; the weather is cloudy; there is a burning wind. The children are at home and we have guests that evening. I go out to shop at the exorbitant Arab's; he doesn't close on Sundays. I pass by the beggars' park. I see the Wolf Lady sitting on a bench; her eyes fixed on a distant point. She is cold; she has pulled the lapels of her coat up and hunched her shoulders. A half-open book is on her knees. A half-lit cigarette is stuck between her fingers; her hair is dirty and disheveled as usual. Her right leg is stretched out; her ankle is twisted and her shoe has come off. Her child is busy playing in the sand. She is so sad and broken I feel sorry for her. I ask myself why she is sitting in this wretched park in this cold, and I remember her letter. No doubt her neighbor has complained and ordered her to take her kid out of the house to play. I realize another Wolf Lady has targeted her; I feel bad. In this opulent building overlooking a church are tens of wolf-like-lambs who are lying in wait to blame each other for their miseries; tired and hopeless wolves, with petty wishes and vague hopes, waiting for better days and things.

I ask myself, Could it be any other way? Could it?

A few drops of rain fall on my face. I walk quickly. The lower-floor lady, confused and disappointed, is sitting there. A drunken beggar has passed out under the trees; or maybe he's dead. No one looks at him. I hurry. I think about my guests, and in the rush of shopping and cooking I forget my question.

PART THREE

How joyful flying

Marcia

Kader Abdolah

Now and then, exceptionally, it happens that some people, having come out of nothingness, enter my life. They stay with me for a moment; then they leave.

They disappear, but in reality, they stay with me forever.

She, Marcia, has left, too.

She may be gone all right, yet she stays near me.

Her desk is unoccupied now, but I still see her in her seat.

Although she is no longer there, I still smell the perfume of her long rippling hair.

Marcia was an intern who came to work for a while at the old public library.

She was Dutch, but her long wavy hair, black as night, betrayed her foreign roots.

I was—as I am now—in the basement, seated in front of my computer. Suddenly I heard footsteps in the hallway. A woman's footsteps.

I recognized the clicking of high heels. That sound was locked away in a corner of the cave of my memory.

A silhouette appeared behind the frosted glass on the door. A second later, the door opened slowly. A young woman stuck her head in.

"Hello! I think this is where I am supposed to be. My name is Marcia."

She set her black napkin on the desk—which is bare today—and went over and planted herself next to the stove.

With a movement of her head she indicated the desk and said: "I hope that's not my desk... it is so ugly and bare!"

I put a pile of old books there, and two or three diskettes next to them.

"Now, it's not ugly anymore."

When she looked at me, I saw she had green eyes. An old memory suddenly came to my mind. I thought: There; another girl who is never going to leave me.

That afternoon, returning home, I felt ill at ease. Something was burning inside me like a fire.

In the grip of an indefinable feeling, I went to bed and hid under the covers.

I fell asleep at once and had a dream. I dreamed it was night. Coming out of nothingness, the wind was blowing a veil toward me. When it came closer, it seemed to me that it was my sister's black chador. The chador she covered herself in on the night she left. Now I recognized her long hair streaming behind her. Finally, she herself appeared.

She did not stay beside me long. The night swept her away again. You might say the wind was carrying her far away from me.

Until then I had never dreamed about her. I continued to wait for her, but she did not come back.

How many years was it that I hadn't seen her?

Nine years? A hundred years? Three hundred and fifty-five years?

I have no idea. I just knew that I had not dreamed about her for centuries, and that many more centuries had passed since I saw her last.

The spot where I work is located in the basement, in the hallway of an archival storage place. The library has the use of a vast warehouse where they keep miles of books that haven't yet been inventoried and catalogued; thousands of volumes several hundred years old.

Some are so old that it is forbidden to touch them. They would crumble to dust.

No one knows how they got here. Some come from old libraries that were torn down a long time ago. Others come from private collections. They must all be filed before the public can use them.

I am the only one who makes a record of the books in storage. Every day, I scour the old shelves and pick up a pile of books, which I bring to my office.

I dust them off with a cloth; I use a brush to remove the dust that has slipped in between the pages; after that, I write a synopsis of each book, which I put on the computer later.

My colleagues don't want to work here in this basement. That's why I'm always alone with this old, much-too-slow computer.

Sometimes the interns come to give me a hand. They don't like the place either; they'd rather not be isolated. It's not very pleasant to acquire one's first experience in a basement, and with a foreigner to boot.

But this isn't always the case. Marcia, for example, was different from the rest.

The second day, I went with Marcia through the underground hallway toward the storage place. I wanted to show her everything.

I opened the old brown door to let her through and turned the light switch on. Two or three bulbs lit up, but it was still dark. She had to wait a moment before her eyes grew used to the half-light.

"My, there certainly are a lot of books!" she exclaimed. She scoured the shelves and went from one book to another, reading the titles. I watched her.

Something radiated from her, something connected with my past. But what?

I closed my eyes in order to concentrate for a moment, but again I heard the footsteps, the soft clicking of her heels on the tiled floor. I knew those footsteps...

"In here, I breathe the past," she exclaimed.

I went over to her. With the local daily, she swept away a spider's web between the shelves.

"It's almost inconceivable. People have been putting out newspapers for centuries. In fact those people have died, yet these go on living," she said.

She unfolded one of the newspapers and leafed through it gingerly. She bent over a piece—a poem—and tried to read it.

Above the poem was a drawing; a portrait of the author.

"Listen, when I read this work, the poet comes to me," she said. She stood stock-still, listening intently.

"Do you hear that? He's coming; he's getting nearer to me."

I didn't move, but instead of hearing someone coming closer, I heard someone running away.

"Funny, huh," she said, laughing; "Don't you think so?"

She started going from one shelf to another again until her silhouette melted into the dark.

My sister, too, disappeared that way into the darkness.

With me, that's how it always happens. As soon as I take a person into my heart, they leave me. They fade away in the night.

To tell the truth, I had never had the chance to know my sister well. I don't know if her eyes were always so green.

When she was small, I rarely saw her. She was deep in her own little world. She was just my little sister who was living at home and going to school.

Every time I went back to my parents' house I noticed that she had grown a little more. But she didn't yet have that long rippling hair.

For many years it was impossible for me to return to my parents' house due to the risk of being arrested, assassinated, or betrayed; something that, in my country, was the order of the day.

The situation was too dangerous; so much so that I was forced to sever all ties to my past.

One day I had such a burning need to see my family that I packed my bag and left that evening, in secret, for my native city.

At home, everything had changed. In the interim, my parents had grown very old; the walls were moldering; the windows were dilapidated; the stairs were worn, and the trees had grown.

Every corner of the house sheltered a piece of my past.

In the courtyard, I went up the stairs leading to my old room, now my sister's.

The stove was lit like the old times, my books were still arranged on the shelf I had set against the wall myself, and my clothes were in the wardrobe as before.

I put my suitcase on my old desk and went back down the stairs to my parents.

They were happy I was there, but I read the fear in their eyes, too. They were in dread of a raid by a death-squad coming to arrest me.

Late in the evening, as I was reading on the floor next to the stove, I heard footsteps on the staircase.

Someone was coming cautiously up the stairs. I heard the clicking of a woman's heels.

They were not my mother's footsteps. There was no other woman in our house. Who could it be?

A silhouette appeared behind the glazed door. She stopped, and the door opened slowly.

"You aren't sleeping?" She asked in a low voice.

At the time I didn't even recognize her. It was Marsi.

"Why, is that you, Marsi? What long hair you have now!"

She came in. I saw that she was very frightened.

"What's the matter?" I asked.

"I think you'd better not stay here tonight."

"Why?"

"I think you had better leave."

"Leave? What are you getting at?"

"Listen, it's that tonight... I'm going to do something."

All at once I got goose bumps. In less than a minute I saw what was going on. I understood that she was going to do something dangerous and that she was worried about me.

"I have to leave," she said, and wrapped herself in a black chador.

I got up. I thought I should say something, warn her of the risk she was taking, but I kept silent.

She was now covered from head to foot in the everlasting black chador. You might say the young girl standing there was a stranger, someone I didn't know.

Only two green eyes, familiar, tearful, were looking at me. I held out my arms. She came to me, kissed me on the left cheek, and left.

Standing in the doorway, I followed her with my eyes. I wanted to call her back to see her one more time, but I restrained myself. I stood there until she had disappeared into the darkness; then I slipped into my coat, got my bag, and went noiselessly downstairs, thinking *Something is going to happen soon. Something I can't prevent. Since when has she been in the resistance? What can I do? What should I say to my parents? Do I need to wake them up? No, I'll let them sleep peacefully tonight. Tomorrow, at sunrise, they'll see for themselves what the night has brought them.*

Outside, it was cold. A mysterious silence reigned over our street. In fact, I should have run for it fast, but I couldn't. I decided to go look for her. I shouldn't have exposed myself to the danger, but I couldn't stop myself.

She had to be somewhere in the neighborhood. I wouldn't meddle in her affairs, but if she was in danger I could help her.

I wandered around the streets, bag in hand. Not a sound in the city. You might call it the calm before the storm.

Where could she be? What did she mean to do under cover

of this black, silent night? To get revenge? My God, the reprisals! Into what adventure was she rushing headlong?

Did she mean to kill the assassin with two bullets? To get revenge for the two bullets in our brother's head?

I was listening to the night without moving. Suddenly shots rang out. Somewhere a bullet whistled in the sky. I held my breath. Fresh shots were fired.

I ran in the direction of the street where the largest mosque of the city stood. It was hard to tell where the shots were coming from. I didn't know which direction I should go.

At an intersection, I stopped, out of breath. Suddenly I heard someone running along the street where the mosque was. In the diffuse light of the mosque I caught sight of a woman in a black chador. She fled in the direction of the bazaar and vanished into the night.

Was it Marsi? No, that wasn't her... And yet...

The crisp clicking of her heels echoed down the empty street.

Shit, what was she thinking of, wearing those stupid shoes?

I tried to catch up with her. No sooner did I reach the mosque when I heard shouts.

A group of bearded men appeared, guns in hand. I hid in an alley and saw nothing more, but I heard the boots of men rushing in the direction of the bazaar.

My sister left that night; I never saw her again.

She left like so many others, but she stayed with me. She is still running along an obscure street in my memory.

I have often thought about her these last months, but she hasn't appeared even in my dreams.

No doubt she fled so deep into my memory that she could never reappear.

This was like owning a movie without showing it.

As soon as Marcia came, Marsi came too, but not for long.

Every day, Marcia arrived a little before I did.

She would go to the storage place and bring back a pile of books, which she would put on her desk, and then wait for me to arrive.

One day when we were busy entering the data into the computer, she suddenly stopped reading aloud and pricked up her ears.

"Listen! I hear footsteps above us. Don't you hear that?"

"It's the people in the reading room."

She listened, not moving.

"Great! Before I came to work here, I had a completely different idea of a library. I thought all they had was reading rooms, but now... This is really great! The public doesn't know we're here at all. We hear them, but they don't hear us. Listen! Listen; up there, someone just ran out. Did you hear those quick footsteps, too? A woman's. Did you hear them, too?"

Yes, I thought; I certainly noticed that, but I don't need to listen carefully. The thing is, I always hear a woman running.

Deep in thought, she took a cigarette out of her purse, put it between her lips and lit it with a match. She wasn't used to smoking. For a moment, the smoke hid her face from me. I thought: She's not there anymore; she's disappeared, too.

She came to me one day and said, "I'm leaving... I must leave."

I wanted to ask where she was going, but I didn't. I always knew one day she would have to leave, but the news still caught me off guard.

Surprised, I just stood there looking at her. She came over, kissed me on the cheek and left.

I wanted to follow, watch her leave, but I didn't do anything.

I waited for the clicking of her heels to disappear. Then, alone, I went into the hallway.

It was empty; only the musky fragrance of her hair still filled the space.

I don't believe in destiny, but I am someone who, when he loves a woman, is abandoned by her. She leaves me and never comes back to me.

I believe I am not the only one to suffer such a fate or to have such a past.

In my opinion, Marcia knew that, too.

"I've brought you something from the storeroom," she said one day.

"For me?"

"Yes, for you," she insisted.

She laid an old book on my desk.

I picked it up. It was dusty. I dusted it with a rag. Over the years, the pages had become damaged and loose. I looked for a date but I couldn't find any. The mice had eaten away the date.

The text had been written by hand and bore an old seal on the flyleaf, a sign that the book came from a private collection.

Here in this library, I had learned to read old Dutch, but this text dated from an even more remote period, and it was even more abstruse.

"What is this?"

"A diary, I think."

"Who wrote it?"

"A Portuguese poet."

I leafed through it.

"A Portuguese? In Dutch?"

The pages were of handmade paper. A drawing related to the contents adorned the beginning of every story. This drawing showed a man who was hiding in an alley and watching something. In another drawing there was a group of police in pursuit of someone or something. Somewhere else, a young girl was running away.

Suddenly, on top of the following page, I saw a very clear illustration of this young girl, in black and green inks. A curl of her black hair escaped from the scarf she was wearing on her head.

My heart began to beat wildly. I closed the book.

"Where did you find this?"

"In a dark little corner of this old cupboard."

"What could this Portuguese poet have been looking for here?"

"He had escaped from the Inquisition."

She didn't say anything else.

I had every reason to leaf through the book one more time, but I didn't do it; I didn't dare. I was afraid of coming across the portrait of the poet on one of the pages.

Marcia has gone and the book is in the drawer of my desk. I haven't opened it again. They say history repeats itself. I don't believe it, and yet I am afraid that it is true, at least in my case.

I can no longer control myself. Since I don't believe in destiny, I have no reason to be scared.

I open my desk drawer and take out the book; I switch on the desk lamp and turn the pages. I know the poet's portrait must be somewhere; my hands are trembling, but I continue to leaf through the diary.

I find his portrait on the top of page 49; he is sitting at a table; he is about 38 years old, with graying temples.

An old book is open in front of him; from his attitude one can see he is searching for something.

Translated from the Dutch into French by Anne-Marie de Both-Diez and from the French by the editors

Zarathustra's Fire

Hushang Golshiri

There were seven of us sitting in the living room of the Foundation's housing complex[1] at a round table, with two flasks of tea, five or six glasses, a bowl of a sugar cubes, and an ashtray. Three sides of the room were of glass and on the other side, on the right, was a wooden bar without any shelves behind it; and in the middle there was a door that led to the TV room and a payphone next to a couch and a bookshelf that mostly held the works of Heinrich Böll. On the left side of the door was a fireplace where Banuyi and I had been putting logs made of paper on a pile of wood chips since the early hours of the night and had finally lit the fire, which was now beginning to take and was burning with a low red flame in the middle of the logs.

We, Banuyi and I, had arrived a week ago, and for two or three nights we, with an Iranian painter and his wife, had moved the chairs around the table to face the fireplace and at night we had come there to warm up by the fire. Around us, outside the glass walls, were the silhouettes of a few trees laden with blossoms on a lawn only illuminated here and there.

Apart from us, there was a Russian woman writer by the name of Natasha and a couple from Albania. We only knew the man's name—Yelvi. He had been there for only a couple of months, alone; and then when the Civil War began in Albania he wanted to bring his wife and children out. It was a few days since his wife and his two daughters had arrived and it was the first night they were joining our gathering. The very first day they arrived, Banuyi said, "Their little girl goes back inside their house as soon as she sees me."

I said, "She is afraid of me, too; as soon as she saw me, she let out a scream and went and hid behind her father."

It took her two or three days to get used to our presence.

It seemed she only knew Albanian. Now, with her short, boyish hair, she was in the TV room from morning until noon and from afternoon to night and was apparently answering the telephone; all she would say was *nein*, and then she would hang up. Those of us who were close to the phone, would run to get to the phone as soon as we heard it ringing, before it was disconnected. I don't know from whom—maybe Sylvia, the painter's wife who was French and knew a little Persian—we heard that in Tirana the children and their mother had often been forced to lie on the ground so they wouldn't get hit by a bullet from people going around armed.

Banuyi, a glass of tea in her hand, said, "In the evening when I came to watch the news on the German TV, trying to understand something from the pictures, when they showed a demonstration in front of the German embassy, Anisa said, 'Tirana.' I said, 'Nein, Iran, Tehran.' She yelled, 'Nein, Tirana!' I leaned toward her gently and said, 'Nein, Tehran,' and pointed to myself. She cried, 'Tirana, Tirana!' and she ran out."

We had not drunk our first cup of tea when first Yelvi's wife and then Yelvi came in; after Sylvia invited them to, they sat down. Yelvi turned to Banuyi and said, "Nein, Tirana," and laughed.

Banuyi said, "Nein, Tehran!"

Then she said in English, "I came to listen to the news. Anisa was there, too."

Yelvi shrugged his shoulders and waved his hands and turning to Sylvia said something. Sylvia said, "She doesn't understand English; she only recognizes cognates."

Turning to Sylvia, Banuyi said in Persian, "They might be upset; please explain what happened."

Sylvia said in a broken Persian, "I'm not in the mood. He understands."

Yelvi was a composer; besides Albanian and Russian, he knew German and French and I don't know how many other languages. Banuyi and I knew English, and Morad understood a few words of English, but he spoke only in Persian. Yelvi's wife apparently understood a little English; or maybe she did not understand and simply kept smiling. Natasha knew Russian and a little English. So if Sylvia and Yelvi and Banuyi and I and possibly Natasha were patient it was possible to understand what everyone was saying. But Sylvia looked sick; or maybe she really was sick. I don't know from whom we had heard that she had had an operation on her chest.

When the phone rang, Natasha got up and ran toward the phone and said, "It is from Paris; it is for me."

She had guessed right. She was talking, apparently in Russian. We were sitting quietly looking at the fire and perhaps at the shadow of the blossoming trees on the other side of the glass and listening to Natasha, who was talking loudly. I got up and poured tea for the four of us and signaled to Yelvi, asking him if he wanted any, saying in English, "Tea."

Using his head and hands he signaled that he didn't want any, and he also said something. Sylvia said, "They usually use tea bags."

Yelvi's wife said in English, "Yes."

I poured for her. She picked it up, smelled it, but didn't even touch it. The sound of Natasha's laughter, loud and piercing, came from the next room. Yelvi shook his head and seemed to push the sound back with his hand. I asked Sylvia, "It seems he doesn't like Natasha; maybe he doesn't like all Russians?"

Sylvia said only a couple of words in French to Yelvi. When Yelvi answered her, she pulled the two sides of her shawl that she had wrapped around her thin shoulders and arms and said, "Yelvi says, 'Her voice and movements, I mean, very aggressive, as if she is the only one here.' "

The flame was now growing higher and reached the bank of the logs all around it. We had gone through so much trouble to light it. Banuyi put in chips of wood and I blew on it. And finally we wadded a newspaper and placed it under the chips and leaves until the fire took. When Morad and Sylvia appeared with a log in their hands, we were sitting and looking at the fire which, flickering, was rising from the midst of the darkness of the leaves and the newspaper and twisting around the chips.

Yelvi said something. Sylvia said, "He has heard the news about Iran."

Morad said, "But he talked a lot."

In a tired voice Sylvia said, "For you it doesn't have—how do you say?—oh, anything new. High school and university students, many, have gone in front of the German embassy. They have yelled, very much. About the Berlin trial. They wanted to attack the embassy, but the police were there, they had made a chain, with their hands. Anti-riot police were there. Then they left."

Natasha came in; she was laughing. She leaned toward Yelvi and was saying something loudly and she pointed at her head and her face and her neck and the collar of her white shirt, and her legs, and then she looked like she was holding crutches under her arms and she laughed again. Yelvi wasn't laughing. He bent his head and in his soft voice explained to Sylvia. Sylvia said, "He says, 'Her friend has decided to come and pick her up at the station. He has described everything about himself, then, finally, he has remembered that he has crutches.'"

We looked at Natasha. She looked at us. She was surprised. She explained in English and then again she pointed to her hand and her face, the line above her upper lip and the collar of her blouse and lastly her pants, and finally once again she pretended to be standing on two crutches and laughed loudly. Banuyi and I laughed, too. Banuyi said, "Natasha says she is going to Paris tomorrow. This is the first time she is going there. She called someone she knew only by name to come pick her up. Natasha asked him how she would know him. He told her, 'Well, I'll have a beret on. It's gray. I also have a moustache. My tie will be dark red with blue stripes. I'll be wearing a checked jacket and gray pants.' Then he said, 'Don't be upset if I arrive late. I broke my leg last month and I still have to walk on crutches.' "

Morad and Sylvia and the two of us laughed. Yelvi's wife just smiled. Yelvi seemed to be looking at the fire. Natasha drew a moustache over her upper lip, and said in English, "Moustache." And then she laughed, her shoulders shaking, and finally sat down next to Banuyi. This time Yelvi explained to his wife, certainly in Albanian, and pointed to Natasha, then to his upper lip and to his shirt, and finally pretended to be standing on two crutches. His wife laughed, too, quietly. Natasha laughed loudly again.

Morad said, "Ask Yelvi, what's the deal with this Albanian king?"

Sylvia said something and in response Yelvi pointed to his head with his finger and again looked at the fire. His wife kept smiling.

Morad said again, "Ask him precisely about this king thing; I'm very interested. I hope we don't go back to where we started."

Sylvia asked; then finally she translated, "He says, 'We, our problem is the Mafia, the Russian and Italian Mafia. They have weapons, all of them. Some people are attacking because they are hungry. How do you say? They do (with her hand she grabbed something in the air) whatever they find.' "

I said, "Loot."

"Yes, thanks. They loot, from the houses. The stores—he says—are empty."

Yelvi explained again, then he mentioned the name Anisa and said in English, "My daughter." Then he went on speaking in French.

Natasha asked him something; maybe in Russian. Then they spoke for a while. Natasha stood up and she was shouting. Yelvi, his head down, was answering, still softly.

Sylvia said quietly, "I do not understand; it occurs to me that they have the argument about these Mafias being Russian or Albanian."

"What was he saying before that?" I asked.

"I don't remember."

"He mentioned Anisa."

"Yes, yes. I forgot. They, Yelvi's family, did their sleeping on the ground most of the time. No, not sleeping; they were awake (she pointed to the glass next to her). Fearing the bullet, they are sleeping on the ground. Now, at night, Anisa has dreams and jumps, from the bed; she is thrown, no, she goes herself to the ground, on the ground—how do you say?"

Natasha was now explaining to Banuyi in broken English; first she apologized for having been angry. Banuyi translated, "She says, 'Yelvi is cruel. We often fight. He puts all the responsibility for their miseries on us, the Russians. Well, it's true that there is a Russian Mafia; they are mostly ex-security agents; KGB. Former high-ranking members of the government have now become the supporters of a bunch of thugs. Those same former rulers have divided all the government institutions among themselves; even the factories. Albania was under the rule of the Ottoman Turks for some centuries. It was the last Balkan nation to become independent. And then we Russians went and made them Communist. Then it was the Germans' turn, and then the Russians' turn again. During the events of these past years, Albania was the last country in Eastern Europe to become independent, and it started with a riot. Now the same former rulers have become liberals and democrats overnight. And the Italian Mafia has come, too. There are also hungry young people who are unemployed. A few people get together and loot a couple of houses and they become a gang. Military cadres have also begun looting; so have the police. They don't receive their wages, therefore they loot; they kill.' "

Again Natasha talked to Yelvi. Yelvi also said something and finally turned to Sylvia and translated. Sylvia said, "It's been a month that they do, not fighting, they speak. I do not have the patience to translate these things. Everywhere is the same; like ex-Yugoslavia. There is war. Women are... you understand yourself. You have had a revolution."

I said, "There were no such things in the Iranian revolution. Nobody raped any women. They didn't loot anywhere."

Sylvia said, "They broke bank windows. They threw fire in a movie theatre with everyone inside. I was there myself. They threw acid in the faces of women."

Banuyi said, "Those were exceptions. People didn't attack a place for the loot. They broke bank windows, but we didn't hear of even one case where someone took any money."

Sylvia said, "The books of one of those rich monarchists— Morad was there, he saw it—they threw them in a pool. Most of them were manuscripts. Everywhere is the same thing."

Banuyi's cheeks were red and she was passing the fingers of her right hand through her short hair.

I explained in English for Natasha the way things were then. I told her about my experiences. I had seen a stack of coins in a phone booth, or a woman with a child in her arms and a fruit basket in her hand, standing in front of her house and offering fruit to whomever was passing by. I told her about the men who had a bowl in one hand and a hose in another and were giving water to people at a rally. I told her how the neighborhood children took my can of kerosene and carried it to the door of our house. How at night they stood guard in the alley with wooden sticks in their hands. Finally I told her about a motorcycle rider who had a gun in his hand. The first non-military person who had a gun and I was so happy I cheered. I said, "I understood then that it was our turn."

Natasha asked, "You don't think now that it was your turn?"

I said, "I just thought that people were not empty-handed anymore."

Natasha said in English, "Mr. Yelvi thinks anytime there is

blood and bloodshed the winner is the one who can kill, but I think..."

And then she said some things to Yelvi and his wife, perhaps in Russian. Then Yelvi again in his soft monotone answered something we didn't understand, until finally Sylvia with her sharp voice and hand gestures talked and talked, and then Yelvi talked. Sylvia said, "Again—how do you say?—they have jumped at each other like cat and dog."

And then she said some things in French.

Morad quietly asked Sylvia, "What were you saying?"

"The thing we saw at the beginning of the revolution."

Morad said in Persian, "Sylvia is wrong; she sees all those events from the point of view of a foreigner; every minor incident of violence scared her. When they didn't let her join a rally, she came home crying. After the women's demonstration in protest against the slogan 'Either a head scarf or a blow to the head,'[2] she didn't stay on any longer."

First Banuyi translated for Natasha, then Natasha for Yelvi. Then she said in Persian, "It happened to me, too. I had a hooded overcoat on..."

Sylvia said, "Hooded what?"

"It had a hood for, for example, for snow or cold."

Sylvia said, "Well, then what? Please go on."

"Nothing, there was a woman coming up behind me. First she asked me to cover my head because there were strange men about.[3] She actually came and helped me pull the hood over my head. After I walked for a while my head and neck were sweating, and I threw the hood behind my head. This time the woman, without saying anything, pulled it over my head. Once more I threw it back and said something to her. She was smiling and with her eyes and eyebrows was showing me the men on the sidewalk. I moved ahead two rows and pushed the hood back. Again someone yanked it back over my head. It was she, only her eyes were visible and she was pointing to the sidewalk again. This time I pushed the hood behind my head, under the collar of my overcoat, and pulled the zipper up under my throat. After I went a few more steps ahead I felt a burning sensation on my bottom. I looked behind me. There were a couple of scarf-wearing girls and a few chador-wearing women at my side. Only one of their eyes was visible. Again I went ahead, and again I felt a burning sensation on my body. It was impossible to continue. I came out of the line, but the following day again I thought it had been accidental... Every day something was happening and we kept thinking it was accidental or that they were members of the Shah's secret police throwing stones."

Then she began translating in English for Natasha. She was not listening, she was talking to Yelvi, and now Yelvi was shouting, too, and he was waving the index finger of his right hand at Natasha.

Sylvia said, "Again they are fighting."

She said something to Yelvi in French. Yelvi passed his hand over his face and rubbed his eyes with two fingers; then he lit a cigarette. He whispered, certainly in Albanian, to his wife.

The narrow flame of the fire had now reached the edge of the logs. It was flaring from the body of the logs and there were no blackened chips or black flakes of burned paper down there. The red and pink colors entered each other and ended in sometimes-blue margins, long, narrow, blue flames.

Yelvi was talking to us; Banuyi and me. Sylvia said, "He apologized. He says that one of the compositions from Envar Hoxha's time belongs to him. He was a member of the Party, and a member of the Union of Writers and Artists, then; he said, I composed a piece, very pretty, very very beautiful. I don't know how to say it. They did not let it to be broadcast."

Morad said, "Banned."

"Yes, it was banned, but that piece is broadcast on radio, no, was broadcast, without the name of its composer, Yelvi. He also said, 'I don't remember. It is not important. Everywhere is the same. You have the same things; things like that are many in the world.'"

Natasha said in English, "I tell Yelvi, why does he hold the Russians responsible for everything? The same woe happened to us, too. Our officials, too, acquired millions, real estate, villas overnight. The Mafia, too, is there; smuggling is also there. Sometimes we hear that in cabarets dancers swim in a pool of champagne. Like old times, they light the cigarette with dollar bills. And then women, young girls, go to Dubai, one week, two weeks, and then they come back with food, with money, so their families won't die from hunger."

I told Morad quietly, "And we wasted our youth to reach what ideal?"

Natasha asked Banuyi, "What did your husband say?"

Banuyi said in English, "Things like, I mean, all of us went to prison, sometimes for years, just because of a book or a short pamphlet translated from Russian, so that we could reach you, so that our country could become something like Baku the paradise, Leningrad the paradise. Now..."

I wasn't listening anymore. I didn't listen to Natasha, who was apparently saying something in reply. The clusters of flames, high and low, had merged, and the thin, high flame was blazing toward the hidden mouth of the fireplace's chimney. Pointing to the fire, I said aloud in Persian, "Zarathustra's fire."

Banuyi said in English, "The fire of Zarathustra."

Yelvi laughed, and said something to his wife of which we understood only the word Zarathustra.

Sylvia said, "Zarathustra, yes, fire, it was sacred point, no?"

None of us said anything because we were looking at the fire, at its high, colorful blaze, and perhaps at the breast of the fire, which was red and warm without even one black stain at its center anymore.

No Comment!

Fahimeh Farsaie

Everybody was convinced that something really ought to be done, in response to this horrible, shameful situation; that we must not sit idly by and say nothing and shut our eyes. We should defend these unfortunate, miserable, defenseless people, these foreigners, and show that Yes, there are those who dare to say "No" and demonstrate this not just by words but by actions. How we did it was not important, but we had to do something, even if it was getting into a fight with them in the street. Otherwise...

Since we all believed that it was time to really do something, nobody bothered to predict the dire outcomes of procrastination and of doing nothing in response to that ghastly situation. Because anyway it was clearly obvious that conditions were difficult, complicated and painful, and, as Ingrid said, these conditions had existed in Germany once before; in the years prior to the War, or during it, or something like that; before the War, during the War, but not after the War...

And at this point Martha said "No!" and although we all unanimously believed that we should say "No" and that we should say "No" through our actions, nobody agreed with her "No." And since, as everybody knows, in order to start a unified movement, unanimous agreement among all is necessary, we decided before anything else to reach a common, logical conclusion and then take action. Obviously we all possessed a high level of social awareness and understanding, and we were not at all prepared to blindly do something that we couldn't— not something we wouldn't—accept, generally and logically, in its theoretical details. That was why, by repeatedly nodding our heads, we agreed to meet for a few nights in succession in an alternative Kneipe[1] and discuss the issue on a fundamental basis from the historical, political, and cultural points of view, and to exchange ideas so that we wouldn't end up with extremism, digression, regression, ultra-rightism, ultra-leftism, like all leftist groups of all countries. The main and apparently insoluble problem emerged when we all took our calendars out of our bags and to our complete surprise reached the conclusion, mutually, that in the next two months, out of the whole 24 hours of the day, none of us had a single hour that would coincide with others' free time. Because we are so engagé and political and revolutionary that every one of us is an active, irreplaccable member of several men's and women's groups and national and international mixed groups, of anti-war, anti-militarism, anti-violence-and-force, anti-Commonwealth, anti-biotechnology, anti-the-"new foreigners'-law" and anti-anti-foreigners, and...And although we are continuously trying, with the help of our psychotherapists and psychologists, to find a line between private and public life, as well as a specific space for our concentrated and continuous activities in specific fields, we do not succeed in clarifying the real and undeniable importance of this or that issue, or the objective, unavoidable preference for this or that subject so that we can concentrate our constructive effort and abilities. And this is not because we, despite our having a high level of social awareness and understanding, are not capable of simply designing a practical daily, or nightly, plan—at times some of our "activities" last until two or three AM! Of course not because of this, but because of the disconcerting fact that in this totally corrupt world there are so many miseries and disasters and acts of oppression and natural and unnatural catastrophes that we do not know to which group of the defenseless victims of these disasters caused by Heaven, Earth, and humankind we should devote ourselves and our time. Amid all this, Ingrid's situation was worse than everyone else's, although, like all liberated and independent women, she was constantly trying, with the help of her therapist, to evaluate and determine the limits of her power in a realistic manner. All the pages of her calendar were black with various appointments and scheduled programs. And although she had one "Women" calendar, one "Third World" calendar and one "Environment" calendar, sometimes, when there were important meetings—such as our meetings—she was forced to write the time on a notepad and stick it on the blackened pages of the calendar. Besides, she was also suffering from a wearisome preoccupation: she didn't know if she should fall in love with women or with men. Before Christa she had always slept with men, but one day when Christa had to leave the meeting in order to get to another gathering, Ingrid, all of a sudden, felt so sad. This sorrow suddenly led her to the great, unbelievable discovery that her heart beat not only for all men and all unfortunate, miserable and oppressed people and victims of the world, but also for all women! Therefore, like all of us who have learned to face and treat everything, ourselves, our feelings, our bodies, society, environment, she began, quite consciously, to establish a series of relationships with compatriot and non-compatriot—Third-World foreigners—women. And of course this was very important... because it showed that, unlike most Germans, Ingrid does not approach foreigners with prejudice. Obviously not! The consequences, though, of establishing very intimate and non-prejudicial relationships with foreign women—although Kuwait's oil wells were controlled ahead of schedule—caused Ingrid confusion and bewilderment.

My situation was a bit better on different fronts. Because, first of all, I have only one calendar: *Freudin!*[2] It was a gift from a friend and completely devoid of social and political issues. And, I am one hundred percent sure that I can fall in love only with a member of the opposite sex. My fading love for Martin is the best testimony; a love at its last gasp. Martin is a skilled carpenter, but he always wanted to become a famous sculptor and eternalize the bitter realities of the life of simple people, on tree trunks. To get in touch with these bitter realities and to experience them, he even traveled once, with an Entwicklungshilfe[3] group, to Pakistan, and for the poor people of the faraway village of Multan, who like primitive people go into the bushes to answer the call of nature, he built traditional toilets by means of which he taught them how to civilize themselves and make progress. Naturally these practical objective experiences had a decisive and inspirational influence on his ideas and designs. For this reason, almost all of the "things" he makes, meaning all the useable artistic works he creates, are somehow similar to the traditional toilets he once built in villages near Multan: candleholders, vases, chairs, lampshades newspaper racks... the comparatively large bread box that he gave me last year for my birthday is, also, almost a small version of the same toilet design, built specially for me and offered to me with love.

When Martin looks at the things he has made, he involuntarily remembers his desire to become a famous artist and then resolves, seriously, to travel with a group once more to a famous place in the Third World, a place where people do not have the slightest idea of civilization and progress. He will be inspired by their simple and natural life while he teaches them the alphabet of a civilized and advanced life! In my opinion, this idea does not seem vital or even necessary. Because, although he has not become a "famous artist," he has been able to put a decent amount of money in his pocket by selling his "works" to alternative stores such as Bio Möbel[4] and Foton. We have discussed this matter a lot. But he believes that a true artist is successful only when he is constantly in contact with the bitter realities of ordinary people. At any rate, Martin has decided to keep his distance from me for now so that he can think freely and in peace in order to see where he stands in life and what he really wants. My presence in his daily life, since I always carelessly unleash my "strong and natural" feelings toward him, causes him fear and confusion. The degree of my closeness to him makes him disoriented and consequently pushes his "independent feelings" into the context of a relationship where neither side has equal rights. Of course I don't understand his logic and reasoning, but since I profoundly believe in respecting democracy in every aspect, even in relationships between human beings, I had to respect Martin's democratic right to free thought and free choice, and although it was suddenly discovered that the BND (Bundesnachrichtendienst[5]) has been on the verge of deciding to smuggle military equipment to Israel, I agreed to leave Martin alone and curb my strong and natural feelings any way I could. Now, instead of going to Pakistan or some other godforsaken place in this oversized world, he has gone with a group of "Beck Van" followers to Holland so that by taking part in the programs of screaming and yelling and shaking and laughing hysterically and crying out loud and liberated sex he can explore all his complexes and free himself from all the pressures imposed on him by his parents during childhood, by teachers and principals during his teenage years, by coffee shop owners, bosses and managers of places where he worked during his youth. Naturally, this, too, is his democratic right...

In any case, I couldn't, or didn't want to, renounce even one minute of my eight hours of sleep for participation in any meeting, no matter how vital and immediate its reason; an earthquake, a flood, the widening of the ozone hole, fratricide in Yugoslavia... (Someone from our group suggested we meet at midnight, for a short while, in an alternative Kneipe, and talk about the principles of our work in an orderly no-nonsense fashion and reach common ground and so on and so forth!) My therapist also affirmed my resolution. Because my only hope is to see Martin in my dreams and tell him exactly what my heart desires. When I see him in my dreams and unleash my strong and natural feelings toward him, I can then fight all day, calm and poised, for a variety of ignored and even crushed rights. Otherwise, I would be constantly fighting off the cruel crablike claws of revenge, regret, and animosity that are continually scratching my innards and making me sick.

If those two Lebanese kids hadn't been burned in the fire from the Molotov cocktails rightists threw into their homes in the middle of the night, it is not clear how long our discussion would have lasted about the similarities between the current conditions in Germany and its shameful, xenophobic state before the War, during the War, or after it. Although Martha still insisted that before anything else we should all agree on the principle that this country's past, which is marked by shameful and animalistic crimes, has never stopped, that it was continuing at the present time, and that if we didn't take fundamental steps against it, it would lead to the same catastrophic results that it once, specifically, brought about during the War. Sonia had to leave, obviously for another meeting. But she didn't want to leave with her opinion unstated. So, while putting her stuff inside her backpack, she said that she didn't know what happened before, during, or after the War and was not interested in knowing because "all these things" made her sick... Oh, man! We are at war already, the war has begun; an unequal war, whose flames turn innocent and defenseless children into charcoal; an unjust war that hunts its prey from simple and innocent foreign girls, violates them mercilessly and cruelly cuts their veins with the point of the knife... why do we refuse to understand this bitter reality? If this is not war, then what is it?

Thinking about these heart-wrenching images, we all grimaced, filled our beer glasses, and, although there was not even a drop of fresh air in the Kneipe, lit our cigarettes and with deep puffs, tried to relieve our anger and distress. Sonia, whose tears were about to pour down, picked up her backpack, got on her racing bicycle, and, lowering her head against the cruel lashing of wind and rain, went off into the night.

Her departure made Martha sadder than everyone else. Because although they were lovers, recently they had had a tiff. Because Sonia couldn't tolerate the degrading situation anymore. It was natural that she couldn't; that the situation had become intolerable. I don't mean the socio-political situation. Of course the socio-political situation has its effects, but not so much so that it makes her completely confused and distraught and throws her daily life, her routine, and her love life into total disarray. Like Ingrid's case. When one Tuesday at noon Ingrid heard the news about the neo-Nazis' attack on asylum seekers residing at Hoyeswerda,[6] she straightened her back in front of a mirror where she was making a big clay fruit bowl, and without turning off the machine, angrily clapped her red-clay covered hands and, although she was all by herself in the studio, shouted, "*Das gibt doch nicht! Das darf nicht wahr sein!*"[7]

But it *was* true! And so then and there Ingrid closed the door of her ceramics studio, didn't go to work anymore, and committed 24 hours a day of her time, her money, her mind, and her strength to fighting racism. She continued this so much that after a while she was yellow as turmeric, she was blue around the eyes, and she had no more time to spend on her half-broken love affair with a foreign woman. Of course not because she had hidden racist tendencies, as the foreign woman later claimed; quite the contrary, because she immersed herself completely 24 hours a day fighting intolerable racist demonstrations!

At any rate, tolerating the situation had become impossible for Sonia as well. Because, besides her, Martha had a relationship with another woman, Heidi, and considered this relationship to be as beautiful, dreamlike, and indispensable as her relationship with Sonia. Of course Sonia didn't know that Martha, for the sake of variety and also to prove that she had no xenophobic tendencies, calls a foreign woman every now and then; they speak for hours about the collapse of the pillars of dictatorship in socialist countries, the collapse of the anti-humane Communist system, the collapse of the foundations of the American theory of cold war, the collapse of the savage apartheid system in South Africa, and the collapse of people's fear of fighting for their rights, and a thousand other "collapses," and when there was no place left on their coasters for the waiter to mark—to show the number of beers they'd had— they would leave the Kneipe, which didn't have to be an alternative, just close to Martha's house, and would land straight on Martha's twin-size futon. Obviously Sonia didn't know about these things at all, but knowing about Martha's affair with Heidi was enough to make her sick.

Sonia's being sick of "all these things" helped us a lot. It implicitly convinced us not to talk about pre-War and Wartime matters anymore, although this undeclared agreement seemed to be contradictory to the democratic method and conscious approach of those who possess a high level of social understanding. But I suppose each one of us considered it our democratic right to every once in a while veer from our principles for the sake of a more pressing issue. Other than Sonia's being sick, which we all caught as if it were a contagious illness, a dozen first-rate Früth Kölsch beers, and a pocket of tobacco that we bought by pooling our spare change and finished in no time helped us to come to this decisive conclusion. I even ended up a few times, despite my therapist's strong recommendations, going to bed later than usual. Well, that was because the problem was vital; it was about our duty in regard to history, future generations, and all of those for whom if we did nothing later on, certainly, we would be questioned and blamed for catastrophes that might happen in the future. I think that is why Martin left for good and never again appeared in my dreams. When I spoke to Ulla about the crablike claws that shamelessly scratched my innards, she burst out laughing and said, "You are a total ass!... Otherwise you wouldn't have let yourself be enslaved to such a jerk!..." Ulla treats everything very comfortably and logically. That is why she has been with Dietrich for eight years, though recently she has fallen in love with Klaus. She spends the first three nights of the week with the second one and the second three nights with the first one. She spends the seventh night all by herself in her room and thinks about the deficiencies that bother her about each of these relationships. At the same time, she feels very lucky that Dietrich is so liberated and untraditional and magnanimous that he hasn't created any difficulties about her having the second relationship and has not shown the slightest sign of jealousy. It was she who, based on her experience, showed me a solution that even my therapist couldn't think of: following my dreams even when I am awake and telling Martin's image whatever I was telling him in a dream. It wasn't simple at all. At the beginning I had to fight both with the crazy crablike claws that cruelly stuck to my entrails and Martin's image, which often faded away under the horror of scenes of bombing the defenseless people of Croatia. On such occasions, Martin's face would become so crooked and elusive that although I tried, I wasn't able to reconstruct it. I suffered so much because of this. But I tried to reduce this heartwrenching pain by counting on the results of the "Middle East Conference" and by counting on the revelation of the Stasi's secrets and the taking of Hunker back from the miserable Russians. Amid all that, Martha was trying to make Sonia understand that she was not capable of suddenly giving her heart, her bed, and her weekends, which she had divided between her and Heidi, to only one of them. Obviously this could not be done! But Sonia didn't understand and kept getting sick. Our sickness reached Sonia's degree when one Friday we read in *Taz*[8] that Mate Eksi, a 19-year-old Turk, had died. A 23-year-old named Michael, of German origin, had beaten him with a baseball bat so badly that he died, after three weeks in a coma in the hospital.

That was why all of us without any guilt cancelled all of our appointments and scheduled meetings and gathered in the kitchen of a Wg⁹ where Ingrid had a room. Ingrid was suffering so much from the anti-foreigner atmosphere going through all the new and old German cities that the blue shadows around her eyes had reached her temples and forehead. She was saying that a kind of horizontal and needle-like pain was constantly tearing at the skin of her head and face and penetrating it. As if a bunch of lice with their rough antennae and double-sided hooks were stuck to the veins and nerves around her eyes and temples and with their penetrating sting were tearing at them and kept advancing. Ingrid was trying to somehow stop the parasite-like movement of these blind insects by the constant rubbing of Japanese oil on her temples and forehead and also by inhaling the humid air mixed with the microbe-killer steam of eucalyptus leaves. Some nights, when she became totally aggravated with the penetrating, interminable, tormenting movements of those insects, she would take lethal steps. She would sit in front of a lamp that radiated deadly ultraviolet rays, put her face right in front of those invisible waves of light, and while she was obviously disgusted at the thought of the piling up of the dead, dark corpses of those dead lice in the bony holes of her forehead and upper jaw, she would breathe deeply and calmly. In the middle of that, I mean in the short time between those deadly breathings, we all seriously reached the conclusion that definitely, certainly, now, without wasting so much as a single second, we should immediately take action of some kind against this shameful and intolerable anti-foreigner situation. And it was not important anymore who, where, when, what had happened; before the War, after the War, or during the War, and no one had the patience to talk about the high level of social awareness and understanding and democratic rights and the necessity of mutual ground for mutual action, and...

Because all these issues, as well as the question "What must be done?" were way too much for us. Just then the phone rang and Ulla, in a sobbing voice and a tone of apology, said that unfortunately, although she really wanted to participate in tonight's meeting and she knew it was very important, she could not do so because, unfortunately, her bicycle had been stolen. We all sighed sadly and sympathized with her from the bottom of our hearts. Ingrid, while blowing the dead lice in her handkerchief, told her on our behalf that we all understood the situation very well and that it was no problem that she couldn't come this time and that we, at the end of our meeting tonight, or if it lasted longer, which seemed to be the case, tomorrow morning, during the day, or at the latest toward evening, would call her and would inform her of any critical decisions.

We really felt sorry for Ulla. Especially when we wondered how poor Ulla was going to travel the distance between Dietrich's and Klaus' houses: one of them was on one end of the city and the second on the other end. Especially at nights, in this cold and darkness and with the lack of safety! Fortunately Ulla passed a complete self-defense course, and she and Ingrid had been going to a tai chi class for two years... Yes, but artificial danger and reacting to it is one thing, and actually facing the danger and reacting fast and agilely is something else... Anyway, we all expressed our hope that this dire event wouldn't effect the love relationship, that is the love relationships, because that would be really painful. Because if we decided to examine all aspects of the issue, we would see that to a large extent, so large that one has difficulty imagining it, as long as one has not faced the problem, as long as one has not experienced it in practice, to a large extent everything is related to everything else, everything effects everything else, everything influences everything else and most important of all, our daily life and its rhythm influences the body, feelings, affections, thoughts, mind, understanding, capabilities,... and what would happen if this untimely theft of the bicycle created an imbalance in Ulla's love relationships and consequently jeopardized the rhythm of her political activities? And in this dangerous and important time in which all the orders and balances in the world are in a state of mayhem; the balance in the Soviet Union, in the Middle East, in Yugoslavia, in Europe, in our own country after the fall of the Wall, and in the movement of the Left in general, and in the peace movement, and in all movements for the liberation of the Third World... And during this state of imbalance and mayhem and disarray what would happen if even Ulla lost her balance and Sonia kept feeling sick and Ingrid was stuck with those dead lice under her forehead and upper jaw and Martha wandered between two loves and two beds... and the group as a whole lost its balance and nobody did political work?... And all of this because someone stole a junky bicycle! Ah... that would be really terrible!

Ulla believed that she hadn't lost her balance and Ingrid, who had talked to her, believed, or rather thought, or maybe imagined, or maybe had the impression that Ulla understood her situation very well and had dealt with it, and has been able to live with it, more or less, and now she thinks of it, she can say, she cannot swear though, but she can imagine that in spite of the complicated and awful situation and then this cowardly robbery, yes, in spite of all that, Ulla is in her best psychological condition! Besides that, she even made a very interesting suggestion: going on an "educational trip" to experience the Third World life of asylum seekers!

Ulla's suggestion seemed to me quite stupid and meaningless. Because before anything else it reminded me of the toilet-related inspirations of Martin and their effects. Therefore I opposed it very harshly and thoroughly and practically. I had decided that even if everyone voted for it, in order to defend my principles and the legitimate use of my democratic rights, I would withdraw my ideas and thought and power from the group and wouldn't cooperate with them anymore. We were close to getting into a fight. Because some believed that precisely what we needed (in order to understand the wretched situation of the miserable people who have applied for refugee status, in order to understand their feeling) was practical experience! And if by going on an "educational vacation" thousands of kilometers away from artificial life, in a virgin and untouched village, in an isolated cottage made of mud, without water, without electricity, with just elementary and primitive means for a primitive and natural life we can gain this practical experience, then why not? It is not important if this village is not in Kurdistan or a Third World country but in the heart of European culture and civilization, in the south of France. What is wrong with it? After all, we have to support the expansion of "alternative tourism" as well, don't we? And besides that... at such a good price! Although thinking about bringing water from the well, washing our bodies in the river, drinking a tea made from whatever plant and flower we find and sleeping on the hard ground of a mud cottage made us so happy we couldn't breathe (because in fact this is what is called a healthy, natural, humane and "nature-friendly" life), Ulla's suggestion was rejected by a small margin between nays and yeas. Suddenly Sonia, who was seriously getting sick of all the useless and fruitless discussions, opened the newspaper and, her eyes almost out of their sockets, read a piece of news that scared all of us, although we were still affected by the stealing of Ulla's bicycle and were having stomachaches just thinking about it. I had decided to leave the group, and I was preparing myself for nightly sleep without Martin. I just barely heard Sonia's short tearful interpretation at the end of the news.

"There, now, we are sitting here doing nothing and just talking nonsense and they have been shooting at yet another Heim... and it is a Heim that Weizsacker[10] has visited, and only refugees from Lebanon, Kurdistan, and Mozambique live there!"

I was going to cry from anger. Worst of all, I was very tense because we were not allowed to smoke in Ingrid's Wg. How could one tolerate all this misery and pain and all these problems without sleep, without Martin, and without a cigarette? Martha could no longer tolerate the situation and therefore she had told Heidi and Sonia that at this point she could either sleep with both of them or neither of them. From the way Ingrid took her chin in her hand and stared at the wall in front of her it was obvious that she also could tolerate neither that horrible situation nor the constant movements of the lice under her eyes, nor the dizzying wandering of her heart, which was standing at the crossroads of loving men or women. All of us in a state of suspense and wondering, were going back and forth like the clock's pendulum, between personal what-should-I-do's and political what-should-be-done's until, all of a sudden, Ingrid straightened her back, as always, clapped her hands and shouted, "I've got it!... They attack Heims, so it is our duty to defend them!"

At the end of Ingrid's shouting, all of us suddenly found a rare happy feeling that later on, when we told each other about our feelings and moods and talked about our understandings, we realized was a "feeling of stability." Her suggestion drew our wandering pendulum like a magnet and we saw that all of a sudden we were standing on solid ground and our backs also rested against the solid wall of confidence. It was obvious that we were all ready not to sleep a wink the whole night and guard the Heims of refugee applicants. Naturally everybody was ready, especially since... Oh, Martha said, in fact I should not have forgotten! Oh... So many different events take place in this world; but it is not too late now, although this event is not directly related to our discussion, but it is an important issue in itself, although in this inappropriate situation, or perhaps... well yes, it is quite appropriate in this situation. Yes, North and South

Korea have declared that after unification their country will be without nuclear weapons! Just imagine: *Ein atomfreies Land*![11] We all became very happy and felt that the ground under our feet was even more solid. And we kept this feeling until Sonia asked in a thoughtful manner, How and when and with what and in what way do we want to guard Heims. Some said, Actually, oh,... these things are not important at all... we will do it as always, different from others, in an unusual way, as always, in a way that others would notice. Then all said that everything would proceed nicely and the way we wanted it to, without any specific plan, but we would always be ready and alert, so that in case something happened we could take action according to the situation and conditions and means. Only a few placards, a few whistles, a handful of change for the phone, an armful of firewood because it would definitely be very cold, *eiskalt*[12] and we should also wear whatever warm clothes we have. For sure, everything will be done nicely.

No doubt, no doubt. And if Sonia kept bringing up this problem it was because she wanted this time to be better than previous times. And she thinks that this time is a bit different, in fact a lot different, from previous times. For example, previously we didn't have the issue of men and now, this time, well, we do have a problem named men and she doesn't know, and she can't even imagine how she will protect men and guard those men who are seeking refugee status and live in Heims! Obviously she can't!

Everyone thought she was right, because after all we are a women's group and we are working for women's rights and specifically on particular women's issues and even if we consider other issues it would be from that particular women's approach. But anyway we cannot ignore the reality, ignoring the reality does not help us at all because finally and at the end reality will impose itself on us, it will have the last word, and so to a large extent reality determines our behavior and actions and in Heims men and women are mixed and there isn't a Heim where men and women are separate and the Heim to which we frequently go, in Hürth,[13] unfortunately in one sense and fortunately in another sense, the number of women is much less than men! In the end Ingrid suggested that in general and in particular we should set aside the discussion about men and women, because then what about the reality? Nothing could be done about reality and she didn't have the patience to talk about something that cannot be changed. I didn't speak at all because in general I am not in a discussing mood; I am more ready to act. At this time, Martha suddenly said that she was not in a mood to discuss things we have talked about a thousand times. And Sonia, too, had said from the beginning that she was absolutely in no mood to discuss any subject at all. And since none of us were really in a discussing mood we continued our discussion about losing our patience with words until Martha said that she really had a problem with the decision that our group should be mixed with men's groups and guard a Heim where men and women live together, and she inclined her head to the right and in a sorrowful voice said she was very hopeful that our group could come out of this identity crisis healthy, and also that the issue had to do with respecting the principles and following specific goals in our group, and not with one limited and temporary cooperation with men. So far there hadn't been any such identity crisis in the group and the group had always been supporting its identity, and if now the group lost its identity and its balance and fell apart, then what would happen?

And nothing! The sun was rising and we were still in a labyrinth of discussion about men and women, with women and without men, for women and against men, or principally and basically, women with men, looking for a way out. We had emptied all the beer bottles into our stomachs and, after a short while, into the humid and smelly toilet of Ingrid's Wg, our

throats were still dry. With difficulty, with wrinkled foreheads
and raised eyebrows, we were trying to keep our eyelids from
falling over each other, and sometimes instead of understanding
what was being said we were just hearing the sound of a
constant incomprehensible buzzing drilling and penetrating our
confused brains. No one was capable of continuing the
discussion one more second. Voting as a last resort didn't solve
our problem either. Confused and absentminded, dead tired, we
finally reached the conclusion that in this specific case everyone
should do what she thought was right! This suggestion received
the majority of votes while everyone's eyelids closed and our
chins drooped to our necks. Then we all gathered our last bits
of energy and dragged ourselves along the table and chair and
door and wall and got ourselves to Ingrid's room and
unconscious and without clothes, next to, under or over each
other we fell down and slept. We all had one wish: that
everything would go well.

Everything went well: contacting the Heim's managers, the
Hausmeister,[14] the social worker, and the Heim's residents. They
all thought, Wow! What a good idea! Refugee applicants, most
of whom were men, black and African, also put their hands in
their big pockets and said, Well... what could we have against
this?

Naturally Sonia and Martha couldn't participate in our
action: for political reasons and also because of loyalty to
feminist and homosexual principles. Our group was not,
however, small in number. Because each one of us had spoken
to our friends and acquaintances and they cooperated with us
quite happily and without discussion. Besides, Ingrid was given
the responsibility to "move the phone chain" and call all of
those whose names were on the "emergency list." Finally 40
people, women and men, from mixed groups, or from just
women's groups but willing to work with active men's groups,
gathered around and formed three mixed groups that were

supposed to guard from six PM to six AM, in three shifts, a Heim whose walls were still full of holes from neo-Nazis' bullets. I joined the second group, whose shift was from ten PM to two AM. There, when the flesh of our faces was half cooked because of the fire we had made but our bones were still so cold that they clicked with any movement, Ulla told me that Martha, that very night in Ingrid's room, where she was sometimes next to, sometimes under, and sometimes on top of Sonia, had decided to forget Heidi completely. For Ulla, too, it was pretty difficult to live with two loves simultaneously and deal with the headaches and difficulties of two loves, without a bicycle and with one house on this side of the world and the other on the other side of the world. Obviously she couldn't and now she was thinking about seeing whether or not she would like to start a relationship with a man who was on one floor exactly twelve steps and one turning step under her, away from her. Ingrid was also in our group. She was not coughing, nor was she looking for a handkerchief. The lice under her eyes were completely destroyed, and there was no trace of blue on her forehead. Hand in hand with a blue-eyed man with blond hair, a bit shorter than she is, she was going around the Heim, and whenever she reached us next to the fire, she would smile and say, "Everything is going well, very well, isn't it?"

And I would take my eyes off the attractive, sweet, beautiful, dreamlike, and intoxicating smile of a gorgeous woman who was sitting all night in front of me on the other side of the fire and would smile without any reason and say, "Yes... very well!..."

And then I would lose myself in looking at the exciting curves around her lips, which sent a warm thrilling feeling flowing to my heart and warming my bones. Until then I hadn't even imagined that the sweet and lovely smile of a woman could affect me so much!

And in fact everything was going well and we were so

caught up in the situation and attracted to each other that we didn't realized at all that the residents of the Heim, one by one, or in groups of three or four, had left their rooms and passed by our fire and disappeared in the cold and darkness behind the trees of the Heim. It was only when the next shift read its report at the meeting for evaluating our work that took place the following day that we found out we had shivered all night in front of an almost-empty building, empty of the residents whose lives we had been organized to save. Except for a few people who out of sickness or tiredness couldn't move, all the residents of the Heim had gone to a nearby discotheque and in a warm and exciting environment full of music, had danced until morning.

be will come

Said

the telephone rings three times, twice, then once. for seven days i have been sitting at home between 2 and 4 PM waiting for this signal. i don't need to rush. we have time until dusk; now in the summer it comes rather late.

i sit down to write a letter to e. to thank her for her love—wild and loyal. it's going to be a short letter. we have always understood each other—without major explanations. i will address her, using one of her pet names and tell her that i will miss her.

i am putting on my clothes; exactly what i wore yesterday. only the underwear must be clean, just in case. i have changed my shirt yesterday; i can still wear it today. then my well-worn vest, even if it is warm today: i want to be protected. But first empty and pick through all the pockets; nothing wrong should remain there.

two handkerchiefs in the pockets of my pants. the left handkerchief is a kind of spare reserved for special needs; usually i clean my glasses with it. the right one is a hankie to blow my nose. i never carry anything in the breast pocket of the shirt; it gets in the way.

the vest: its lower left pocket has always been reserved for my pocket watch. today i will polish it with silver polish. i open the lid of the watch and also clean it inside. a glance at the photo. i am four years old with a lice-defying crew cut. i close the lid, wind the watch, stroke the face with the palm of my right hand and put it into the left pocket of my vest.

right lower pocket: this is the place for small change. Left upper pocket: for banknotes. i count them. there is a bit of money in the bank account. i will withdraw some on the way. today i want to have the feeling that i can spend money as i please.

the right upper pocket: it's reserved for receipts and notes. today i no longer need to keep receipts. and at last: a day without notes.

i put on my jacket. right inside pocket: the place for calendar and address book. i don't need the addresses any more and neither do i need the entries for the next days.

left inside pocket: the wallet. i open it and take everything out. the commuter pass for streetcar, bus and subway; i am going to walk only, i have time. the credit cards? i cut them in two and throw them on the table as well. i won't be handing anybody my business card anymore. i put them on the stack on the shelf. i also can do without checks. they know me at the post-office, where i have had a mailbox for over 30 years, and i can withdraw up to dm 400, even without an ID. then the press card, the social security card, the card for the public libraries in the city, the media union card, the card for the state library; today i am under no obligation to identify myself. the childhood photo in my pocket watch is sufficient—even for the police.

the small upper pocket on the left: the railway pass i don't need; i shall remain in town. i also put down the telephone card; today i am not making any calls. i hate the telephone. one by one i throw the cards carelessly on the table. i want to see where they land and how they juxtapose themselves; perhaps a picture will emerge: a kind of tarot.

i pat down the outside of my jacket. the ballpoint pen still is in its proper pocket, on the upper left. i pull it out and put it across the notepad. today i am not signing anything personal. there is a cheap pen in the post-office that i usually refuse to use.

my shoes stand in front of the door; i put them on. to the right on the radiator lies the key to my post-office box. i pocket it. i could pick up my mail one more time, then open it in a café like on any other day, and maybe there will be even a beautiful letter in it.

before i open the door, i first cast a glance through the spy hole. only then do i turn the key; i always lock the door from inside. i step out. i want to lock the door from the outside, but i don't; today i want to change everything. do i still need the apartment key? into each pair of pants i have had a little pocket sewn especially for this key—inside, invisible from the outside. i step back and look at the closed door. the pale-blue paint is flaking off. i decide to jack off on this ugly door, i want to say good-bye to it. i open the zipper, take out my dick and close my eyes. i get closer to the door, the drops of cum are now slowly running down. i stick my dick back into my pants, turn my back on my door for good and walk down the hall. i decide to take the stairs, after all, i wanted to do everything differently today.

all my pockets are empty, except for the little, sewn-in pocket inside my pants. now the key to my post-office box is there. the key to the apartment i hold in my hand. i open the entrance door; one look to the right and one to the left. i turn to the right and go to the nearest mailbox. i kiss the name on the envelope and slip it in. i cross the street and discover a garbage pail for my apartment key.

i go past one of my cafés: angela, the waitress, with thick, red hair and full lips. of short stature and with a resolute gait. her ass jiggles as hard as if she wanted to knock over chairs with it. small, firm breasts that always tremble. her eyes are pale-blue, dripping cum.

i walk on and think up a love scene with her. its opening eludes me. i change sides of the street. i put both hands into the pockets of my pants and fondle two clean handkerchiefs.

in the post office i open my box: magazines, newspapers, bills. i leave them where they are. nothing should point to a possible identity. a single letter is among them, sent by an unknown woman from leipzig.

i withdraw money, without an ID, without any problems. the woman knows me and we exchange a few words. i leave the post-office with money in my pockets; now i only need to get rid of the key to the post-office box. i decide to throw the key into a mailbox. but not into the one in front of the post-office. that one gets emptied hourly. somebody might get the idea that it was my key. i find a mailbox on the next corner.

i don't carry anything in my pockets, except for money, two clean and ironed handkerchiefs, my pocket watch with my childhood photo and the letter from an unknown woman. of course, i will tear it up, after i have read it. it, too, could point to a possible identity. and the childhood photo in the pocket watch? could someone identify me through this picture? i don't want to part with this photo.

now i only have to find a café, where i can have my espresso and open my mail. i won't read the paper today, to drop another ritual. for years i have been reading a different newspaper each day; so as not to develop the kind of attachment many people show toward a certain newspaper. i wonder where to have my espresso today? i decide to go to a café that i don't know. i decide to go to a part of town i have never been to.

the café: middle class with empty seats by the window. chances are that the espresso is horrible here. but the location and the quiet in the café please me. most importantly: no muzak, none of this aggressively continuous exposure. i look for a place by the window. a real lady with a wonderful czech accent waits on me. i would have loved to dine with her, letting her talk just to be able to savor this accent. she is in her mid-forties, can tell a story or two, as well as listen tenderly, and is likely to have good taste.

i drink the espresso, tear up the unread letter and put the shreds carefully on top of each other.

i call my lady over and ask for cigarettes and matches. we start up a conversation. she comes from marienbad. i tell her i once spent a day in marienbad. she listens attentively. then she excuses herself; she has to wait other tables.

i light a cigarette and watch the passers-by through the window. most of them are in a rush. because they are loaded down with all kinds of stuff? because they feel guilty? i am not likely to ever know. i only know that they are happy because they exist. and that they are ugly, most of them. many are yawning. and then there is the way they walk. the men don't have a walk of their own at all. the women are more independent. but mostly their gait is ruled by their asses. in that case their way of walking just wants to excite and that way gets ugly. still, they are happy without knowing why. an old man walks into view. he holds an ice cream cone in one hand, in the other one he carries his purchases in a cloth bag. the ice cream is enormous. the man sticks his tongue out to a great length and licks the iceberg, slowly and with relish.

i turn my attention to my lady from marienbad. she struts between the tables without jiggling her ass. i decide to give her a big tip. but immediately I discard the idea; it could come across as somewhat suggestive.

a little jerk enters, his hair oiled and greased, his gait borrowed from hollywood. he sits down, waves, orders, pulls out his cell phone and starts to speak loudly.

just at this moment a child begins to wail. i hadn't even been aware of the child. it is tiny, with blue eyes. and it wails so loudly that my ears hurt.

the mother is tall and beautiful. she has long dark hair and has her strong legs crossed. she is leafing through a magazine and sipping her coffee. she neither allows the wailing child to disturb her nor does she attempt to calm it. the man with the cell phone continues to talk.

i put some money on the table, get up, and leave the café. but in the little curtained-off entry way before the door i stop and piss and look at the posters stuck on the wall. the piss is running warmly down my legs, soaking my socks and shoes. i walk out and turn left down the street. i stop in front of a camera store, put both hands in my pockets and look at the photos. people who threw themselves into poses supposed to depict happiness but which disfigure them.

i reach into my left upper vest pocket; i could throw the money into a mailbox. but i have imposed on them already enough

today. give it away? it would look like showing off. i must buy
something with the money, something useless, unimportant.

my shoes. i hate shoes, i have always hated them. i take my shoes
off and also my socks. i stuff them into the shoes, which I tie
together by their laces. i hook the laces over the middle finger
of my left hand and walk on. i swing the shoes back and forth
until another mail box comes into view; i force them inside. i
loosen my tie and open the buttons of my vest. the tie hangs
down on both sides like donkey's ears.

i could buy something to eat; but i don't feel hungry. i will buy
silk; white. i love white silk. i need to feel this material and its
warmth. soon i find a store. In front of it is a telephone booth;
i reject the idea, i enter the store and find white silk. i show the
sales person all my money. she is old and dignified. she doesn't
ask any questions, she measures the material and sells it to me.
a few coins are left. i don't dare to offer this rest as tip to the
woman. i bow and say "good-bye," she smiles and says "see you
again!" i lean forward, put my finger on her mouth and say
slowly "good-bye." she nods, without losing her dignity. i bow
again and leave her. i keep the coins in my hand.

i drape the material over my shoulders. it is long and reaches
down to my hips. i must look like the widows in mediterranean
countries, but in white. outside, the telephone booth again. i
gaze up at the sky, there is still a lot of time left until dusk. i
stroll down the street. the tie is loosened, the vest is open, i am
barefoot, with that beautiful white shawl around my shoulders
and jingling the coins in my hand.

i step into the next telephone booth. i pick up the receiver, put
in some coins and dial an arbitrary number. i let it ring three
times, interrupt, then press the redial button and let it ring

twice. interrupt again. this time I let it ring only once. i hit the cradle softly and put the receiver on top of the phone. i open the door of the box and step outside. a cool breeze hits me; i shiver. i wrap the white silk shawl tighter around myself.

Translated from the German by Cheyda Abadian

We Disappear in Flight

Mohammad Asef Soltanzadeh

They have killed my father, or perhaps my brother. I don't know which one, but I know for certain they got one of them. Because other than those two I had nobody in Kabul. The rest had managed somehow and left the city, which had by then become an inferno. Those who had a few worldly goods left and had remained safe from war and pillage could pull themselves out of the whirlpool and leave the city. It was said that as soon as the fighting died down a little, you would see people with bundles of household necessities in their arms, shepherding their children in front of them, in fear and trembling, crawling out of their burrows and fleeing to the outskirts of the city. Only those without the money or the means to do that much stayed in the city. Unless something tied them down. My father could have gotten out of Kabul, as others had, but why didn't he leave? Maybe because he had an attachment to something, maybe there was something he loved there.

They have killed my father, or my brother; or maybe they just got killed by themselves. There is a difference between someone who they have killed and someone who gets killed by himself. The first, you see, someone stands him against the wall and lays him out cold with gunfire; in the second case, he is just sitting at home when a mortar or missile comes in and finishes him off. It means one cannot know who his assassin or assassins are; that one cannot go and collar someone and say *you did it*.

They have killed my father, or my brother, or perhaps both of them. This is what my uncle, who is standing in the doorway, told me. Uncle didn't say it, but he is about to. I mean, first he wants to take me to his house, and then he will tell me, Yes, man! May you always be healthy; they have killed your father or your brother. The same way, three months ago, he brought me the news of my mother's death. Or, to be more accurate, the news of my mother's having been killed.

Exactly one hour ago, after ten at night when I came back from work, tired and worn out, I was so tired I could not even eat dinner. I just put everything back and spread out on my bed to sleep, when all at once somebody knocked at the door. I thought it was my next-door neighbor who always comes back from work late, like me. I paid no attention and continued to lie down, but they knocked again. A moment or two later the door opened. I heard footsteps coming, coming toward my room. Feet were dragging along on the ground. How familiar those footsteps were. I had heard this kind of walking before. I recognized it. Quickly I turned on the light. Uncle had reached the doorway.

Why has he grown so gaunt, in the few days since I saw him last? How white his hair has become. His shoulders are sagging, as if they are under a heavy load. His slender body looks even thinner inside his clothes. Exactly like the uncle of three months ago.

Uncle didn't wear a smile; he went over and sat down. He tried to moisten his dry lips with his tongue. I sensed something unpleasant must have happened. A few days ago I had heard that one of the relatives had recently come from Kabul. My brother brought Uncle a glass of water.

"Uncle! I hope the news is good. This time of night?"

While he tried, shamefacedly, to avoid looking at us, he said, "The news is good…" And continued, mumbling, "You know, one of the folks came from Kabul two days ago. He's just come to our house… the rest are there, too. Why don't you come by too; we'll ask how the family's making out." I had not been able to bear it and had left the house and started pacing around in the courtyard to calm my heart. The night was humid, and it was difficult to breathe. I looked up at the sky. It was cloudy. From far away one could hear the yowling of two cats fighting. My brother came into the courtyard, too. No doubt he too realized from Uncle's state that there must be bad news.

"Brother, I think there must be bad news. I hope to God Mother and Dad are safe in Kabul."

After all, the older brother should take care of the younger brother. Mother said the same thing when we were on our way to Iran from Kabul. As she wiped her tearful eyes with the corner of her chador, Mother said, "I trust my son first to God and then to you who are older. You must not let him undergo hardship."

And she had cried. Even in her letters she admonished me to take care of him. In her last letter she had written:

> My sons, you saw how quickly the dark night passed and the morning dawned. Although the separation from you was hard for us and this night was very long, the hope that the day would come when we would see you here again eased that hardship, for I knew all these things would pass. Yes, the time of fear and suffocation passed... Compulsory military service is no more, since there is no war. How good peace is because our children can be with us. Yesterday I unlocked the doors to your rooms. I opened the windows and swept the dust from the house. How empty and dull the house is without you. Come back as soon as you can. Take care of your younger brother. I know he has grown up, but for me he is still the same loveable little child.

I mustn't let my brother undergo hardship. I had to bear the burdens by myself. That is why I told him, "No! nothing has happened. Everything is all right. Don't worry; it's nothing."

Brother began looking in my direction with penetrating eyes in the darkness of the night under the only light coming from the window of the room. He was definitely trying to read my mind. Like Uncle, I fled from his eyes. Uncle, too, came outside and said, "Why are you talking here? Hurry up. Let's go;

everybody's waiting for you."

I caught hold of Uncle's hand and took him to a corner of the courtyard. I had to be sure my brother wouldn't hear us.

"Uncle! Can't we go early tomorrow morning?"

I was worried for my brother. Poor thing, after a few nights working the night shift, he had come to have a good night's sleep.

Uncle said forcefully, "No! It can't be done. We must go tonight."

"Listen, Uncle, my brother is very tired and worn out, and I am in no better shape than he is. Give us this one night. Tomorrow we will do whatever you want."

"No, it can't be done. We must definitely..."

I understood something had happened. To whom? Father or mother? Or both? I did not know. Brother came closer. His eyes were wide with fear.

"What should we do?"

"There is no way out; we've got to go."

Uncle is still standing in the doorway. My heart sinks when I see him. Ever since that night when he had come to our house to bring us the news of my mother's death, every time he came to our house, I was scared as soon as I saw him. I thought he would say right away, "Let's go to our house, I have something to tell you." He, too, knows that I am scared when I see him. That is why every time he comes, he smiles. Meaning, *Do not be afraid! There is no bad news.* And little by little I would calm down. But why isn't he smiling now? Maybe... I am panicking. In the doorway, Uncle says, "Aren't you going to ask me in?"

His voice is drowned in sadness, and there is shame in his tone. He is definitely ashamed because once again he is bringing bad news. Without waiting for an answer, he comes in and finds himself a place and sits. He picks up a book from a corner and starts flipping through it. I know his mind is not on the book. He looks at it, but I know he doesn't see it. His look is empty of seeing. His hands are trembling. He realizes that and tries in vain to hide the trembling of his hands from me.

"Uncle, I hope the news is good. This time of night?"

"It is good news... You know, one of the folks came from Kabul two days ago. He's just come to our house... the rest are there, too..."

I cannot bear it anymore and go out into the courtyard. I wish my brother were here. Now, I am standing in front of Uncle, completely alone, all by myself. My brother is not here. I know something new has happened. To whom this time? To father or brother? I know other people have come recently and have brought unpleasant news. What a world we have. We are afraid of people who come. We know that as soon as they open their mouths they will talk about death, destruction, devastation, sickness, and famine. I turn angrily.

"Listen, Uncle! If you have come to bring me bad news, I don't want to know. I told you before."

And I had told him before, after the mourning rites for my mother, when relatives brought us back from the mosque to Uncle's house and then Uncle brought us to our own home. Our room was so cold. My brother and I were shivering. It was not because of the cold. We felt such a strange loneliness. I thought a corner of my heart was empty. I was unhappy that they had told us. Uncle said, "What was I to do? You had to know one day!"

I had told him angrily, "You should have waited for the day when we go back to Afghanistan."

"Maybe we don't go back, not even twenty years from now. What then?"

"We would wait; it makes no difference."

What I said hurt Uncle. He said angrily, "Fine, and then what would people say? Wouldn't they say this fellow isn't man enough to hold the mourning rites for his sister-in-law, and you are not man enough to pay your respects to your mother? You owe it to your mother, as I owe it to her."

I had asked him, "Why did you take us to your house and then tell us the news?"

"What could I do? Here in your house it couldn't be done. This is a bachelor's home. A few relatives and friends come to see us. There should be someone who makes some tea and sets some dates before them."

I had broken the silence that followed these words. "It is past now. But from now on, whatever happens no one has the right to bring me the news. Understand? Let people talk as much as they please."

"If the situation continues like this, every once in a while we have to go to relatives and bring them news..."

"I will neither bring others news, nor should others bring me news."

Uncle comes over and takes my shaking hands. His hands are shaking too: It's nothing; there's no bad news. Only my wife's cousin has come from Kabul, and relatives have gathered and are asking how their families are. I thought it wouldn't be a bad thing if you were to come, too. Ask them about your father and brother.

When he says your father and brother, he chokes up; he understands that I am aware of that.

I say, "You go ask how they are. I don't want to come. I am afraid of you, of him, of all of you. Please go and leave me to myself."

He stands up and pulls me by the hand, "Don't be crazy! What will people say?"

There's no help for it. I must go. I lock up the room and we set out. How brutal and unjust the laws laid down among relatives are. They don't think that at least when someone is weary and worn out, just coming back at night from work, we ought not to bring him the news of the killing or death of his family members. And by the way, why should it be anybody's business whether someone is holding mourning rites for his family or not?

Alone, Uncle and I are going to his house. Uncle is hunched up in one corner of the cab and I in the other. I am looking out the window. Streets are passing before my eyes but I don't see a thing. The last time when we took a taxi to Uncle's house, Brother was seated between Uncle and me. The driver tried to show what a jolly fellow he was; unlike the drivers of Tehran, who are nervous wrecks. He started to kid around, "Nighttime is the right time for going out and about, isn't it?"

When we didn't answer, he looked at us in his rearview mirror; we all had stony, cold faces. He frowned, too, and didn't talk anymore. Obviously he realized that something unpleasant had happened to us. In the upper right-hand corner of his rearview mirror was written in exquisite calligraphy, *Mother, don't ever die.* In my heart a suspicion rose: Maybe my mother had died. When we got out in front of the alley of Uncle's house, the driver said, "May God grant you patience."

Later on, Brother said, "When I read 'Mother, don't ever die' in the taxi, a thought crossed my mind: *My mother has definitely died.*" And that is just what happened.

The driver takes out his cigarette and lights it without any fuss. Silence has erected a wall between us. Curiosity tempts me to glance in the driver's rearview mirror. Maybe this time, too, there is something written that will let me know who I have lost. No, don't look: I don't want to know. Look. No, no, no. Finally I cannot help it, and out of the corner of my eye I glance quickly at the mirror. From behind a curtain of smoke, the driver puffs out of his nose and I see it reflected in the mirror, I read the writing on the mirror: *No smoking allowed.* I feel like I am suffocating and I roll down the window. Eagerly, I breathe

the air outside. Years ago, in the same spot, in front in the taxi, they put up the following sign: *No political discussion allowed*. But they have removed it now, which means that years ago political discussions were heated but now they have cooled down.

I am glad that my thoughts have gone elsewhere. I forget myself, and I am distanced from my past. This forgetfulness gives me such pleasure; more than any narcotic (although I have never used one). But I know that anyone who goes in for them wants somehow or other to forget himself. Forgetfulness is such a blessing... I wish the distance between our house and Uncle's house would go on and on to the end of the world. Even beyond the end of the world: forever. I wish we would never arrive. And that I would never find out which one of my family is lost. And I would not find out that my father or my brother...

Ohh, forgetfulness! Let me think about other things, things other than myself. What can I think about? Like a moment or so ago, for example, about the sign *No political discussion allowed*, which I miss. Why? Perhaps people are not in the mood for such things anymore. Or maybe they think it is futile, that it goes nowhere. Or maybe in the past some people would take someone's side and others would take someone else's side and in the end they would jump on each other and beat each other up and break each other's heads. Like our own Afghanistan where this group is going after that group with guns. My thoughts make their way to the other side of the border. Where there was war and passionate political people, who had learned from politics only how to be passionate, and after the passionate political discussions would go off to join the army and go to war. And since they were themselves in solid fortified trenches, they themselves didn't get hurt; only the innocent were wasted. Like my mother, who three months ago was lost under the rubble. How the need for that sign *No political discussion allowed* was felt there.

My thought again arrives where I don't want it to be: they

have killed my father, or my brother, and now we are going where they will tell me the news. I come to myself again and fear overtakes me. I am shaking and my teeth are chattering. I feel such cold! Maybe it is a cold night. We arrive at the alley where Uncle's house is. This driver has brought us here fast. We get out. I cannot stand on my feet. When we go toward the house my feet are dragging along on the ground and moving ahead with difficulty. Uncle senses this, because he comes and takes my arm. Now he is pulling me along with him. Uncle is silent, and I do not say anything either. I am a prisoner led before the firing squad. I don't want to go, but Uncle, like a soldier, has taken my hand and brings me along with him. I have the striped outfit of a prisoner and they have gagged me so I won't talk. Even if I could, I wouldn't have anything to say. I have already done the begging, and it has been useless. We arrive at the place of execution. Uncle opens the door to his house. When we enter the courtyard, through the window of Uncle's house I see that relatives have gathered. Maybe they have come to watch someone's execution. I see Uncle's wife's cousin, who also has come. How old and worn he has grown. Certainly he must have undergone many hardships during these years. But haven't I grown worn? Haven't I undergone hardships?

If I enter the house, after we all exchange greetings, the newly-arrived traveler will come closer and say, May you be healthy. They killed your father, God bless his soul, or, they did such and such to your brother. Or, God rest both of them, they were lost under the rubble.

When we went inside Uncle's house, the newly-arrived guest from Kabul moved over and said, "Come here, my son, sit next to me."

I went straight over and sat next to him and my brother came and sat beside me and Uncle sat next to him. When I looked at my relatives their faces were blurred. I don't know if it was because the light in Uncle's house was poor or if it was my eyes. I couldn't see whether there was sadness in their eyes, or pity, or both; or perhaps neither. Maybe happiness was surging behind the pupils of their eyes. The kind one feels when one sees an unfortunate person and is happy he is not is his place. Or maybe they are happy because they have pulled themselves and their families out from that abyss. Or maybe they were proud of their foresight, proud that they had come here many years ago. And it was out of pride that I didn't cry when he said, "There is news my son, which is very difficult to tell..."

"Tell it and be done with it."

"During the battle a shell hit your house, and your mother..."

Brother had put his head on my shoulder and was crying. My throat was burning; the lump in my throat was preventing me from breathing and my eyes were red with tears and lack of sleep. The silence imposed on everyone was ringing in my ears, and even my brother's and Uncle's sobs didn't put a stop to the ringing. My head was swimming. Although the windows were open, the air in the room was heavy and stuffy; I couldn't stand it anymore and I left Uncle's house and quickly passed through the stuffy, deserted alleys and reached the park nearby. I fell onto the first bench. I let myself go and allowed the lump to burst and the tears to pour down.

"Why did you stop? Go on."

I looked at Uncle. He wasn't that armed soldier anymore. I was that prisoner, but my hands were not tied and the gag was gone. Like the prisoner who makes a last effort before they place the noose around his neck to find somewhere to run to. That is why I turn back quickly and leave the courtyard and start to run down the deserted alley. Uncle's voice pursues me. *Where are you going? Wait! Where can you go? No matter where you go, they will catch you.* Maybe he wants to give me advice and consolation. Like that night he came to the park and said, *Don't cry. Everyone travels along this road. We all have to go through it.*

"I am crying because they have forced us to go through it."

And Uncle, caressing my hair, had said, "Let's go home. When friends and relatives come to see you on Friday, in the mosque, it will be a comfort; don't cry."

I don't know how many hours of the night passed by the time I reach the terminal. Slowly the taxis near the terminal have started to drive away. Not a passenger is coming nor a bus arriving anymore. One of the last buses leaves the terminal's exit. Maybe it is the last bus. The terminal is about to close. I run toward the bus and hold up my hand. The driver slows down; his boy sticks his head out the window. When they get closer, he asks, "Where are you going?"

I want to say, *Nowhere. It makes no difference to me where I go. I just want to flee Tehran. To wherever. To a place where no one knows me and no one will say, Man, they have killed your father... you know, your brother was with him too.*

A thought crosses my mind, *Why should it be other people's business what kind of injustice you have endured?* That is why I say, "To wherever this bus goes."

The boy recites the cities on their route: Qom, Esfahan, Shiraz, Bandar Abbas. I say, "That's right, these are the very places I am going."

As he opens the door he asks once more, "Where to?"

"To one of the places you mentioned."

He moves to one side so I can get on. I feel he is looking at me suspiciously. I pay no attention. There are a few passengers on the bus, and there are more empty seats. When I reach the first empty seat, I sit down. As he is starting the bus, the driver looks me up and down cautiously in the mirror. Maybe I look like one who has escaped the gallows. I ignore him and settle down in the seat. The seat is over the wheel. I don't attach any importance to that. I could go back a few more rows and sit in a more comfortable seat. I don't want to. Comfort is no use to me anymore.

Man, take care of yourself; you are getting skinnier by the day.

My brother used to say that. I said, "After mother, it doesn't make any difference whether I am fat or thin. It was only for her sake. I didn't want her to be sad when she saw the pictures we sent with our letters. I didn't want to have her say sorrowfully, *How thin my son has grown.*

Yes, that's true; nothing was important to me anymore. Nothing inside or outside was attracting my attention. I had become indifferent to everything.

I was afraid your younger brother's life might be turned upside down, and I wanted you to help him and protect him in the hard times. But now I see that it has affected you even more.

That's what Uncle said, and he was right. It had affected even my job. I was working only for the bare necessities. No more no less. My employer was aware of my situation and didn't say anything. I knew he was troubled because I wasn't working enough, that it was causing him to lose money. Several times he tried to preach to me, "Look, man, what's past is past. We should get on with our lives. It is true that... But life goes on... It seems you are somewhere else."

"Uh... ? What did you say?"

This life was not a life anymore.

I look out the window. Gradually the city gives way to the desert. In the darkness of the night the sleeping landscapes pass as fast or as slow as the bus goes. Where is this bus going? Wherever it goes. Even if it goes to Kabul?

I want to go to Kabul. I want to know why they have killed our mother, my brother would say. And I replied ironically, carelessly, "So go pick up a gun, too, and kill the mother of whoever has killed our mother."

"I don't want to pick up a gun. I hate guns. I am only going because I don't want people to say, 'How gutless those two are. Their mother has been killed and they are still there, strolling happily about the streets. They don't care at all.'"

"It's nobody's business what we do."

"And besides, every time there is a report from there I feel I am going to die here. I keep wondering if one of those missiles they fired has hit our house."

"Look, be like me. When there is a news program on TV, change the channel. When they broadcast the news on the radio, turn it off. Don't look at the newspapers anymore. If someone new arrives from Afghanistan, don't go see him. If a letter comes for you, don't open it. Throw it away. There may be unpleasant news in it..."

"How long are you going to stay indifferent? We should be there. Being inside the disaster is better than being outside it. You are there and you see with your own eyes what is happening to you. But far from your home, your mind reads the story of that disaster it has heard from others a thousand times a day. This is so painful."

"Fine—if you are going to Kabul, go and bring back with you our father, who has been left alone.

But Father wouldn't come, would he? How could he leave his love whom he had buried? She who had stayed with him through the worst times and not left him. His heart was there.

Without one's heart, no one can go anywhere.

Father had written that in a letter. I am sure he was responding to me, who had told my brother, *Bring him back with you.* He continued, *If you want you can come, too. The three of us will rebuild the house. Even if they destroy it over and over.*

My heart is wrung with sorrow. Now there was neither my father nor my brother. How would it be if I were to go back and see what had become of them? If I were to go back? No! Where are Uncle and our relatives now, and what are they doing? What has what they are doing got to do with me? Until when should I escape? Until... until the future. The future toward which this bus is going so fast. I look outside through the front windshield. I can't see more than a few meters ahead. The road is stretching out in the darkness. I don't know how far it will go. Certainly, my destiny, too... Whatever happens will happen. We are not talking about the future, but about the past. See what has happened to you. I don't want to know what has happened. Until when? Until anytime. Until what time, for example? Until we go back to Afghanistan. Well, in the end you understand; one day, now, or any other time. You must learn how to deal with events. You should learn how to confront them. Leave all this for when we go back. When you go there, there will be so much suffering you will be disoriented. It might even break your back, like a tree that is broken in a storm. So, then you should hear the news of disaster little by little. As much as you can tolerate. Let's assume I tolerate it, what then? Really, what then? Why have they written our destiny like this? Two events in three months. It's very hard. Why are we always waiting for someone to come from Kabul so we can gather around him and ask, *What's new, man?* About death and dissolution? Who is still alive? Who is in good shape and who is wounded? Is our house still standing or has it been bombed? I want to think about whether one should be afraid of events or welcome them. I mean, should we be afraid of newly-arrived relatives or should we hurry to greet them?

The bus slows down, and, after a few moments, stops. I look up and I see that we have reached the highway patrol station before the exit out of Tehran. A few weary officers and soldiers are busy inspecting the cars. An officer comes toward our bus. The boy opens the door, and the officer comes up and stands in the front. Although his eyes are tired, they are penetrating. He stares at each passenger and then shifts to another one until he reaches me who am sitting right next to him; on his left. My face and appearance attract his attention: "Are you Afghan?"

"Yes, sir."

"Where are you going?"

"I don't know."

He is suspicious, and I quickly correct myself, "I don't know what time we reach our destination."

He comes closer and stares at me, "I didn't say *when*, I said *what* is your destination?"

"Bandar Abbas."

"Do you have a permit? A transit permit? A permit from the highway office?"

I remember that in order to go from this city to another one we must have a transit permit.

"I don't have it; I mean, I didn't know where I should get it."

The officer, who was looking at me angrily, changes after he hears "I didn't know." Or perhaps he pities me. He assumes a fatherly expression and begins advising me, "You see, my son, when you are going from one city to another you must have a permit. In order to get one, you must go to the governor's office, which issues those permits. Do you understand? You have your ID card, don't you?"

"Yes, sir."

And hurriedly I get out my card and show it to him. As he looks at my card, he continues, "Your card was issued in Tehran. You cannot leave Tehran. I mean, you have no other place to go to unless you have a permit. Now come down and go back to Tehran."

We get off the bus. God bless him, he was one of the good officers, otherwise, according to the law, they had to leave me over the border. My mind was too tired to be able to think why he let me go. The boy sticks his head out, "Hey, Mister! What happened to your fare?"

The driver says something to his boy and then signals with his head, *Go on in good health.* Maybe I look like one who has escaped the gallows and that is why they pity me. This troubles me.

Now that the fate is pushing me toward Uncle's house, I know what to do and how I should escape it. I am going back to Tehran, but I will never go to Uncle's house, or even to my own house. I know they will find me there. I will go and disappear somewhere in this huge city so no one can reach me. Why should they force me? I don't want to know what has happened to me and whether they have killed my father or my brother or both.

I have not yet gotten across the highway to the other side going toward Tehran... when a car pulls up right beside me. I recognize Uncle next to the driver. I am sure other relatives are in the back seat of the car. Uncle and two of the relatives get out and come toward me. I am standing there frozen. Uncle doesn't know whether he should be angry or whether he should have pity or sympathy for me. His voice is trembling with anger and pity, "I told you there is no place for you to go, I told you I would find you."

And two relatives take my hands. I don't know whether I should resist or go with them. We get in the car. What can I do? My mind is tired and doesn't answer. It is crippled. It is not working. And what can it do? If only I could build a high wall around myself so they couldn't reach... Or if I could change my face in such a way that they couldn't... Then they would go and forget me somehow... I wish I could sleep; it is at least a way of separating from this world. Have I closed my eyes, or is it the world that is growing darker? Streets, houses, people, they all scramble in the darkness. Like photos of an unhappy memory under light.

I open my eyes. I don't know where we are going. Now I don't know anymore why this man sitting in front turns every now and then and glances at me and says things I don't understand, and I don't know why two strangers, one on each side of me, are holding my hands very tightly... And by the way, me, myself, who am I?

Anonymous

Ali Erfan

Taking refuge in the warmth of the café's heater, the writer stared at the stone lions on the Place Daumesnil; they looked ready to spring. From their mouths they were spraying cold water into the late winter afternoon air. The wind pounded the icy rain on the head and face of a passerby running in his hurry to get somewhere.

The writer was sunk in contemplation of the gloomy sunset. He was waiting and confused, too. He had lost his calm an hour before with the anonymous phone call. After two months, he had gone down five flights of stairs, and on each floor he had stopped for a moment, debating with himself, No!—I should go see what he wants, and then he had gone down another floor.

Like old or tired people who catch their breath anew on every floor as they are going up stairs, the writer, as he was coming down, had been hesitant and unsure, and had talked to himself: Well, I don't know this man! Why did I agree to meet him? And he had gone down another flight.

Inside the café, he was staring at every new arrival: Maybe this is the anonymous man! It wasn't. Why didn't I ask him what he looks like? I could at least have given him some sign by which he would know me. He thought that maybe they were making fun of him; maybe someone knew he hadn't left his room for a long time and wanted to draw him out. Or maybe it was just a joke. But once again he remembered the anonymous voice, miserable, begging and imploring, "God knows if it were not for urgent need on my part I would not have bothered you. Please allow me to see you!"

Overwhelmed, the writer had refused Anonymous's request several times: "At least tell me what it is you want; perhaps I can help over the phone!"

"No. Please! We must meet face to face. It is very important. Please!"

"Very well. Then let's make an appointment for..."

"This very day. In one hour. Wherever you say. I have a pen and paper. Only please spell the address! I don't know French!"

When he saw the street sign, he realized he had put two letters in the wrong place and forgotten the letter "S" completely. That's why I hate whatever you write but can't read, he thought. No doubt Anonymous will not be able to find the square.

In his heart he was happy; he had had a cup of tea, taken a little walk: and now, his mind at peace, he would go back to his room, and embrace the beautiful woman of his novel, which he had left half finished.

"Hello, sir!"

A young man, thin, tall, polite, standing on the other side of the small table and looking at him expectantly. His face was red from the cold, but the writer thought it was red from embarrassment and shyness.

"Did you telephone me?"

"Yes, sir."

And he sat down. On the phone, Anonymous' voice had been fuller, older; now it was bold yet friendly. Several minutes passed; he saw that Anonymous was not speaking. He told himself, What a quiet, bashful person! But if he doesn't want to speak, then why has he insisted on seeing me?

Both of them were quietly listening to the music and to the washing of the coffee cups and beer glasses. The waiter was standing by the table, ready to take their order. He remembered that Anonymous didn't know the language. He asked politely, "Would you prefer coffee or tea?"

He saw Anonymous' shy smile, and his eyes with their childlike brightness.

"With your permission, wine!"

He forgot his dizziness and ordered wine for himself, too. Again they both remained silent, each waiting for the other to start the conversation. The waiter set the wine glasses on the table. Thirsty, Anonymous drank half his wine in one gulp. The writer held the glass of wine in his hands to warm it. After a few seconds, the stem of the glass between his fingers, he brought it to his lips.

"Is winter always this cold in Paris?"

"Colder than usual, this year."

And he took a sip. Once again they both stared at their glasses in silence. Without attracting Anonymous' attention, he glanced around. He was afraid there might be a conspiracy. He was bored, too. But Anonymous, who seemed to be in no hurry, was calmly playing with his cigarette pack, which made the writer even more sluggish and confused.

"Is there something you want to tell me?"

"Yes, but first I wanted to thank you for agreeing to meet me, and I also wanted to apologize for being half an hour late. You know how it is! I'm a stranger here, and I don't know Paris. I had difficulty finding this place; otherwise I would have been here on time."

He was happy that Anonymous had finally opened his mouth and broken the silence.

"It's not important, sir! Please tell me what I can do for you."

Anonymous looked at him reproachfully. His mocking, ironic stare caused the writer to ask himself if he had said anything out of the ordinary. Was Anonymous waiting for him to guess the whole story?

The voice of Anonymous saved him.

"Writing is your profession, is it not?"

The writer thought, I write about the things I know. I am not a fortune-teller! But he said, "Please tell me what it is you want."

"Before I say anything else, I must tell you I am in trouble. You know how it is! At any moment they may deport me, and if another country doesn't accept me, they will have to send me to Iran. You know the rest! They will execute me... in front of a firing squad."

The writer thought, Well, what has that got to do with me?

"Why?"

Anonymous sniffed with such an ironic air that he felt ashamed.

"There is no why! They execute you in front of a firing squad. You know that!"

"I mean, why would they deport you?"

"Because I don't have a residency permit; in fact, I don't have any documents. That's why I need your help. Indeed, I am seeking your protection. I have no other recourse. You know how it is! Yesterday my application for refugee status was rejected for the second time."

Dumbfounded, he stared at Anonymous' mouth. He waited for him to drink his wine.

"I beg your pardon! Why have you come to me?"

"I have gone everywhere. I have knocked on every door, and I have come to realize that no one can help me."

"Not even political organizations? Aren't... ?"

"Well, yes... But it is better not to talk about the Organization. It is not worth talking about it. In fact, I have been having problems with the Organization. Perhaps one day I shall tell you about it. But now I am in hurry, and I think only you can save me from death."

The writer shivered. He tasted his wine and said, "But I, too, am a stranger here, like you. I don't know anyone. Besides, I'm not such an important person here that a letter of recommendation would have any effect."

"I don't want you to recommend me!"

He had become even more confused. Compassionately,

impotently, he said, "Then what can I do for you? Believe me, I want to help!"

"Thank you. You are so kind. I will tell you... You know that in order to be a refugee one must file an application and submit documents..."

"I am unaware of these processes."

"So much the better! It's far better that you don't know. In that case you can be of even greater help to me. Frankly, my case was ruined by the very people who knew the details of the process and all the norms. They kept holding up my case. I didn't know. They wrote whatever they liked. Of course they called me in for questioning a few times. After all, among the documents, you must submit a detailed account of your circumstances in order for the Commission to go over it and grant you refugee status. How was I to know? Where would I have heard about it? I gave them the honest outline. The first time I gave them the honest outline. I didn't want them to find out the first thing about me. They were strangers, and caution was essential. It wasn't more than one page, but the Commission rejected it. Everyone was approved except me and a few others, and no one could tell why! The very same people who had been guides said, It was because you wrote so little! One must write in detail! They had written it themselves. It was not my fault... you know how it is! My problem is the French language; otherwise I knew how to go about things. The second time I wrote a detailed account; fifteen pages. Of course, I didn't state all the facts. I put a few pieces of my life together with a few pieces of other people's. I hope you understand my situation and do not judge me harshly!... I had no other recourse. I could see that my biography would be short; not more... it had nothing to do with political life... Besides, it cannot be told. It is my life. You do understand, don't you? I was therefore obliged to put different things together so it would be a long, absolutely acceptable account. This time they were confident, too, the ones who translated it. But two days ago when I went to the office of refugees for their response, I found I was the only one turned down by the Commission. You can imagine how I felt at that moment!

The writer took a deep breath. As if he had just got through writing a long introduction. In a low voice he said slowly, "I understand!"

"Might I ask you to please order another glass of wine? I'm thirsty."

At a loss, embarrassed, he showed the empty glass to the waiter.

"But you haven't told me how I can be of assistance to you!"

Anonymous stared at him, surprised. Then, he waited for the waiter to fill his glass. This time he drank it down in one gulp and said, "You know, my misfortune began with that very statement. Because they make their rulings based on individuals' stories. And in my opinion, the two statements have been the cause of my failure and misery. They are badly written and no use to anybody.

The writer interrupted Anonymous. "Yes... Yes... I understand, but what does this have to do with me?"

"You are a good writer. Believe me, although I have not read your stories, I do admire you. I have heard so many good things about you. Frankly, political work left me no time for reading literature, although, when I was a child, I longed to write stories and novels. Unfortunately, Fate had other things in mind. There were many stories in my head but no time to relate them. Besides, my compositions weren't any good either. Now I understand what a gift I have lost. You really are a fortunate person! If I had started to write in those days, at least I wouldn't be a wanderer and an exile today and, wouldn't be facing death at every turn. I could write a proper autobiography. Do you follow me?"

"No, I'm sorry! You're not making yourself very clear."

"Look, you are an accomplished writer and storyteller. And you understood my problem, too! Not having an absolutely acceptable story; I mean, let's assume that my life has no story. It's completely empty; like a sheet of blank paper... Write my story! Do you follow me?"

The writer covered his ears so he wouldn't hear. The wine had done its work and dizziness had overcome him. He shook his head violently a few times as if he was shaking it to get rid of anything extraneous and irrelevant. And he grew sad. He said to himself, He imagines storytelling is a joke or a game... What an arrogant generation!... Damn the Revolution. They fool with everything sacred. And glowering, he said to Anonymous, "I am sorry, sir!"

And he signaled the waiter over. He took out his wallet. Quickly Anonymous said, "Forgive me! I am thirsty—another wine, if possible."

The writer was so startled and at a loss that, involuntarily, he pointed out the two empty wine glasses to the waiter and turned his embarrassed face toward the stone lions. Cold water still cut through the air. His uninvited guest said, "I guessed that for you storytelling is a very serious matter."

Ironically, politely, and quickly, he answered, "You don't say! So in your opinion a story is serious?"

"It is not enough that it be serious! It is vital... You see, for me, a story means breathing instead of facing a firing squad."

The writer shook his head again. He should not have touched the wine, but since he had started drinking, he shouldn't stop. Unconsciousness is better than dizziness. He closed his eyes to shut out the spinning in front of them. He heard the voice of Anonymous continuing, "I wrote a few articles in the Organization's journal about the role of literature—I wrote that literature is the savior of humanity."

Eyes closed, he answered, "I don't share that opinion.

Writing is a private affair."

"But all these stories you've written, they're not all stories of your own life! How many stories does one person have? Surely you have written about other people, too!"

The writer shouted, "Not just any other people!"

Silence. He wanted to open his eyes and see that Anonymous had given up in despair and gotten up, intending to leave; but he also had a fear of dizziness. What if all the things in the café were to start spinning around him? He felt like a blind man who, in the darkness, might turn toward a person addressing him without being sure whether he was there or had left. He said to himself, No doubt he got my drift and has gone off in a huff. But I didn't hear the sound of a chair scraping.

As soon as he heard a wineglass hit the table he realized that Anonymous had downed his wine. In the darkness he felt around the tabletop for the glass. Anonymous helped him, "Here you are, sir; it's here! You need to concentrate."

Without fear of dizziness, he drank his wine and, his face hot and red, trembling with anger, said harshly, "Listen, sir. What you have written is not important to me; nor what the duty of literature is; nor what the role of the story is. I am not one of those people who is impressed by slogans. For me, the story and the people in the story have their own meaning."

"But I did not disagree."

"Hear me out! I have never written a story for no reason. I must have an issue in order to write. I must have an issue myself. Do you understand? I don't write stories on demand."

His voice trembled with anger. Anonymous waited for him to continue, and when the silence lasted, he asked calmly, "How does something become 'an issue' for you?"

"How should I know how it begins?! I suppose I see someone; I get involved; I find I have a problem with him. You don't understand, do you?"

"Well, but you have seen me! Now you are angry with me

and you quarrel with me, too!"

He was so flustered and angry that he forgot his dizziness. He opened his eyes and shouted, "How else can I put it? You are not a character in a story!"

Everybody was looking at him in astonishment. Even the waiter had come a few steps closer, fearing the writer might throw the wine glasses. Like the other customers in the café, Anonymous was staring at his red face. He himself was more dumbfounded than any one else; he knew he was dumbfounded because his dizziness had fled. He could see perfectly well; objects were not spinning in front of his eyes anymore. For the first time in years everything was clear and alive. Brightly he told Anonymous, "I thank you; I am in your debt."

Anonymous smiled gently. "Then, you will write my story?"

Suddenly the writer came to; he realized he was trapped. "Look, sir. I understand your situation. I hope you appreciate mine. I'm in no position to do this. How can I put it? Writing a story has its rules. I don't know you! You understand? Saying you are a blank sheet of paper on the table is not accurate. One cannot construct a story out of nothing."

Quickly Anonymous said, "Then I will tell you about myself. How about that?"

Nervous and trapped, the writer twisted around. He was looking for a way out; a note of entreaty entered his voice. "Would you please pay attention to what I am saying? I cannot do it. Believe me, for years and years I have been cursed by this one and that one demanding to know why I don't write about the lives of real people. What can I do? I hate copying. It's not creative."

Anonymous, overjoyed, interrupted him, "That is precisely why I've come to you. I don't want you to write my real life. Rather, I need the story of someone who ought to be granted asylum as a refugee. That is why I brought up the... blank sheet of paper... That kind of writing is more likely to save me. But it was you, sir, who said that one must know the person in the story."

His mouth was open in surprise. His eyes fell on the wine, and he drank it without fear. Then his lips parted in a smile. Anonymous continued, "I have a solution. Of course, if you agree!"

"Do go on."

"First, if you permit, let us fill up our glasses!"

Anonymous didn't wait for an answer. He used what he had learned; he raised the two glasses and showed them to the waiter. Then, laughing, he said, "You learn how to speak faster this way."

The writer had grown more taken with him, more fascinated, but he was still afraid. Anonymous continued, "The problem for both of us is clear. I need an absolutely acceptable story for refugee status. You do not make an exact copy of reality, nor do you construct something out of nothing. Very well! I shall give you a desultory account of things. And I should also remind you of the storytelling laws for the office of refugees."

The writer said quickly, "The laws of that office in regards to stories have nothing to do with me."

"You are right. But still, in the end you must save me! Otherwise, they will reject me again."

"But I have no knowledge of their laws. I don't even know whom they mean by refugee!"

The waiter set the glasses on the table. Anonymous, who had been waiting, drank his wine and lit a cigarette, "Look, 'refugee' means someone whose life is in danger because of his religion, the color of his skin, or his opinions. That sums up the rules! It is not difficult. Of course for America a few other rules must be observed, too."

Surprised, the writer asked, "Have you applied to America, too?"

"Yes, I had it in mind too, and I still do. Frankly, I need a universally applicable story; because with all the cares taking up your time, it would be difficult to reach you. It would be better if you write a story that would work with every embassy."

The writer laughed. After so many years the wine had made him tipsy. He raised his glass, "To your health!"

"Long life to you! There are just a few American rules I'm going to mention. I mean, there are some people who cannot go to America. Those who have been members of a Communist Party or who have communist ideas; those who want to go there and spread communist propaganda; those who have evaded military service. That is the summary of the rules. As you can see, they are not complicated! And many people, although they broke these rules, have gone there. Now, will you permit me to begin?"

Shocked and frightened, the writer said, "I didn't promise anything! Since you are talking, I am listening."

"But you said a few minutes ago that you have to get involved and that it has to become an issue for you so that you can write."

"Yes, I did say that."

"Then please listen! Perhaps you will get involved. And here is pen and paper, if you need any! This is my case: I was born into a poor family. My father was a taxi driver."

Pen in hand, the writer sat there. He interrupted Anonymous, "Excuse me! What has a taxi driver got to do with ideas, religion, or the color of one's skin? You said the regulations of the office of refugees do not number more than two or three!"

Anonymous listened to him with consternation, sadly. Then, he sighed and said, "You see the sort of major mistakes that were in earlier stories? Like those who wrote the texts, I thought being the son of a taxi driver or stonecutter or shoemaker means the right to be a refugee. But how fortunate it is that this question arose. You should be informed about the two earlier texts; to make sure the mistakes will not be repeated. At the same time, your story should not be too far removed from the earlier narratives; otherwise they would find out... or, no,... don't trouble yourself! Write freely! The earlier ones are not important. I am applying under a different name!"

Surprised, he asked, "Under another name?"

"Yes. I am not a famous person. I don't have an identity card, either; that means I have no identity. Choose whatever name you want! I don't have a birth certificate or a passport. If I am accepted, they will give me a new passport and identity card, with the name that I—or, sorry, you—will choose."

The writer whispered involuntarily, "How interesting this is!"

"So it's not important in which city and into what kind of family I was born, or that I grew up in the midst of family quarrels. You are right! These things have nothing to do with ideas and life-threatening dangers. Many people's mothers have been killed by their fathers; this is not a reason for being a refugee."

"Was your mother killed by your father?"

"No! I was talking about one of the comrades. The same catastrophe was about to happen in our house, too, but I prevented it. I didn't talk about that in any of the earlier texts. You shouldn't write about it either. The first text was one page long. In that one a bank seizure and a few other operations were mentioned in a very concise, brief fashion."

"Were you involved in armed robbery?"

"Revolutionary confiscation! My role was a very minor one. I was on a motorcycle, at an intersection, acting as lookout, guarding the team leader and a few armed Kurds. In the second text I represented myself as the team leader, and I described the event in a few pages. I think that was a mistake on my part. I had to write the truth. I didn't even explain how I became active in politics. I didn't know where to begin. Frankly, I never could tell what it was my heart desired. In France I've tried to pull myself together. But I couldn't think at all, while everything had become an issue for me; I had trouble drinking the water; I couldn't even hear my own voice. Do you follow me? I felt weird about myself. I tried to remember my whole past, and indeed to get into the mood and atmosphere of the past. What kind of person did I use to be? What did I use to think about? I locked the door on the inside and sat down. When someone knocked, I didn't answer. I drew the curtains. I wanted to be in the mood and atmosphere of the old days, when I was five years old, say. What was important to me then? What feelings did I have? Then, what happened to me? Why haven't I talked about another issue? For example, about my mother, or Nahid or Parvin? How were my feelings formed? I wanted to find out. And I never found out. Why did I become politically active? One could finish high school, be friends with a girl, get married and not have these sensitivities. For example, not cry over the separation in the Organization and its breaking up. You know, I was very sensitive. When the Organization broke up and the movement fell apart, I cried. I couldn't do anything else. After the breakup, at the meeting of our cell, in front of our team leader and two other people, I wailed. But the circumstances were not mentioned in either of the two earlier texts. I'm only telling you about them. Do not write them. They are of no use to the office of refugees. And your wine is finished!"

The writer came to himself. He signaled to the waiter and asked Anonymous, "How did you prevent the killing of your mother?"

Anonymous laughed and replied, "It seems to me that private affairs or love affairs are more important to you. You are right. But you are not going to mention them anywhere! Certainly not for the office of refugees! Let me summarize, because your time is limited and we should write the main story. I had just gone to school. One day I fell sick in class. When I came home I heard the sound of my mother's laughter. I went upstairs. You can guess that she was with my father's friend. They both sat there, scared. And I ran to the courtyard, sat in a corner and cried. My mother came. Although I had a fever she gave me money to go and buy an ice cream. At night my throat got infected. It might be of interest to you that I didn't want to see my father. I was afraid of his eyes. Fortunately he was busy with his opium brazier and didn't notice me. He just knew that I had a high fever. If I had told him he would surely have killed my mother. Of course I have never told these things to anyone. I mentioned them since they were of interest to you, otherwise they are of no use to the office of refugees. They are looking for something else."

"What, for example?" And despite the fact that he had quit smoking a year earlier, he stretched his hand out toward the cigarette pack. Anonymous held the lighter under his cigarette.

"They look for three things: first, the nature of your political activity and its exact description; then, how you left, and lastly, what dangers are threatening you. In the second text, I wrote that I was selling books in front of the university. Hezbollahis[1] rushed in and burned all the books. And then I joined the Organization. That was a lie. I'm telling you the truth. I was already in the Organization; in the practical action section. Once when friends came to Tehran, it was decided that we would rob a jewelry store. They had already targeted one and had checked out different opportunities. They had also gotten hold of a motorcycle. These events took place before the 30th of Khordad.[2] I was supposed to wait on the motorcycle with a machine gun. I had never used one, but I was supposed to fire if necessary. They had told me how to shoot. They asked if I could ride a motorcycle and I told them I could. I did not write this. I didn't know what was going on. I said, 'Sure, I know how to pretty well.' I had never ridden a motorcycle before. They said, 'You are to be the motorcycle rider in this affair.' I said, 'What is the affair?' and that's when I found out it was robbing the jewelry store. I was in the middle of this event. But for the office of refugees I wrote that I was the leader. Imagine; I was supposed to ride the motorcycle very fast and at the same time open fire on the *komitehchis*.[3] Of course we had someone in charge, and a planner. The driver of the car was from their own people who had come from the Kurdistan group. He was a good driver. The group that had been sent to Kurdistan had returned to Tehran. Not to rob a jewelry store. They planned to assassinate a few *jash*.[4] I wrote Hezbollahis instead. They were looking for them. In the midst of all that, a mutual plan was set up with our people. Basically, with me. It was decided that we go halves on the money. They were in charge of the operation. I had not done anything like that. Besides, I didn't believe in shooting anyone. I did write that. In fact, someone suggested I write that. And in the end the operation was not carried out. The plan had been exposed. When we arrived, the jewelry store was surrounded by Pasdaran.[5] We found out that another group had robbed the jewelry store. Someone inside had betrayed us. One day, in a house, they came up with another plan and asked my opinion. I didn't have any information to base an opinion on, so I was silent. They said, 'Why are you so quiet?' I said, 'What can I say? I have never stolen more than a bottle of Pepsi from the grocery store in the alley. I don't know what to do! I have never robbed a bank or a jewelry store.' Their plan was to rob the house of a wealthy doctor. They wanted to kidnap and hold one of his children hostage, and then take the money. You know, all the Organization's money was from these kinds of robberies. I have not written this either. But I told that to the people of the Organization. Because they tried me. When we came abroad they tried me. They said, 'The betrayal of the jewelry store was your doing.' Imagine that! I was not on the central committee so I would know everything. I am telling you the truth. I have never seen the people in the Organization up close. In my cell, too, I knew only our leader. The other two people always sat facing the wall. I heard their voices. Then, here, I saw everyone up close."

Anonymous fell silent. The writer showed him his glass and in a friendly tone said, "Have a drink!" And as Anonymous, with eyes shut, was drinking his wine and calming down, he asked, "Why were you tried?"

"Well, you don't know the story of Parvin. In the text I did not talk about that. I just wrote that I am married and the father of a two-year-old child."

"Do you have a child?"

"It is not my child. It only looks that way. When the child was born I was not yet separated from Parvin. You know, when we arrived here, everything changed. I found the leader of my cell. I had married Parvin on his orders. An Organization marriage, you follow? Of course, I have furnished an account of an ardent love to the office of refugees. But you should know, and don't write this, that it was a mandatory love. Of course we liked each other. Before that, I was crazy about Nahid. In the second text, I wrote about Parvin what I really wanted to write about Nahid. I had seen her in front of the university, during the night of a sit-in. I have written this. We were together all night. Then we would be together at comrades' houses. But Nahid was from another organization which, temporarily, was in a coalition with our organization. After our paths diverged we lost each other. The leader said: 'Marry Parvin!' But here everything collapsed and I couldn't understand the reason for it. There was no talk about the Organization's money yet. Parvin confessed. She said she was pregnant and that she was in love with my leader from Tehran. There was no other way out. We waited for the child to be born. You know there is a mosque here, too. She divorced me and married the leader here. Then the two of them set out for Greece. They decided to go to America. A few months later she returned. She said she was still interested in me; that she loved me. But, a while later, she missed the leader again. She said that she was at a loss; that she didn't know which one of us she should choose. I said, 'Parvin! This won't do!' You know how it is! These days she is very nervous; she cries all the time. She is a broken woman. In fact, several times she seemed about to have a heart attack. The veins in her neck stood out. She falls down. You know, she is trapped, and it cannot be explained to the office of the refugees. I have written in the text that because of torture and psychological damages, my wife is now ill. Unfortunately nobody pays attention to these words. Look! It is snowing."

The writer turned his head. Outside it was dark and a heavy snow lay on the ground. He squinted. The fountains had been turned off. It seemed to him that the stone lions were asleep, crouched and old, fallen behind a curtain of shivering white. But the pleasant warmth of the heater and the wine had changed his mood. The café was empty of early evening customers. Next to the table, the waiter was anxious to bring the bill. The writer, apologizing, asked him to fill up the glasses for the last time. The waiter was impatient and tired, but he came over. Anonymous couldn't take his eyes off the fast-falling snow. The writer brought the wine glass to his lips. He was tipsy, and he had a desire to kiss the thin edge of the glass. Without taking his eyes off the scene outside, the writer listened to a voice that seemed to be coming from his own throat.

"In the second text I wrote that I left Iran in 122-degree heat. You know that in the summer in Chah Bahar fire rains down from the sky. We were burning. But there was nothing else for it. The fear of getting caught and dying was stronger. Passengers were made to disembark the plane in a military zone, outside the airport. Near the waiting taxis we were looking for our smuggler, and of course we also made a mistake.

Based on our agreement, he had to come forward and start talking. But everyone came forward and someone spoke. We thought it was him. The conversation began. But the real smuggler who was standing to the side realized that we had made a mistake. He came forward. In fact, we were saved, especially me, who was the only one out of the ordinary around. You know that over there everyone has tanned, dark skin, and my white, fair skin stood out. Then and there I felt I was outside; outside Iran. They were speaking in a local language, Baluchi. A foreign language, like here. I did not understand anything. I made them understand by signs and signals. I could not accept that this place was part of Iran. I was in no mood for an excursion. I'm saying this only to you. I have written something different in the text. I wrote, 'My only wish was to stay in Iran.' But then, I was thinking more about leaving. At that time I wanted to leave Iran forever. I wanted to leave everything, even those people, although I was wearing their clothes. I had put on Baluchi clothes so the patrols wouldn't notice me, although they did not match any of our faces, and mine less than anyone else's. The others were at least a little tan. But my white skin had nothing to do with being Baluch. I saw myself in the mirror, in the hotel, in a white cloth, no, it was beige, and I started laughing. I had wrapped a shawl around my head. Only my eyes were visible, so they wouldn't notice. We got on a truck. I know I am boring you but the office of refugees wants an exact description of how and from which border you left. To tell you the truth, I didn't feel the border. I said this earlier; even before leaving I was over the border and a stranger. And even before that. Please don't write this! But I have to tell someone. Just think about it! Many hours in a truck. A small child, with sunstroke, was crying. We were suffocating under the shawls. The sun, hot and burning. Suspicion of Pasdaran in front of a coffee house. Then, long waiting next to a pond. Again in another truck. This time, the child and the mother next to the driver and the rest of us, eight people, from everywhere, on top of the load and bouncing around. And every moment the shouting of the driver pointing to a few ramshackle houses, naming a village, on a barren sand desert, and that the Pasdaran have hit the place! They have hit that place and it was not clear why! Walking a couple of hours on the sand-covered ground and then pointing out a hill in the middle of the road, with a few dried trees, and saying: Border patrol; and then moving fast, and disappearing in the midst of the hills and at the end saying, 'It has been one hour since we crossed the border!' How do you expect me to remember which border I crossed and how!"

Tears filled the writer's eyes. Anonymous drank his wine in one gulp. He was in a blithe mood. He laughed and continued, "But I wrote in the text, 'When I crossed the border I kept looking at Iran, which was moving further and further away. The color of the dirt and the ground, even the air, was different. The humidity in the air had changed. I was looking. I was feeling. There was nothing particular in my view. It was a simple sort of nature. Pure dirt and sand was moving away, as if everything was there. It was beautiful.' Those things, someone here suggested that I write them, but they were true, too."

The writer was in a good mood. He was warm and didn't want it to be finished. That's why he asked the waiter, who was standing there with an expectant look, to fill up the glasses. Anonymous witnessed the writer's entreaty and his squabble with the waiter. He asked, "What is his problem?"

"He says it is late and he should close. He is tired. I asked him to have patience for one more glass. You saw that he accepted with displeasure. Talk faster now, there's not enough time."

Anonymous didn't wait for him to finish his sentence and quickly continued, "At night, bruised and tired, we arrived at Basandeh,[6] a city next to the sea. The smuggler's wife brought us food. We had dates and bread. I was anxious to call Tehran. I had to call and let them know I had arrived safely. I said, 'I want to go and see the city. I'm interested in seeing how foreigners fish.' They said, 'It is night now, and besides, you should not go outside. People will inform the police. There will be problems.' But I couldn't control myself. I said, 'I have to go to the bathroom.' They said, 'There is no bathroom in the house. You have to go out to the alleyway, on the side.' People in Basandeh go in the alleyway. And nobody cleans them. They get dried. I had seen that in the darkness on the way. They squat on the side or near a tree. Without any shower or cleaning up after. They go to the sea. But the sea is full of sharks. This was the first time I squatted in an alleyway. Like what we have back home in the north, in the corner of the garden. Do I have to say these things too?"

The writer, excited, said, "Talk about the trial! And take your time drinking your wine! It will last longer. Don't you see the waiter is in hurry? Go on!"

"About the wine, I am sorry. I can't. I have to gulp it down."

And he gulped it down and continued, "The trial has a prologue. Everything got into a mess in Basandeh. It was night. I was in the courtyard. There was a kind of dew—no, I'm sorry, it was sultry. My whole body was wet. It was hot. The comrades summoned me. They were in the room. All of them were there. But behind the curtain. They still didn't want me to see their faces. The leader and I were on the other side of the curtain. There was talk about money. They said, 'Is the Organization's money with you?' I said, 'Yes.' They said, 'We should divide it.' I said, 'In Europe.' I have not written these things. Remember, these are the secrets of the Organization. Besides, I was lying. I had no money. I thought if I said I didn't have any they would leave me there and they wouldn't get me a passport. I didn't have a ticket. I said, 'I will give it to you in Europe.' A voice from the other side of the curtain said, 'We want to split up.' I said, 'Then you don't have any right to the Organization's money.' They said, 'No, we want to go to America from here.' I had no way out. They had already paid the smuggler. I saw that I had no other recourse. I said, 'Those who are going to America should take from those who are going to Europe, and I will give everything in Europe.' I was lying. I didn't have any money. Some of them, believing that, paid for my ticket and passport. Of course it was not their money. It was the Organization's money. When we got here, I said, 'What money?' And they tried me. They said, 'It was the Organization's money.' I said, 'It fell apart.' They said, 'We don't care about these things; you owe us 2,000 dollars.' I said, 'I don't have any money.' But let me tell you, even if I had I wouldn't have paid. Why should I? That was the Organization's money. Even if it wasn't money gained from robbery, it was money made by the hard work of the lower-ranking members of the Organization, all of whom either stayed or were killed or are in prison. Only high-ranking members and leaders left, because the money was in their hands. Please don't write this either! They said, 'Back then you were inactive; now you have become a thief, too! You must be tried.' I said, 'You should be ashamed of yourselves. Get out!' And finally a fight broke out. They said, 'You should return the passport; we bought it.' I said, 'I won't give it back.' They said, 'We want to sell it.' I realized things were getting serious and they meant to beat me. I gave up my passport. I had no other recourse. It was complicated. There was also the case of Parvin. I couldn't speak. Do you understand? In Iran, they were all behind the curtain. Here, I saw them all, without a veil! What the hell does this man want from me?"

He shouted the last sentence. He was pointing at the waiter, who was standing next to the table. The writer's face was hot and wet from perspiration. The pen had fallen from his hand, and he was whispering to himself, "They want to close. They should be kept busy. This should be continued. There might be time for one glass."

Sadly he looked at the waiter. He was light-headed, drunk. Politely he thanked the waiter, who had taken him under the arms so he would get up from his chair. The voice continued, "My misfortune has always been the shortage of time. Always, right here, my statement is cut off. That is why I have been rejected a few times. There hasn't been time to relate another story."

The writer was leaning on the waiter, heading for the door. The proprietor was turning off the lights. The door opened. He felt the frozen air on the burning skin of his face. He still heard his voice. "But this time I will summarize it. Write! They arrested me for reading books. I used to sit in the corner of the room and just read. The President's books. Although I have written before that I disrupted his meetings several times. I tell you, if I have the opportunity, I will do it again. But don't write this!... no... It's not enough to read..."

The writer apologized to the waiter once more and walked on the snow. He kept turning around, as if he had lost something. He looked at the ground; he saw nothing else but whiteness; and he heard, "Write! I was working with moderates. In fact, write that I have been a proponent of human rights. But no... I don't know anyone. I don't know how to deal with my misery. You are not paying attention to me either."

For a moment, the writer felt he was flying. The feeling was brief, though, and he landed in the snow. His body hurt. Desire for a deep sleep on the frozen snow was tempting him. He whispered, "My heart is thinking about you, believe it! But one cannot be saved by what you have recounted so far. You know? It cannot be. With tens of lies, it cannot be done. One has to come up with a basic idea... And where are you? Where are you?"

The writer raised his head. Snow was coming down fast. The Place Daumesnil was hidden under the snowfall. He tried to remember how he had reached this point. He vomited at the foot of the stone lions. An hour later, he stood up. He collapsed again, and finally he put his hand on the wall. Slowly, slowly, he

stepped along on the slippery snow. An alleyway later, he cried.
He wanted to sing. Under the barrage of blizzard and midnight
snow he sang:

> I took my shadow to the tavern.
> I poured and poured; he drank;
> He poured and poured; I drank.[7]

Biographies

Kader Abodolah was born in Iran in 1952. He completed his education as a physician but worked as a journalist in opposition publications before and after the 1979 Revolution. A few years after the Revolution he left Iran and went to Holland as a political refugee. Since 1989 he has published a number of collections of short stories in Dutch including *De Adelaars* (The Eagles) and *De meisjes en de partizanen* (Young Girls and Partisans) and a novel, *The Cuneiform Writings*. In 1997 he won the Dutch Media Prize for his journalistic works.

Tahereh Alavi was born in Tehran in 1959. After finishing high school she began working on children's literature. In 1986 she moved to France and studied there for six years. During this period she translated many books for children and young adults. After returning to Iran she began writing for an older audience. She has published a number of collections of short stories including *Zanan-e bi Gozashteh* (Women without a Past) and *Man va Heidegger* (Heidegger and I).

Reza Baraheni was born in Tabriz, Iran, in 1935. He completed his Ph.D. in literature from the University of Istanbul and in 1963 was appointed Professor of English at Tehran University. During his long literary career he has taught at many different universities inside and outside Iran and his work covers many different areas, including literary theory and criticism, poetry, fiction, and social issues. He was a founding member of the Writers' Union in Iran, an organization that promoted the freedom of expression for many years. Baraheni has also been very active in introducing modern literary criticism in Iran. He is the author of hundreds of articles and more than 50 books including *Ruzgar-e Duzakhi-ye Aqay-e*

Ayyaz (The Infernal Time of Mr. Ayyaz), *God's Shadow: Prison Poems*, and *Azadeh Kanom va Nevisandeh-ash* (Azadeh Khanom and Her Novelist). Many of his works have been translated. He is President of PEN Canada and teaches comparative literature at the University of Toronto's Massey College.

Ali Erfan was born in Esfahan in 1946. He lived and worked there as a cineaste and writer until 1981 when he left Iran and went to France as a political refugee. Since then he has published a number of collections of short stories and novels, many of which have been translated into French. They include *Le Dernier poète du monde* (The Last Poet of the World), *Ma Femme est une Sainte* (My Wife is a Saint), *La Route des infidels* (The Road of Infidels) and *La 602eme nuit* (The 602nd Night). Recently he received the title of Chevalier Arts et Culture from the French Ministry of Culture.

Fahimeh Farsaie was born in 1952 in Tehran. She worked as a journalist and a literary critic in Iran. After the 1979 Revolution she moved to Germany (1983) where she continued her work as a literary critic. Her works include *Mihan-e Shisheh-i* (The Glass Homeland), a collection of short stories, and *Die Unendlicheflucht* (The Endless Escape) written in German. She lives in Köln.

Ghodsi Ghazinour was born in Iran in 1941. She finished her education in the Department of Fine Arts in Tehran. During her long literary career she has published 36 books, most of which are for children. Among her most recent works are *Na Abi Na Zard* (Neither Blue nor Yellow) and *Dokhtar-i ba Pirahan-e Surati* (A Girl with Pink Dress). She is the recipient of many awards, including the Hans Christian Anderson Diploma. She lives in Holland.

Hushang Golshiri was born in Esfahan in 1938 and studied Persian literature at the University of Esfahan. He began his literary career by publishing poems and short stories in various literary journals. Golshiri's first collection of short stories, *Mesl-e Hamisheh* (As Always) was published in 1958. A year later he published his most famous book, *Shazdeh Ehtejab* (Prince Ehtejab), a short novel, which is considered a turning point in modern Persian fiction. During his long literary career, Golshiri was invited to many different countries for lectures and participation in cultural and literary activities. His experience with Iranian exiles, after the 1979 Revolution, led to a number of literary texts including *Ayenehha-ye Dardar* (Folding Mirrors), a short novel. Golshiri's works have been translated into many languages and he has been the recipient of numerous awards including the Erich–Maria Remarque Prize. In 2000 Golshiri fell ill with a lung abscess and died at the age of 62.

Farkhondeh Hajizadeh was born in the village of Bazanjan in 1953. She later moved to Azarbaijan, where she continued her education, completed her degree in Persian literature, and began working as a librarian. During the past twelve years she has written five collections of short stories and a novel, including *Khalaf-e Democracy* (Contrary to Democracy) and *Az Cheshmha-ye Shoma Mitarsam* (I am Afraid of Your Eyes). She is managing editor of the literary journal *Baya*.

Dariush Kargar was born in 1953 in the city of Hamedan in Iran. He studied communications in Iran. In 1984 he was forced into exile in Sweden, where he studied graphics and linguistics. His books include *Zendani* (Prisoner) and *Inak Vatan Tab'idgah Ast* (Now the Homeland is an Exile) published in Iran. Among many of his books published in Sweden is *Bagh, Bagh, Bagh-e ma* (Garden, Garden, Our Garden). He lives in Uppsala.

Nasim Khaksar was born in Tehran in 1943. He has published works in many different literary genres. His works include collections of short stories *Diruzi-ha* (The People of Yesterday), *Mora'i Kafer ast* (Morai is an Infidel) and *Akharin Nameh* (The Last Letter), a play. He has also published four children's books. He lives in Holland.

Farideh Kheradmand was born in 1957 in Tehran. She completed her education in drama and dramatic literature. Her writing career began in radio. From 1988 to 1990 she worked as a playwright, director, and actor in the Persian Gulf area. In 1992 she left her work in radio to devote time to writing. She has written several plays and has published several works in children's literature. Her collections of stories include *Parandeh-yi hast* (There is a Bird) and *Aramesh-e Shabaneh* (The Nightly Tranquility). She has now migrated to Canada.

Mohammad Mehdi Khorrami was born in Iran in 1960. In 1982 he left Iran and continued his education in France and the United States. During his graduate studies he specialized in Persian and French literature. He teaches Persian language and literature at New York University. His most recent works include *A Feast in the Mirror: A Collection of Short Stories by Iranian Women* (with Shouleh Vatanabadi) and *Modern Reflections of Classical Traditions in Persian Fiction*.

Pari Mansouri-Kianush was born in Tehran in 1936. She holds a BA degree in English and English literature and an MA in social sciences. She has written and translated several books. Many of her short stories have appeared in Persian journals. Among her works are a novel, *Balatar az Eshq* (Above and Beyond Love), and a collection of short stories *Mehmani dar Ghorbat* (Entertainment in Exile). She lives in England.

Mehrnoush Mazarei was born in Tehran. After graduating from business school she moved to California. She is the founder of a Persian literary women's magazine, *Forough*. She has published three collections of short stories, including *Boridehha-ye Nur* (Streaks of Light) and *Klara va Man* (Clara and I). Two of her stories were among the top 100 stories chosen in the Writer's Digest Competition. She lives in Los Angeles.

Marjan Riahi was born in 1970. She is a graduate of Tehran University in business management. She also holds degrees in screenwriting and acting. She has published several short stories in different literary and women's journals in Iran. Her collection of short stories, *Eshareh-ha* (Points) was published in 1999.

Said was born in Tehran, Iran, in 1947. In 1965 he went to Germany as a student. There he combined his literary interests with political-democratic engagements, thus making his return to Iran impossible. After the fall of the Shah in 1979, Said visited Iran, but, faced with the regime of theocracy, he saw no chance for a new beginning and returned to exile in Germany. Said has published a number of books in German, two of which have been translated into English: *Be to Me the Night*, a collection of love pomes and *Landscapes of a Distant Mother*. He is also the recipient of numerous awards, including the Jean Monnet International Prize for Literature.

Sirus Seif is a graduate of theatre studies. He started his work in Iran as a playwright and director in Iranian television. Among his works are *Avaregan-e Khabgard* (The Dreamy wanderers), a novel, and a collection of short stories, *Tabestan Shod* (Summer Came). His plays include *No'i Mard, No'i Zan, No'i Kabus* (A Kind of Man, a Kind of Woman, a Kind of Nightmare) and *Aram-Shahr* (City of Tranquility), which is translated into Dutch. He lives in Holland.

Azar Shahab was born in 1955 in Tehran. She has worked as a painter, poet, and story writer. Her published works include "Laleh-ye Abi" (Blue Tulip) and "Bazgasht" (The Return). She has been living in Germany for many years.

Mahasti Shahrokhi was born in 1956 in the city of Malayer in Iran. She is a graduate of theater studies from Tehran University. She migrated to France in 1984. There she continued her studies in comparative literature. She has published many articles and short stories in literary and artistic magazines inside and outside Iran. Her last novel *Shali Beh Derazay-e Jaddeh-ye Abrisham* (A Shawl as Long as the Silk Road) was published in 1999. She lives in Paris.

Mohammad-Asef Soltanzadeh was born in Afghanistan in 1964 and completed his BA degree in Pharmacology from the University of Kabul. During the civil war he moved to Iran (1986) where he lived and worked. During this period Soltanzadeh published a number of short stories in literary journals and his collection of short stories, *We Disappear in Flight* won the Golshiri Foundation's best prize in 2001. In 2002, when Afghans were not allowed to stay in Iran any longer he moved to Denmark. Since then he has published another collection of short stories, *Nowruz Faqat dar Kabol Ba-safa-st* (New Year's Day is Pleasant Only in Kabul).

Goli Taraghi was born in 1939. She studied philosophy in the United States and upon return to Iran she taught at the Department of Dramatic Arts in Tehran University. In 1980 she went to France for a short visit and with the start of the Iran–Iraq war she took residence in France with her children. Her direct experiences of migration are reflected in most of her writing; in fact, her work has served as an introduction of the theme of migration in the contemporary Iranian literature. Her writing began with a collection of stories, *Man ham Che Guevara Hastam* (I am Also Che Guevara). Since then she has published a number of collections of short stories and novels. Among these works are her novel, *Khab-e Zemestani* (The Sleep of Winter), and her collections of stories, *Khaterehha-ye Parakandeh* (Scattered Memories), *Do Donya* (Two Worlds) and *Jayi Digar* (Another Place).

Shouleh Vatanabadi was born in Iran in 1955. In 1978 she left Iran to continue her education in the United States. During her graduate studies in comparative literature, she specialized in Middle Eastern literature. She teaches Middle Eastern culture and civilization at New York University. She is the author of several articles on Iranian and Azerbaijani literature. Her most recent work (with Mohammad Mehdi Khorrami) is *A Feast in the Mirror*, a translated and edited volume of short stories by contemporary Iranian women.

Mehri Yalfani was born in Hamadan, Iran. Her first published collection of short stories was *Happy Days*. Since then she has published her works in many Persian and English language publications. Her most recent works include *Afsaneh's Moon*, a novel, and two collection of short stories written in English *Parastoo* and *Two Sisters*. She lives in Canada.

INTRODUCTION

[1] This is a line from a poem by Ahmad Shamlu (1925–2000), one of the most celebrated Iranian poets. The title of the book as well as headings used in the Introduction are taken from this poem, which sums up the different stages of displaced and exiled existence. The translation of part of this poem is the epigraph for this book.

ANXIETIES FROM ACROSS THE WATER

[1] Kelardasht is a city in northern Iran.

[2] *Khoresh* is a kind of stew eaten with rice. *Fesenjan* is a particular khoresh made with pomegranate juice, walnuts, and chicken.

[3] *Khanom* means "lady."

[4] *Umma* refers specifically to the Muslim community.

[5] *Manteau* refers to a long coat that women who do not use chador are required to wear.

[6] Ash-e reshteh is a thick soup of noodles, herbs, and beans.

[7] *Kashk* is a milk product usually eaten with *ash-e reshteh*.

[8] *Sigheh* refers to temporary marriage or to the woman who enters into this contract. It is allowed in Shi'ite tradition of Islam.

THE LAST SCRIPTURE

[1] The story takes place in different places. The italic style indicates the parts which occur in Iran. The regular style indicates events in Turkey.

[2] Boyuk Bazaar is Turkish for Grand Bazaar.

[3] The *salavat* is a prayer to praise God and bless the Prophet Mohammad.

[4] The *takbir* is a glorification of God by saying "God is supreme!"

[5] Eslami Nadushan is a famous literary figure in Iran.

[6] Sheykh Sohrevardi was a 12th-century philosopher.

[7] Van is a town in Turkey near the Iranian border.

[8] Yuksokova is a town in Turkey near the Iranian border.

[9] In 1953, a US-backed *coup d'état* in Iran restored the regime of the

Shah Mohammad Reza Pahlavi.

[10] Karbala, a city in Iraq, has great religious significance for Shiite Moslems. It is the site of a massacre and the martyrdom of Hussein, the Third Imam, in the seventh century.

[11] A reference to 72 Islamic Republic officials killed in a bomb explosion on 28 June 1981.

[12] *Gelecek* is Turkish for "He'll come."

[13] Kyoh is a town in Iran, near Turkey.

THE RETURN

[1] It is part of the Hajj ritual to circumambulate the Ka'aba seven times.

[2] A chador is women's outdoor garb; it is also worn at prayer time.

[3] *Val* is a very thin, expensive silk.

YOU'RE THE JACKASS!

[1] A *ghelman* is a male angel.

POSTCARDS SIDE BY SIDE

[1] "Dayeh Dayeh Vaghte Janga," or "Mother, Mother, it's time to fight," is a folk song from the Iranian area of Lurestan that was very popular during the years of the 1979 Revolution (because of its revolutionary content).

HOURGLASS

[1] *The Blind Owl* is a very famous twentieth-century Persian novel by Sadeq Hedayat (1903–1951). Hedayat committed suicide in Paris and is buried in Pere Lachaise.

[2] "Solitude is dangerous for working intellects... when we are alone for a long time, we people the void with phantoms."

[3] Gholamhosein Saedi (1934–1985), another famous Iranian writer, lived in exile in Paris and died partly because of overindulgence in alcohol.

[4] "Leave the beautiful women to men without imagination!"

[5] Zahir al-Doleh is a cemetery in Tehran where many Iranian artists are buried.

[6] "Dash Akol" is a short story by Sadeq Hedayat.

[7] The main character of the same Hedayat story.

[8] "You do not know how fortunate you are; you are never as miserable as you think."

[9] Reference to a scene in Hedayat's "Three Drops of Blood."

[10] Reference to the central image in Hedayat's novel, *The Blind Owl.*

[11] The author is referring to a poem by Ahmad Shamlu (1925–2000) in which he says, "We endured the unbearable punishment for so long that we forgot our sacred word."

PIR

[1] Yazd is an old city in southern Iran.

[2] Hafez: a 14th-century Iranian poet.

[3] Moulavi: a 13th-century Iranian poet.

[4] Ferdowsi: a 10th-century epic poet of Iran.

[5] Attar: a 12th-century Iranian poet.

WITHOUT ROOTS

[1] *Chelleh,* the first night of winter and the longest night of the year, is celebrated by Iranians.

[2] *Noruz* is the Iranian New Year.

[3] Traditional Iranian stew, *fesenjan* is made of walnuts, pomengranate paste, and chicken, and *qormeh sabzi* of herbs, beans and meat.

CLOSE ENCOUNTERS IN NEW YORK

[1] Nizami, or Nezami (1141–1202), a great Iranian poet, whose *Seven Domes,* or *Seven Images,* is one of the greatest of Persian poems, comparable only to *A Thousand and One Nights.*

[2] Esfandiar, the son of a legendary king of ancient Iran, was anointed by Zoroaster, becoming invulnerable, but he closed his eyes when he was being washed in the Water of Life, and Rustam, the famous hero of Ferdowsi's *Book of Kings,* shot a two-headed arrow into his eyes, killing him.

[3] Throughout the story, whenever Rahmat talks to the cops, his words are in English in the original Farsi text.

[4] The poems are in Azari Turkish, a dialect spoken by millions of people in Iran, particularly in the Iranian Azarbaijan and Tehran.

FAROKH-LAQA, DAUGHTER OF PETROS, KING OF FARANG

[1] The word "Farang" is derived from "Franks" and later, "France," and was used especially in old Persian texts to refer to Europeans. In many cases, especially in old popular novels, it refers to foreign lands generally.

[2] Literary, "born to an Emam." Emamzadeh is mausoleum where it is believed a descendant of an Emam is buried.

[3] Shahcheragh is a famous mosque in Shiraz.

[4] Hazrat is an honorific title usually used for very important religious figures.

[5] A *parasang* is about twelve kilometers.

[6] The painting refers to the battle of Emam Hosein and many members of his family against the Ommayad Caliph Yazid and his army leader, Shemr. The battle took place on the ninth and tenth days of the month of Moharram in 680 CE.

ORIGINAL POSITION

[1] A Persian expression used to indicate the impossibility of an innocent relation between a girl and a boy.

[2] A Persian expression used to indicate desire on the one hand and the inhibition on a woman to initiate a relationship with a man on the other.

THE WOLF LADY

[1] Referring to Europe, or to the West in general.

[2] In Islam it is the Angel Israfil who is to blow the last trumpet.

[3] Mahmoodiyeh is an affluent district in north Tehran.

[4] Shemiran is an area in north Tehran

[5] Darband is a mountainous area in north Tehran

[6] The Komiteh is an armed force instituted after the 1979 Revolution to enforce law and order and Islamic values.

[7] Farangestan, like Farang, refers to Europe, the West.

ZARATHUSTRA'S FIRE

[1] Hushang Golshiri wrote this story when he was living at the Heinrich Böll Foundation in Germany.

[2] This slogan in Persian is "Ya rusari ya tusari" which means exactly "Either a head scarf or a blow to the head." Shortly after the 1979 Revolution a government-backed group of people used this slogan during their demonstrations and also during their confrontations with women who did not cover their hair. Soon after that, Islamic covering became compulsory.

[3] According to Islam, people of the opposite sex not related to each other either through marriage or family relationships are considered strangers to one another, and women are supposed to wear their Islamic cover in the presence of strange men.

NO COMMENT!

[1] In German, *kneipe* is a bar-café.

[2] *Freudin* means girl friend; also the name of a fashion magazine in Germany.

[3] *Entwicklungshilfe*: economic aid to developing countries.

[4] Bio Möbel is a furniture store that uses only natural materials.

[5] BND: the West German secret police.

[6] Hoyeswerda is a city in Eastern Germany. In 1992, Neo-Nazis set a refugee shelter on fire for 24 hours. Police and security officials did nothing to prevent this act.

[7] *Das gibt doch nicht! Das darf nicht wahr sein!* This is not happening! This cannot be true!

[8] *Taz*: a leftist newspaper.

[9] *Wg*: a communal house.

[10] Weizsacker: the German chancellor at the time of the story.

[11] *Ein atomfreies land*: a country free of nuclear weapons.

[12] *Eiskalt*: ice-cold.

[13] Hürth is a city near Cologne.

[14] *Hausmeister*: house or building manager; superintendent.

ANONYMOUS

[1] Hezbollahi means follower of the Party of God. In Iran this term refers to the hardline followers of the conservative faction of the government.

[2] On Khordad 30, 1369 (June 19, 1981) the Islamic government of Iran attacked a large demonstration organized by the opposition. Many demonstrators were killed, arrested and executed. This was a turning point in the treatment of the opposition by the government.

[3] Komitehchis are members of Komiteh (see note 6 in "The Wolf Lady").

[4] *Jash*: a Kurdish term referring to those who collaborated with the government, betraying the Kurds' uprising.

[5] Pasdaran: the Revolutionary Guard.

[6] Basandeh is a city in Pakistan.

[7] This is a passage from a famous poem by Mehdi Akhavan Sales (1928–1990).